Ghost Writer's Inn

BAKER CITY: HEARTS & HAUNTS 6

JOSIE MALONE

GHOST WRITER'S INN
Copyright © 2025 by Josie Malone

ISBN: 979-8-88653-403-0

Published by Satin Romance
An Imprint of Melange Books, LLC
White Bear Lake, MN 55110
www.satinromance.com

Published in the United States of America.

Cover Design by Lynsee Lauritsen

Ghost Writer's Inn is dedicated to my sister writers who inspired Mac MacGillicudy and Lilly Bryce as well as this story.

PROLOGUE

Seattle, Washington ~ September 2016

Lilly Bryce loved the Carnegie public library in Seattle. It'd always been a sanctuary, a safe place to flee from the various orphanages and foster homes where she lived. She'd spent hours reading there and never minded when she had to wait for a chair because the seating was so limited. The smell of books and the sight of the written words always comforted her. The librarians looked out for her more than any other adults did in her life.

They shared their lunches, and one frequently brought her cookies from home. Another gave her a coat and knitted gloves for her. On cold winter nights, they didn't "remember" to find her and send her outside before locking the building. When she was older, they helped research scholarships for her to attend nursing school. She eventually earned her degree, then went to work in a local hospital, visiting the library on her days off and seeing her old friends.

She didn't hesitate to answer the call of her country after the bombing of Pearl Harbor when the U.S. entered World War Two. She joined the Army Nursing Corp and eventually ended up in Italy where she died in 1945, when the hospital was bombed by the

Germans. She could have roamed anywhere, but she was ready to go home. So, she returned to her favorite place in the world, the old library.

She watched as it continued to evolve and expand through the years. She wasn't the only ghost who enjoyed the atmosphere and preferred books to most people. Her childhood friends passed away and moved on, but she stayed. She liked seeing new people discover adventures in books and the library continually added different resources for the many guests, films, music and eventually computers. Those took away her favorite card catalog.

Many of the ghosts she knew left for other branches after the building was remodeled in 2004. Granted, Lilly favored the classic brick style of the first Central Library from her childhood, but she wasn't inflexible—she could adapt. The futuristic architecture of the latest structure always made her think of a spaceship that had landed in the heart of downtown.

Visitors raved about the huge, four-story book spiral, the auditorium, the various labs, music practice and meeting rooms, a Writers' Room for resident artists, world languages collections, local history archives in the Seattle Room, and the distinctive open spaces. It was far larger than the comfortable building where she learned to read almost a hundred years before.

Today, she'd wandered into the computer room where she discovered Mac MacGillicudy, one of the newer patrons, sitting at a station. He scowled at the monitor in front of him and she happily floated closer. He was working away on his next action-adventure romance, and she always enjoyed reading over his broad shoulder. She wished he could hear her comments when he used a contemporary metaphor in lieu of an accurate description of the era where and when she lived, but that was why he needed her help.

His stories featured flawed protagonists, complex plots, and gritty settings in 1940s Seattle. The hero, Titus Mason, was a private detective who lived on a houseboat on the eastern shore of Lake Union. His love interest and secretary ran the small, second-story office near

Eastgate. She frequently pointed out important pieces of evidence to Titus, albeit with some assistance from Lilly.

Flecks of gray threaded through Mac's short dark hair, a close-cropped beard emphasized the firm jaw and rugged features. In the old combat, jump-style boots he usually wore, he was barely six feet. Faded blue jeans tucked into the boots, a black sweater with epaulets, he carried himself as if he was still an Army Ranger. Since he retired last year, he visited the library several days a week to write on one of their desktop computers. She wasn't sure why because he could have taken his laptop and gone to a coffee shop, but their loss was her gain.

Lilly heaved a sigh as she read the opening scene between Titus and his newest client, a blonde 'femme fatale' who definitely didn't deserve the hero or the author. Mac's cell phone distracted him, and he picked it up to answer a call. Taking advantage of the situation, Lilly added a quick sentence to the story and had the secretary ask a pertinent question that would provide more information for the new case.

It wasn't the first time she'd intervened, not that Mac realized she'd changed the ending of his debut novel and allowed Titus to save the woman he hadn't realized he loved. She didn't deserve to die simply to suit the writer's ends.

Besides, I do like a happy ever after resolution. And so will readers when his book hits the store shelves!

Mac MacGillicudy normally let calls go to voicemail and answered them later, but this one was from his literary agent, Gwen Talbot, a former Army officer who'd served as a liaison to his old combat unit when they were in Afghanistan. Two weeks ago, she'd told him she really liked the changes he'd made to his manuscript, *Evergreen City Murders* and intended to send it around to some of her favorite editors at different publishers. "Got a sitrep, Gwen?"

"Yes and you'll love it. I told you I was sending it to six people. I gave them a deadline and five of them responded with offers. The sixth wanted another three days to consider it."

"I hope you were polite when you refused."

"You should know me better than that after our time in the *sandbox*."

Mac chuckled. Actually, he did. When Gwen provided a cut-off or suspense date, it was set in stone. She often quoted the scientist, Bob Carter, saying that "Poor planning on your part does not necessitate an emergency on mine." If she was irritated, she'd opt for a cruder expression from her military days. Her snarky attitude and sarcastic quips flavored the secretary's character in his book, although he'd drawn the woman's physical attributes from a picture he'd found in the library's archives.

Gwen began to provide details of the various offers. When she finished, Mac asked which she thought was the best choice and her reasons. The conversation ended with her promise to email copies of the book contract when she received it. Meantime, he agreed to send the first three chapters of the next book to her as soon as they were ready.

Gotta get back to work, he thought and turned his attention to the monitor. He read through the scene and frowned when he noticed a comment from Lillian Burroughs, the secretary. *Damn it! Why did I do that? She's dead. I killed her off at the end of the last book. Hmm. Wait a second! This really works. I can use this—*

When he retired after his last assignment in Washington State, he wasn't ready to find a permanent place to live. He was done following orders and giving them. Instead, he traveled around the country, couch-surfing with different buddies from his Army days, most of whom put up with the fact that he wouldn't drink with them. He didn't stay long.

After hanging out for a week or so, reminiscing and playing poker, he was ready to move on and did. He'd made a brief visit to his mother and her family in Colorado. Since she and his stepdad didn't have room for him in their McMansion, Mac stayed at a nearby hotel for two days before he headed west to California.

In June, a former sergeant, Jimmy Penrose, who owned a tavern in Ballard, a waterfront neighborhood showcasing Scandinavian heritage in Seattle, invited Mac to stay as long as he wanted. Jimmy worked hard from open to close at his trendy pub. He was rarely home, which meant it could have been a quiet place to write except his many girlfriends floated in and out of the house in various stages of dress and undress. Mac wasn't interested in any of them, so he went to the library to research details for the final draft of his book.

He spent hours in the archives. And he found her! The perfect woman for his book!

Lillian V. Bryce, a World War Two Army nurse who died in Italy. The photo with her obituary was black and white. It only revealed her head and shoulders—and definitely didn't do her justice. Her hair was light, so it must have been blonde or possibly auburn. He couldn't tell the color of her eyes. In those days, her military uniform would have been dark blue until later in the war when the Army switched to brown. She wore a jacket with gold insignia on the collar over a blouse and necktie.

At twenty-eight, she was too young and lovely to die the way she had so he brought her back to life in his first book. He tweaked her name a bit, so none of her relatives would recognize her in the story, although the obit claimed she was an orphan. Granted, being raised by a single mother who eventually married a widower with kids of his own and no patience for his wife's son hadn't been a walk in the proverbial park either, Mac thought. *I'm thirty-seven and I learned to handle drama a long time ago. Did she?*

The lights flicked overhead, and he glanced at the warning that popped up on the monitor. The library would be closing in five minutes. He saved his work on a flash drive and shut down the computer. "Okay, time to call it a night. See you tomorrow, Lillian."

"I've told you a hundred times before, Mister MacGillicudy. It's Lilly."

CHAPTER ONE

Seattle, Washington ~ November 2019
Three Years Later

The cold winter rain cut short his early morning run through the residential area of Ballard. Back at the two-story house, Mac took a hot shower to warm up, dressed in faded jeans and an old gray T-shirt before he headed to the kitchen. He was putting together savory crepes for Sunday breakfast when Jimmy Penrose came in the room and headed straight to the coffee pot.

He hadn't dressed for the day yet, but still wore the clothes he slept in, dark blue board shorts that matched his eyes and a sloppy gray T-shirt, advertising Guinness ale. Spikes of his sandy-brown hair stood on end. "I'm going to miss you when you leave me again." Yawning, Jimmy topped Mac's cup. "I'll have to cook for myself."

"Let me know if or when that happens." Mac tossed a grin over his shoulder at the wiry, lean, muscular man who'd shared his last two combat tours. "I thought it's why you brought home sandwiches from the bar."

"I do when you're not around." Lines of amusement wrinkled

around the blue eyes. "So, tell me more about this new adventure of yours."

"You know what I do." He'd stuffed the crepe with mashed hard-boiled eggs, cooked bacon, green onions and cheddar cheese before he fried it. Mac flipped the first one onto a plate and slid the second into the waiting skillet. "One of my distant cousins tracked me down to let me know she, her sister and I inherited the family home in Baker City, Washington. It's so big that it actually was the town hotel for a while."

"Have you been there before?" Jimmy slapped a spoonful of sour cream onto the crepe before he wandered over to one of the stools near the center island. "I tried going on the Internet to investigate it when you emailed me a few months ago. It's way out in the boonies, about three hours from civilization."

Mac grinned appreciatively and dished up his own breakfast. "Yeah, so it will be a fun place to visit. I dropped a note to my mom, and she said it's an old, hardscrabble logging town. She hightailed it out of there when she left for college forty-plus years ago and didn't see any reason to return."

Jimmy smirked at him. "What are you going to do after you check out the hotel?"

Mac shrugged and cut into his crepe. "I have a book to finish. I sent my new computer there. I found some interesting furniture during my last book tour, so I shipped that too. Dominique says one of our other cousins has a cleaning company so they G.I.ed the place. My stuff will be waiting in the manager's apartment."

"It will give you a home base." Jimmy stood and went after the coffee pot. "I always close the pub for a vacation from Thanksgiving to New Year's. Got room for company in a few days?"

"It's supposed to be a hotel." Mac chuckled. "There's bound to be an extra room or two. Don't be surprised if I hand you a paintbrush."

"No worries." Jimmy high-fived him. "I've got this. And I won't leave the TV on at night. I don't want to interrupt your Jane Austen marathon—"

"What?" Mac gaped at him. He preferred crime dramas so what the hell was Penrose talking about?

Jimmy continued. "Don't leave on the light in the laundry room or your laptop up and running. I never touch your computer, but I always shut down the other stuff when I get home from the bar. I won't be there to watch your six for a while, so look out for yourself."

"I will." Mac rubbed his jaw thoughtfully. He didn't remember doing any of the things that Penrose mentioned, but oddly enough it didn't come as a surprise. *I always chalked the strange happenings at various hotels, or my computer updating on its own, or getting the weirdest suggestions from Netflix over the past three years as problems with the wiring.*

"Whoops, my bad." Lilly hitched up onto the third stool and listened to the men talk about Mac's plans. She always enjoyed drifting through Jimmy's Craftsman style house after Mac went to bed, and she liked streaming different shows on the big flat-screen in the living-room.

Next time they visited the former soldier, she'd have to be sure she turned it off before he arrived home. Okay, so it was silly to enjoy playing with the new washing machine and dryer and other gadgets, but they were so much fun compared to the ones she'd used in the past. And of course, she had to read through the latest manuscript at night and correct all Mac's mistakes.

When he pulled out his phone and scrolled through emails to show the hotel to Jimmy, she drifted close enough to see pictures of a large Gothic wonder behind a black wrought-iron fence. The building had two-story wings off each side, but the main structure was three floors with dormers in the attic. The elaborate hotel had a covered wrap-around porch, a stone staircase, double doors and big bay windows that extended from the ground floor to the corner towers. It looked like a haunted mausoleum, and she hadn't even arrived yet.

Two hours later, Mac loaded his Jeep Wrangler-Sahara. She followed him through the house as he checked the guestroom and bathroom one last time. "Okay, Lillian. Let's hit the road."

She heaved a sigh, shaking her head. Oh sure, he always acted as if he knew she was really there, but to be honest, he didn't. He'd invited her to join him when he left Seattle a little over three years before and she had.

She didn't regret it for a moment. She enjoyed seeing America from the passenger seat of his SUV. "I just wish you called me, Lilly."

Although she'd spent much of her after-life in western Washington State until she went on the road with Mac, she'd never actually visited Baker City in the Cascade mountains before. Mac drove north on the freeway for almost three hours. They passed various exits for Liberty Valley and continued toward the Canadian border. Finally, he turned onto an east-bound highway. It narrowed from four to two lanes after they passed through the town of Lake Maynard, but Mac kept going.

Fields, evergreens, and farms frequently dotted with grazing beef cattle lined the winding road. Mac slowed down to observe the new speed limit obviously lower because of the rural setting. Occasionally, Lilly glimpsed Cedar Creek through the pastures and trees before the stream vanished from view. Thick layers of snow covered most of the distant mountains.

As they headed into Baker City a short time later, she spotted a large barn on the right-hand side of the street. A sign painted on the building proclaimed, "Summer's Feed and Tack." On the left, was another large structure, the Baker City Mercantile. More cedar shake buildings of varying sizes including two bars, the church, a cemetery, and a vintage schoolhouse lined the road.

Mac found a parking space near the café across the street from the church. "Dominique said she'd meet me here. Time to go check it out and meet a few of the natives."

"Sounds like a winner." She'd been dead for more than seventy years, so Lilly didn't need to wait for him to open the passenger door. She could float through it and join him, but she didn't see the point.

One diner looked so much like another, and Mac hated what he called plastic food at chain restaurants. So, she'd wait for him here. He'd return sooner or later.

She hadn't been in the SUV long when a group of people crossed the street from the church. One of the young girls, a redhead elbowed the one next to her and the pair turned to stare at the Jeep. Then, they headed for the rig rather than joining their friends who waited on the sidewalk for them.

The first girl smiled and beckoned to Lilly. "Come on. We want to talk to you."

"What?" Lilly gaped at the child through the closed window. Granted a few toddlers had seen her at the library and in the occasional bookstore, but this stranger had to be about nine or ten. Too old to see what most folks would consider an apparition.

Well, she wouldn't learn anything sitting here. Lilly drifted through the car door and eyed the pair. Back when she was a child, the nuns insisted she dress up for church, but apparently the rules were different in Baker City. These two wore jeans, sweatshirts and boots.

"Hi. You're new here." The first redhead nodded and smiled politely. "I'm Sophie O'Leary-Hendrickson. Who are you?"

"Be polite." The other girl poked her in the ribs. "We're supposed to say we're glad you're here before you ask lots of questions."

"I'm doing that, Samantha." Sophie looked Lilly up and down. "So, we're glad you're here but you gotta follow the rules or Momma and Daddy will send you to places you don't want to go."

"I'm Lieutenant Lilly Bryce and after dying in a war a long time ago, I'd rather stay here." She stared at the twins, still amazed they saw her. "I came with Mac MacGillicudy, and he went to meet his cousin in the café. What rules are you referring to?"

"The mayor doesn't come to church that much. He's in the cocktail lounge. Go ask him 'bout the rules." Samantha gestured to the cedar-shake building and the second door. "Or you can talk to Mrs. O'Sullivan at the school. She'll tell you."

"I should wait for Mac."

Sophie heaved a sigh. "You can catch up with him later if you want. Baker City isn't that big."

"Anyway, you want to meet the other ghosts and most of them will be talking to the mayor and his friends. They do that every Sunday." Samantha smiled at her. "Besides, we can tell Mister MacGillicudy where you are."

"He won't believe you." Lilly glanced past them toward the door, longing to go inside and see if there really were others like her in town. "He can't see or hear me. It's so strange that you do. I don't understand why."

"We're O'Leary's." Samantha heaved a sigh. "In Baker City, they say we have the *O'Leary Gift* of sight. It means we see and talk to ghosts all the time."

"You must get lonely when you're just around the living," Sophie added. "That's what our first teacher here says. She tells us everyone needs company. Go make some new friends."

"I will. Thank you."

The old-fashioned bell over the door jangled when Mac walked inside the small restaurant. He glanced around the room, noticing he was one of the few customers. Booths with old-time vinyl seats lined the walls, while the adjacent windows provided views of the town. Tables and chairs took up most of the center. Stools squatted near the long counter dividing the dining area from the kitchen.

An elderly man holding a stack of menus came out of the kitchen and around the counter to greet him. "Did you want a table or a booth or a seat at the counter?"

"I'm meeting someone. Dominique MacGillicudy."

"She isn't here yet. She'll be along after she does her 'meet and greet' routine at church, drumming up new clients. I'm Pop MacGillicudy, one of her dad's cousins. Is she showing you a property here?"

Mac held out his hand to shake the older man's. "I'm Mac

MacGillicudy. She emailed and said I inherited the hotel. I came to see it."

"So, you're the writer." A friendly smile warmed his careworn features and Pop gestured toward a table. "Grab a seat before everybody gets here after church. Do you want coffee? Lunch?"

"Sounds good." Mac walked to the end of the room, pulled out a chair and sat down in the corner. It provided a good view of the place. He liked having his back to a wall. Pop had barely brought him a mug of strong, black coffee and a menu before the bell rang again and more customers arrived.

It took time for them to settle in different booths and Pop bustled around the room with more drinks and menus. One of the men who held a flowered diaper bag stood still, listening to his daughters, strawberry-blonde twins who weren't quite tweens yet. Something about the way he carried himself screamed prior service. He signaled for the girls to sit in a booth with their mother who held a sleeping baby, leaving the bag behind. Then, the tall, cowboy type with the typical 'high and tight' military style haircut walked toward Mac.

"Hello. Welcome to Baker City. I'm Rob Hendrickson." His dark eyes narrowed. "Got a minute?"

Mac shrugged. "For now. I'm waiting to see my cousin, Dominique. I'm Mac MacGillicudy."

"I know." Rob dragged out the second chair and sat down, not waiting for an invitation. "You know anything about our town?"

"Not really. My mother says she left for college almost forty-three years ago and hasn't been back since. She never talked about the place and barely did after I told her about the hotel."

"Okay. Quick sitrep. In February 1910, it snowed until there were drifts more than ten feet high. Clouds couldn't get over Mount Carmody. A foot of snow fell each hour, and it continued day after day, night after night. Valentine's Day, it suddenly warmed up, and the snow changed to rain. Then, the avalanches started."

Mac grimaced. "How many?"

"Five in total. Two big ones hit the town, wiping out the train station, the hotel, the school, three shops, and five homes. Sixty people died. It took months to dig out all the bodies. The last funeral was for Mrs. Doireann O'Sullivan, the schoolteacher who'd come from Ireland. After her husband died in a farming accident, she'd returned to teaching and remained at the school until her death."

Mac shook his head. "Wow. Wait a moment. That happened more than a hundred years ago. The hotel was rebuilt, wasn't it? Otherwise, I'd inherit an empty lot. Why are you telling me this old history? Why does it matter?"

"Because all of the dead didn't leave." Rob folded his arms. "Baker City is known for its ghosts. And you brought a new one with you."

"What is this? Harass the new guy in town? Are you nuts?"

"Nope." Rob pushed back the chair and stood. "Your ghost is in the cocktail lounge. Pick her up when you leave. Oh, and if you have issues with the ones at the hotel, let me or my wife know. We'll help you out until you adjust."

Mac froze in his chair for a moment and watched Rob start away. "Okay, say I believe this crapfest. What's my ghost's name?"

"Lieutenant Lilly Bryce. My girls told me she was wearing an old Army uniform and is very nice. We won't have to send her away. Glad you two are friends."

"As long as she's good-looking, we get along just fine."

Shaking his head, Rob walked away. "It's your funeral, Mac. Never mess with the dead."

How could this guy know about the woman I found pictures of in the archives? Mac reached in his flannel shirt pocket and removed the smart phone. He sent a quick text to his mother. '*What do you know about Baker City?*'

He didn't expect an instant answer, but she'd get back to him later rather than sooner. A new arrival came through the restaurant. The tall, slender blonde woman in her mid-thirties greeted Rob Hendrickson with a kiss on his cheek and spoke to his family before she headed toward Mac. She was a perfect fashion plate in a light blue dress that clung to every curve, skimmed her knees and matched her eyes. Dark blue stilettos made her as tall as he was.

He stood as she drew closer. "Hello."

"You must be Mac. I'm your third cousin, Dominique. Did you have any trouble finding the place?"

"I reconned before I left Seattle. Had to use a map because my GPS cut out halfway here."

"Sounds about right. We don't have a lot of towers up here and the weather interferes with cell reception. I wanted to talk to you about the landline at the hotel before I had the phone company restore it." Dominique sat down and nodded at the middle-aged, brown-haired woman who approached with a tray containing a ceramic teapot, a cup and a coffee pot. "This is Pop's daughter, Linda, a distant cousin. She had her cleaning service start on the hotel, but—"

"The main building has three stories, and we didn't finish." Linda placed the teapot and cup in front of Dominique. "Made you a chef salad because you always whine about my burgers. It's not on the menu yet, so let me know if you like it."

"How many MacGillicudys are there?" Mac asked.

Linda and Dominique shared a glance before the younger woman took the initiative. "Some of the old-timers try to say we're not part of the founding families because the MacGillicudys are Scots-Irish newbies who didn't get here until the 1940s."

"Seriously?" Mac laughed, then sobered when he realized his cousins weren't joking. "I didn't know that. My mom never really talked about her relatives. She told me I was named after her dad, my grandfather, but that's it. And I never met him."

"What does your mom do?" Linda topped Mac's cup with fresh coffee. "My dad encouraged me to go to college, but he's different. The rest of the MacGillicudy clan think women should marry out of high school and start popping out babies."

"Yeah, my dad's a chip off that particular block too," Dominique agreed. "My parents were divorced when I was accepted in the graduate art program at Reed College in Oregon. All hell broke loose. Things got worse when other colleges in California wanted me too, but my mom couldn't afford the tuition. My dad made too much money, so financial aid wasn't an option and the court ordered support ended when I turned twenty-two."

"Herman's never been one to let you kids follow your dreams." Linda focused on Mac again. "And your mom?"

"She was a large animal veterinarian in Colorado, specializing in horses before she retired. My stepdad owned the hunter-jumper operation where she worked most of the time. His kids have taken it over now."

CHAPTER TWO

It took all Lilly's courage to drift through the door and enter the cocktail lounge at the café. Even when she was alive, she hadn't been super social, rarely going to dances or accepting dates from overly eager men who couldn't keep their hands to themselves. Death didn't change her all that much, so she didn't miss the newer spirits when they moved on from the library. She hadn't seen that many ghosts when she and Mac toured the U.S. during the last three years.

She decided she wanted to meet the ones in Baker City although it was an adventure she hadn't expected. As soon as she entered the room, she realized the lounge wasn't open for business yet. It was empty—of living people—but filled with other ghosts. She looked around, seeing women in pioneer dresses, a few in flapper attire from the 1920s, and more in what she considered regular civilian clothes. Most of the guys dressed as loggers and miners. Others wore various military uniforms, some like hers dating back to World War Two.

One older man wearing a dark suit sitting in a corner booth seemed totally in charge. That must be the mayor. When she drew closer, Lilly spotted the black fedora on the table in front of him. A gray-haired man in a red plaid shirt that jarred with his orange suspenders sat across from him. Both men turned their attention on her as she approached, sliding out of the booth and rising to their ghostly feet in what used to be considered courtesy.

"Hello. The O'Leary-Hendrickson twins told me to come see you, Mayor—"

"O'Connell." He studied her for a moment, then introduced his companion. "This is Newt O'Leary. He's related to the twins if you go back a while. When did you get here, Lieutenant Bryce?"

"About a half hour ago. Please call me, Lilly." She flicked a glance around the room. "I had no idea there were so many of us here. The girls told me to see you to learn the rules. What are they?"

"There are only a few." He held out his hand toward the booth. "Join us and we'll bring you up to speed."

Once they were seated, the mayor took a deep breath. "One of the first mediums set forth the rules for the spirits who come here."

"She was my great-grandma," Newt said. "The O'Leary's have always had the gift to talk to the dead. Now, it's Cat's job as the town medium to control ghosts. She'll be along soon, and we'll introduce you. Rules are pretty simple. If we break them, she handles the consequences and none of us like those."

"The big one is not to scare children. No blood or gore," the mayor said. "Cat's grandma used to say that if we didn't act like it's a Disney movie set, she'd send us away. And there's no coming back if Cat or her husband, Rob, evict you."

"We help a little if she needs us, but usually she doesn't." It was Newt's turn to add information. "If nobody liked those kind of folks when they were alive, why would we want them around when we're dead?"

Lilly laughed. "That makes perfect sense. What are the other rules?"

"Acting like a poltergeist is allowed as long as you restrict your activities to harassing adults," the mayor said. "No throwing objects, breaking windows, or slamming doors if there are children around."

"And you need to have good reasons for tormenting the living," Newt added. "Otherwise, we won't back you up."

Lilly nodded. "What else?"

"Some of our folks like flashing strange lights, disembodied laughing, screaming and shouting, stomping on wooden floors and stairs so people hear them, ringing doorbells, and playing musical instruments." The mayor grinned. "We don't have problems with that as long as—"

"It's only done to adults," Lilly repeated. "I understand. I don't have a problem with your regs after haunting the library in Seattle until I joined Mac on his travels."

"Who is Mac?" Mayor O'Connell asked. "He must be new here too."

"Mac MacGillicudy. He came here to see the hotel he inherited."

"Oh, we've heard about him. He's the writer." The mayor beckoned to a slender red-haired woman in an olive-drab uniform and the ghost came across the room. Her friendly smile warmed dark gray eyes. "Lieutenant Bridget McElroy joined us after she passed away in Vietnam. She was a nurse too. Our visitor is Lieutenant Lilly Bryce and—"

"I didn't make it home from World War Two." Lilly nodded politely at the other Army officer. "It's nice to meet you."

"Bridget, would you show Lilly around and introduce her to everyone? Be sure she has a chance to meet Cat and Rob when they arrive after church."

On Sundays, church in Baker City was a must. Cat O'Leary-McTavish sat at one of the smaller tables in a corner of the social hall, her husband, Rob, close by, holding their infant daughter, four-month-old Claire. Their older girls were off visiting friends around the room and would return shortly with Devon Sweeney-Barrett and Penny Sinclair.

Cat smiled at Rob. They'd developed a strategy over the past year of using this social hour to let the residents of Baker City share their concerns. After they listened to the living ones, they'd go to the café and visit the cocktail lounge to deal with the ghosts who were even more talkative. The baby woke and began to fuss. Cat reached for her. She took a moment to settle the infant against her chest. In a few minutes, she'd have to discreetly arrange to nurse Claire

Many older spirits admitted Rob had been one of them since he died at Hamburger Hill during the Vietnam War. He'd taken her husband's body when Frazer left it behind following a fatal car accident. As far as most living inhabitants of Baker City and her attorney were concerned, Cat had opted to reconcile with her soon to be ex-husband instead of continuing with the divorce. A few of her close friends knew the truth and accepted it.

When she first moved to the dude ranch, a destination resort on the outskirts of town, Rob had still been in his ghostly mode, determined to haunt her. After dealing with several of his spooky antics, the culmination had been when he played games with the lights, turning them on and off while she attempted to prepare supper. It'd shocked the twins when she'd sent him to his room for two hours.

Of course, Cat decided she was dealing with an imaginary friend. Turnabout was fair play, she thought, eyeing the ruggedly handsome man across the table from her. It'd amazed her to discover he was real and now they were parents again. Cat opened her blouse, arranging it and her bra so Claire could nurse, gasping when the hungry baby latched onto her nipple. She arranged the shawl over her shoulders to be discreet.

An hour later, after lunch at Pop's Cafe, Cat took the opportunity to head for the restroom, leaving Rob to supervise the twins and take care of Claire who slept in her carrier. She was such a good baby. Instead of turning left and immediately returning to the restaurant, Cat turned right and walked into the cocktail lounge. She glanced around the room and spotted one of her oldest ghostly friends.

Lieutenant Bridget McElroy sat at one of the tables near the frosted front windows. Master Sergeant Raven Barlow, a thin, dark-haired wraith in camouflage fatigues and combat boots had joined her as well as a new spirit, well new to Cat, although the twins had mentioned her at lunch. The stranger was a strawberry blonde in a World War Two, dress Army uniform. When Raven said something, the other woman laughed. Amusement lit her stunning features and the hazel eyes that almost matched her brown jacket.

Deciding to start her rounds with the female veterans, Cat crossed the room, smiling at the newest arrival. "Hello, I'm Cat O'Leary-McTavish. I think you've already met my daughters."

"Sophie and Samantha? They were so nice, and they told me how to find everyone else. I'm Lilly Bryce." The ghostly woman gestured to her companions. "Bridget and Raven have been telling me stories about Baker City. I never thought I'd meet other haunts here."

Cat smiled and sat in the empty fourth chair. "Where are you from?"

"I grew up in Seattle." Lilly tilted her head to one side, obviously thinking of something she hadn't considered before. "My parents died in the Spanish Flu pandemic in 1919 when I was two, so I ended up in foster homes and orphanages. I don't even remember them, and Heaven knows if they came here."

"I'll ask around," Cat said. "I've only been here fourteen months. I haven't met everyone yet."

"At some point you joined the Army, Lilly," Raven said. "Just like me and Bridget."

Lilly nodded. "I was a nurse, and I volunteered after Pearl Harbor. I died when the Germans bombed the hospital in Italy where I worked."

"My turn to share. I grew up in Baker City, on the family farm," Bridget said. "I wanted adventures, not a husband. When the war started, I had to wait until I turned twenty-one and then I enlisted."

"The mayor said you were a nurse too." Lilly tilted her head, curious. "You're an officer, aren't you?"

"Now, I am. I saved my pay so I could go to nursing school. Once I graduated, I returned to the Army as a commissioned officer and went to Korea. I was one of the first nurses sent to Vietnam to teach the techniques I learned nursing in combat and died in a helicopter crash." Bridget glanced at Raven. "I know about you, but Lilly doesn't."

"I enlisted to get money for college too. My best friend and I wanted to be teachers. Farming hasn't changed that much. Our folks couldn't afford college either." Raven shrugged a ghostly shoulder. "Went to Afghanistan on my last combat tour. Didn't make it home. An IED took me —." She paused, then shook her head. "We always said to 'embrace the suck' and—"

"What does that mean?" Lilly asked.

"We'd have called it a SNAFU in our war," Bridget told her. "Situation Normal, All Fouled Up."

"That's about right." Raven nodded. "Although, we never said, "fouled." We were as crude as the guys. I come to Baker City to hang out with my BFF, Sully Murphy and her family too, especially my namesake—the baby she named after me."

Cat slipped away when the women began defining more acronyms used in the military, most of which included various profanities, particularly the 'F' word. She could have remained longer, but other ghosts wanted to visit with her, and the mayor always had news to share. It certainly seemed as if Lilly Bryce wasn't a problem. She appeared to fit in fine and if that wasn't the case, Cat knew she'd hear about any issues later. Just because some of the local residents were dead, it didn't mean they were quiet.

Over lunch, Mac heard more about the town. Dominique explained Baker City was established by the O'Learys, the McElroys, the Sweeneys, the O'Connells, the Garveys, the O'Neills, and the O'Sullivans. Seven Irish boys met on a ship bound for America in the late 1880s and came west to Washington Territory. Since two Murphy men served with their descendants in World War One, they made their way here too.

"Some of the Murphys run an organic farm. When we decide what we're going to do with the hotel, we may want to consider having them as suppliers." Dominique stirred a spoonful of honey into her peppermint tea. "I'm not sure about how to attract guests."

"Who came in the past?"

Dominique shrugged. "We won't get the same ones. Due to climate change, we don't get a decent amount of snow, and the ski resort closed years ago. Most hikers only do day trips. Baker City is more of a bedroom community now. A lot of residents work elsewhere, leaving early in the morning and coming back in the evening."

Mac rubbed his jaw thoughtfully. "What kind of festivals does the town have?"

"The only time we really see a lot of visitors is in October when the Baker City Business Association hosts the Haunted Town Festival to raise money."

He drank the last of his coffee. "I've heard of haunted houses, but never a town."

"We started last year and then expanded to more buildings this year. Everybody jumps in to help. I let them use a wing of the hotel for the event." Dominique paused for thought. "It's a lot of fun. Next year—"

"I met Rob Hendrickson, and he claimed there are several ghosts here."

Relief swept across Dominique's face, and she relaxed. "Okay, that makes things a lot easier. He's married to *The O'Leary*, the town medium and the two of them handle the spooky stuff. It's easier to go along to get along when things start bouncing in the night."

"I thought he was just hassling the new guy in town."

"Oh no, Rob wouldn't do that." Dominique tilted her head to one side and laughed softly. "He steps up even when the local haunts do their thing in the daylight for that matter. Are you ready to visit the hotel?"

"Let's do it." Mac picked up the check and followed her toward the counter.

Granted as a writer, he had an active imagination, but he didn't believe the ghost stories he'd heard today. Of course, he wouldn't tell the people here that they had a credibility gap. He'd wait and learn more about the community. Maybe there was something in the water they drank, the food they ate from local farms or the air they breathed that created so many fantasies.

Outside, Dominique gestured toward her fairly new four-wheel-drive Jeep and suggested he follow her to the hotel. He agreed. She knew where they were going, and he didn't. Before she reached the vehicle, a petite blonde approached. She had to be in her early thirties, but she didn't dress like it. She wore a tight-fitting sequined tube-top that displayed her full breasts and faded, glued-on, slashed jeans tucked into spike-heeled, bling-covered, western boots. Bright lipstick on the full lips matched her red fingernail polish.

If she'd been taller, she could have been a model. Her face reminded him of the quote, "Is this the face that launched a thousand ships?" She was beautiful and undoubtedly knew it. Golden hair framed a stunning face with high cheekbones, angled dark reddish-brown eyebrows, a heart-shaped and dimpled chin.

Dominique hesitated and then introduced the younger woman. "Mac, this is my sister, Veronika. She's the third owner of the hotel."

Veronika flashed a brilliant smile. "Did Dommi tell you our dad wants to buy the place? He'll pay for it as-is and we won't have to waste time or money fixing it up first."

"And he'll demolish it." Dominique stiffened, her hands knotting into fists. "He plans to bulldoze the town and turn it into a gravel pit."

"Don't be such a *Debbie Downer*. Come on. Baker City is falling apart and even you can't find buyers for every house here."

"I can try."

"You're being silly." Veronika heaved a dramatic sigh. "This year, you used the money from the trust to repair the roof, buy mattresses and other furniture and update part of the wiring. Now, there's nothing left until the next installment in January." She turned to Mac. "If you and I agree, we can control what happens. Selling that crappy hotel to Daddy makes sense."

"I have to see it first." Mac nodded at Dominique. "When you emailed me about those repairs, I agreed. Now, let's go do a walk-through and see what's next."

She relaxed slightly. "Okay. I know Veronika has fits whenever I get another building on the state historical register, but I really think it'd be a great promo opportunity. The school, church, café, and mercantile already have their plaques. The feedstore should have one next year."

"You only do that to annoy Daddy."

"And to save my hometown." Dominique turned away.

Amused, Mac suppressed a smile and headed for his SUV. Behind the wheel, he glanced at the passenger seat. He didn't know if a ghost was there or not. He decided to speak to her the way he had for the last three years. "All right, Lillian. Let's go check what may turn out to be our new home."

The large hotel took up a city block. Mac parked between Dominique's Jeep and Veronika's Subaru in front of the 'U'-shaped building. Well, it was more of a horseshoe shape, not truly a traditional 'U', he thought. The photos Dominique sent hadn't truly done justice to the old, moss-covered, brick structure. Some of the mortar was deteriorating and the bricks separated from each other. The place needed a power wash.

He walked beside his cousins through the gate toward the wrap-around front porch. He glimpsed a circular driveway lined with evergreens. It curled through the neglected lawns to the main entrance. "Why didn't we drive up?"

"Several trees fell in the last big windstorm and blocked that road." Dominique gestured to her right and then to her left. "The gates on the exit lane need repair."

"Daddy says you should sell them for scrap."

"They're wrought iron, designed by our great-grandmother and made by her oldest son, the first MacGillicudy blacksmith. I'll have them restored as soon as I find a craftsman to do it. " Dominique glared at her sister before leading the way up the wide stairs. "It's family history."

Mac made a mental note they needed to add a close-in parking lot for guests if they decided to re-open the hotel. For now, he was just on an inspection tour. "So, where did people leave their vehicles? There isn't enough room on the main street."

"You can't tell from here, but there's more parking behind the hotel. Once we're inside, you'll also have a view of the delivery area near the kitchen."

Veronika heaved another dramatic sigh. "Back in the day, their drivers dropped off guests at the front door. After the staff unloaded their luggage, the chauffeurs drove around to park in the back. Like Daddy says, Baker City doesn't attract that kind of clientele anymore."

"Maybe not, but it doesn't mean the town is totally dead yet." Dominique unlocked the ornately carved front doors, pushed one open to reveal an elaborate foyer. "We have twenty guestrooms on this level, thirty on the second floor and twenty-five on the third for a total of seventy-five."

Winter sunlight streamed through the skylights and Mac gazed at the domed ceiling three stories overhead. "Now, that's what I call an architectural feature."

Dominique laughed. "You haven't seen anything yet."

"I'll keep that in mind." He turned his attention to the room. To the far left were two reception counters with old-style luggage carts nearby. Adjacent to that, he spotted an elevator. A matching one was off to the right, apparently for the other wing. Like most hotel lobbies, this one had tables and chairs as well as couches and loveseats. The stone fireplace provided a focal point for most guests. The chimney undoubtedly needed to be cleaned and would require some kind of maintenance.

They walked through the lobby. A large, grand staircase to the upper regions demanded attention, but a wide hallway granted access to the rest of the main floor. To his left, he saw a library complete with an old-style, antique wooden ladder that allowed someone to reach the top shelves. To his right, there was a huge parlor, and he could almost imagine ladies in historic gowns, gloves and fancy hats gathering for afternoon tea.

Back on his left, he spotted an office. He recognized the rolltop desk along with the oversize rocking chair he'd found on his travels and saw boxes containing his new desktop computer. During the tour, Dominique pointed out several bathrooms that still needed repairs or updating, all of which simply had toilets and sinks. She explained the actual guest bedrooms had ensuites with tubs. A few had been modernized and even had showers.

Twin dining rooms were on either side of the hall, and then a professionally designed chef's eat-in kitchen with a big butler's pantry and adjoining laundry room. French doors opened onto the wraparound porch.

Veronika led the way to the next set of doors. "This is the manager's quarters, but Dommi had our cousin, Linda clean it for you. If you decide to live here, there are bigger, nicer rooms upstairs."

"Fair enough." Mac entered the suite, scanning the small living room. A couch faced the fireplace with a flat-screen TV above the mantel. A matching recliner sat next to a table complete with a lamp, perfect for reading. There was even a desk for his laptop with a sliding door close by. It gave access to the porch, suitable if he wanted to drink his morning coffee outside. Of course, he'd have to go into the kitchen to make it.

He walked across the room and glanced into the bedroom. A king-size bed, dresser, a walk-in closet and an ensuite bathroom. This one had a waterfall shower. A door on the far side of the bathroom revealed access to the office.

Mac looked over his shoulder at the two women. "This is better than I expected."

"Welcome home." Dominique flashed a quick smile. "I forgot to tell you about the other inhabitants here."

Mac chuckled. "More ghost stories?"

"Nope. Well, I'm not sure about them. But you're going to discover we have a feral cat colony." Dominique gestured toward the kitchen. "There's food in the pantry for them. Since you live here, please feed them."

"Our cousin, Robin is a veterinarian." Veronika gave one more dramatic sigh. "Dommi and I keep telling her she should take all of them away for good, but she won't. She brings them back as soon as they're fixed and have their shots."

"Linda's son, Dray is taming them and finding permanent homes for the entire kitty clan." Dominique shot another glare at her sister.

"Stop trying to piss off everyone in the family. None of us want them dead and that's what would happen if they ended up at a shelter."

"Hey, you're the one who has fits about stray animals and kids that destroy property values," Veronika retorted. "When people argue with you about the critters, you always offer to have the county Animal Control officers come in and remove them."

"It's how I make the family step up and stop bitching at me."

"Don't threaten me, Dominique." Mac held up his hand. "I don't mind feeding them. One of the hotels where I stayed on my last book tour had cats for rent. I didn't intend to pay extra to have one share my room, but I didn't have a choice after one of them decided I was her buddy."

CHAPTER THREE

She'd spent so much time hanging out with the other ghosts in the cocktail lounge at Pop's Café, it came as no surprise she hadn't noticed when Mac left. Bridget gave directions to the hotel and Lilly headed there. Like most experienced ghosts, all she had to do was think of where she wanted to be, and she arrived a short time later.

She spotted Mac's Jeep Wrangler-Sahara and glanced inside. His suitcases and old Army duffels still filled the rear compartment, so he hadn't moved into his proverbial new home yet. She floated into the building and glanced at the reception counter. She nodded at the silver-haired ghost behind the front desk. "Hello. I'm Lilly Bryce."

"Donal MacGillicudy." He nodded and smiled. "Do you need a room?"

She drifted closer. "I came with Mac MacGillicudy, and I enjoy haunting him. That isn't a problem, is it?"

"Not for us. He's in the manager's apartment with our great grand-granddaughters, Dominique and Veronika. My wife, Florence is escorting them around the place."

"I'll go find them." Lilly waved at him before she headed off to see everything in her new home.

It was so spacious. One room flowed into another. She paused to look in the library and imagined the shelves filled with books. In the kitchen, a calico cat came out of the pantry to escort her. They followed the sound of voices and discovered Mac in a suite of rooms close by. A gray-haired woman in a pink flowered house-dress stood watching the three living people who apparently didn't have a clue she was there. She turned a blue-eyed gaze on Lilly when she came through the door.

"Good afternoon." Lilly advanced to greet her. "I'm Lilly Bryce. Are you—?"

"Florence MacGillicudy." The older ghost studied her for a moment. "You're new here. Why don't we leave this bunch and go find my other guests? The ladies will be gathering in the parlor for tea. Not that we drink it anymore, but we still enjoy our little rituals."

"I'd enjoy that." Lilly flicked a glance toward Mac.

Flecks of gray threaded through his short black hair. His close-cropped beard emphasized the firm jaw and rugged features. As always he wore faded blue jeans tucked into the beloved old combat, jump-style boots, and a black sweater with epaulets over a white shirt. She wasn't the only one who enjoyed looking at him. The two blondes followed him around eagerly like lovestruck teenagers.

Why do I have to share him with these two bimbos? He's not really interested in them, is he? Lilly shook her head. *Okay, time to stop being silly. I'm dead and at some point, he may find someone to share his life. It won't be me. Grow up. I'll enjoy what I have for as long as I have it. And him!*

Dominique's first stop after she left the hotel was her real estate office, a one-woman show on Sundays. After she locked the front door behind her, she did a version of the victory dance she reserved for big sales. She hadn't expected her distant cousin to be such a hunk of rugged masculinity or for him to willingly move into the hotel right away. Yes, she'd arranged to have the manager's suite prepped for him and stocked the kitchen. Was she naive to hope he shared her dream of saving the hotel and Baker City?

Some real estate brokers had separate offices, but she preferred the desk at the back of the main room so she could supervise her agents and greet the clientele. She turned on her computer and pulled up her emails. She deleted the advertisements and political solicitations, then proceeded to answer questions from clients and potential clients. With Thanksgiving only a few days away, it'd be a short work week. And she had a buyer who planned to open an auto-repair business as soon as she found a garage and a nearby house for him. He'd be in town for the holiday and wanted to view properties next Sunday.

The next message that popped up was from her old college friend and sorority sister, Claire Rocklin. They had a lot in common since both of them were in real estate. "My place. Dinner at three o'clock on Thursday with the senior tenants. Bring wine and sparkling cider for those who don't drink. Connor's cooking so if you're not here, I'll send Tony after you."

Dominique laughed, shaking her head before she typed a response. "I'll be there. Don't let the boys make you crazy."

Claire operated her very successful brokerage, Rocklin Properties, and had several offices around Seattle. Her former stepbrother, Tony Baldusi had been investing in the company from the day Claire started the business twelve years before. When he retired from the Army six months ago, he'd shown up at the main headquarters and demanded to be put to work. Claire sent stormy emails and texts on a regular basis, complaining about him or her twin brother, Connor.

Dominique didn't take the bitching too seriously. If Claire didn't want to tolerate the men in her life, she certainly was strong enough to send both of them packing. Even if she didn't admit it, she loved them dearly. However, Dominique knew better than to point that out.

She added the liquid refreshments to her shopping list. She already planned to pick up the tempura or poster paint she'd ordered at the hardware store, and she could swing by the mercantile for the wine and cider. One of her favorite holiday traditions was painting winter scenes on the windows of the various businesses in Baker City. *I already know what Pop wants at the café and Maxine Garvey at the general store also told me what she does, but I still need to talk to Summer at the feedstore. I'll do that tomorrow. I'll stop by the hotel and ask Mac what he thinks. Do we want to do Santa, his sleigh and all the reindeer on the windows closest to the main drag?*

Mid-afternoon, Veronika headed out of town. She usually spent time on Sundays with her father, Herman MacGillicudy in nearby Lake Maynard. It worked out well for both of them. She told him the latest gossip about what was happening in Baker City, and he gave her money for her living expenses, enough that she didn't have to work like her older brother and sister. *Yes, I'm his favorite child and life is good.*

When she pulled into the drive of the large house in a gated community, she saw a late model, black Lexus parked next to her father's white Cadillac. She grimaced at the sight of Liam O'Leary's vehicle. She hadn't seen him since last summer, but her dad's best friend always made her skin crawl. It didn't do any good to bitch about him or his sleazy investment company.

Her father always reminded her that he and Liam grew up together and had been buds for more than sixty years. It didn't matter if the guy was persona-non-grata with the Baker City medium, his daughter, Cat. Nothing he did offended Herman, or so he claimed. Yet her father wasn't all bad, Veronika thought. He was the one who ratted out Liam for abducting his granddaughters last year in an attempt to force Cat to give him the dude ranch she'd won in a contest.

Veronika debated leaving and checking in later, but the front door opened, and her father strolled out on the porch. He waved a greeting and beckoned for her to join him. Taking a deep breath, she parked her Subaru and climbed out. She grabbed her leopard-print jacket from the passenger seat and slung it around her shoulders. She wouldn't stay long. All she had to do was tell him that Mac had finally arrived and was looking over the hotel. Tall, gray-haired, in an expensive dark suit, white shirt and tie, Liam O'Leary sauntered out to stand next to her father, a stocky man with neatly trimmed silver blond hair.

A broad smile filled Herman's ruddy face and warmed the pale blue eyes. "Hey, baby girl! Come in and share your news."

Hours later, classic country music poured from the jukebox when Veronika entered the cocktail lounge that night. She glanced around the room, checking out the guys at the pool tables. She'd stopped by her apartment and changed clothes, opting for a short denim skirt, a skimpy, white lace crop-top, blue fishnet stockings and high-heeled western boots with lots of bling. She always flaunted all her assets. She'd learned a long time ago that men preferred talking to her chest, rather than looking her in the face. And if letting them stare at her boobs meant they paid for her drinks, well it was a cheap way to get free booze.

Her cousin Linda was behind the bar waiting on the few remaining customers who'd probably leave before the place closed at midnight. Her dad must be closing the adjoining restaurant. Veronika hitched up on a stool and waited. She preferred Canadian whisky and strong mixed drinks, but after her last DUI ticket, she'd tapered off on those. She ordered a beer when Linda reached the end of the bar.

"Did Reverend Tommy or his wife, Virginia find you?" Linda put the glass on a napkin. "They missed you at church today."

"I'm not much for being preached at." Veronika took a small sip of beer. "It's never been my thing."

Linda frowned, resting one hand on the counter. "Virginia's not going to sign off on your community service hours unless you actually do them, Ronnie. And they have to be completed before Christmas."

"Daddy's lawyer says he'll get me an extension." Veronika swallowed more beer. "This town is enough to make anyone crazy. Everybody knows everyone else's business."

"It's because we're one big extended family." Linda wiped the old wooden bar with a damp towel. "Do the right thing. You don't want Chief O'Connell tracking you down and taking you to the food bank to help prep the Thanksgiving baskets tomorrow and seeing to it that you're there on Tuesday when it's time to pass them out."

Veronika grimaced, slid off the stool and sauntered to where Jack Madison waited until Ted Fenwick, the local tech guy racked the balls on the pool table. Dark brown hair curled around his shoulders to the purple Huskies sweatshirt he wore. His faded blue jeans were nearly as ragged as her favorite ones, but she doubted he'd bought them at the mall like she had.

The twenty-somethings were two of her favorite guys. She often wondered if they knew she'd slept with both of them at different times, but she didn't say so and neither did they. She put her glass of beer on a nearby table. "Okay if I join you?"

"Only if you promise not to run the table." Ted laughed and winked at her.

"Don't give her any ideas." A sunshine blond, Jack grinned, his smile warming the spring green eyes. In a flannel shirt, hacked-off, ankle-length jeans and lace-up boots, muscled from years of logging, he hated dressing up and she knew he'd undoubtedly worn that outfit to church and Sunday dinner at his parents' house.

Her father had offered a bonus for getting Mac on her side to ensure he agreed to sell the hotel. She'd invite Jack to come home with her tonight. He wouldn't complain. Then after breakfast tomorrow, she'd convince him to take his chainsaw and help Mac clear the driveway in exchange for some of the timber. Jack usually complained about the logging company he worked for always closing Thanksgiving week. This would provide the opportunity for him to sell firewood to the locals, and she'd look like a good person to Mac. It was a win-win for everyone.

Before she left, Dominique showed Mac the driveway that led to the parking lot at the rear of the hotel. She'd given him keys to the front and back doors, along with an old-fashioned master key to the various guestrooms. She explained the individual ones were kept at the reception desk. Once he moved his Jeep closer to the rear entrance, he unloaded his gear.

He spent the afternoon unpacking. He hung his jackets, shirts and jeans in the closet. The rest of his clothes went in the dresser. A long-haired calico sat on the bed and supervised. When he went into the kitchen to make a cup of coffee, the cat followed. Two half-grown kittens, a tortoiseshell female and an orange male arrived, and the trio escorted him to their dish in the pantry. He filled it with dry food from the sack Dominique had left.

He heard vintage swing music start playing and saw a radio sitting on a shelf near the farmhouse sink in the kitchen. One of his cousins must have it on a timer. He left it alone, enjoying the magic of Doris Day's voice, promising to take a 'Sentimental Journey'. He glanced around the room.

It'd been upgraded to commercial standards. White walls, white ceiling, brown cupboards, fluorescent lighting, laminate wood-planked floors, plus natural light from the large windows during the day. A breakfast area with an older wooden table and six matching chairs were close to the French doors that opened onto the outside deck.

The counters were topped with granite and so was the large matching center island. The room even had new appliances, thank-fully white rather than stainless-steel ones because he hated polishing those. He liked the commercial-grade, six burner electric range with its large oven. There were two more ovens set in the wall. He could prepare some amazing meals here.

When he inspected the refrigerator and cupboards, he found the makings for his favorite chocolate chip cookies. He stirred up a batch while the disc jockey played 'Boogie-Woogie Bugle Boy' followed by

'Chattanooga Choo-Choo' and other popular songs from the 1940s. With the first tray of cookies in the oven, he started a grocery list.

Sure, Dominique had provided the basics, but she didn't know he preferred butter to margarine, or to grind his own coffee beans or to bake bread rather than buy it. Now that he had a real kitchen of his own, he could prepare his sourdough starter. He used it for pancakes, breads, rolls, desserts and anything else that appealed to him.

The timer buzzed and he removed the cookies, sliding a second tray into the oven. When he was growing up, his stepdad always made fun of him for liking to cook, saying it wasn't very manly. Mac pointed out there were many male chefs. During his Army days, he visited his mother's family when he was on leave. When his stepdad or stepbrothers taunted him, Mac simply said that cooking distracted him from memories of what he and his buddies called, their 'sixty-second solutions'- how long it took them to sneak up and kill someone.

His mom asked him to stop sharing such gruesome stories and Mac agreed, provided everyone else remembered their manners. When they didn't, he headed off to the neighborhood bar and played pool with the locals. He usually won because they were drinking beer while he stuck to sodas. He hummed along with the radio, wondering how Dominique or her sister knew he liked old-time melodies. Had they read his books? Was that why they realized he preferred the world he'd created for his stories to this one?

Lilly perched on a stool at the center island and watched Mac putter around the room. When she finished visiting the ghosts in the drawing room, she'd come looking for him. She'd turned on the radio and found a favorite station. She wasn't surprised to see him start baking cookies in the kitchen. Other guys might tinker with their cars in the garage or build stuff in a toolshed or even play video games on their phones. That wasn't Mac's style. For him, it was baking first, followed by cooking elaborate breakfasts, lunches or dinners.

"If I was still alive, I'd pig out on those even if I prefer your version of Peanut Butter Blossoms." Lilly breathed in the delicious scent of the first batch of large chocolate chip cookies when he took them out of the oven. "I'd have to join a gym, and I don't think Baker City has one of those."

That idea reminded her of the amenities in the different hotels where they stayed when they roamed throughout the country. Many of them had swimming pools and work-out facilities for their patrons. The memories prompted her to rise to her ghostly feet and go exploring. Florence MacGillicudy had shown her most of the rooms on the first floor, but the building was huge. There had to be more to discover.

After she left the kitchen, Lilly drifted through the wall of the pantry and found herself in a hallway that led to a locked door. It didn't stop her. When she went through it, she was on the wrap-around porch. She returned inside. She spotted another door. When she floated past it, she found a staircase. It made sense that one flight went up because there were three stories, but why did another go down? There must be a basement.

Time to explore, she thought, and headed down the flight of stairs. If she wasn't dead, she'd have to duck several cobwebs or brush them away from her face. She was, so she didn't.

When she entered the basement, she found several rooms. One was a huge laundry where the staff must wash the linens for the bedrooms. A second held cleaning supplies. A third had maintenance equipment. Once she was past the staff area, there was a media room with theater style seats and a large screen on the wall. And finally, she found a gym. After jaunting around America with Mac for the last three years, she recognized the equipment. There were various kinds of cardio machines, weight machines and strength training devices from treadmills to stationary bicycles, to yoga mats to jump ropes.

Did Mac know about this level of the building? If not, how could she show him?

When she started back the way she came, she found an elevator near the restrooms. Hurray! Fun times awaited. She loved playing with new toys. Inside it, she studied the wall panel and chose the letter, 'M' for the main floor. It took a minimal amount of energy to send it flying upward. Yippee!

The doors slid open and revealed the reception area. She waved at Donal MacGillicudy who sat behind the counter waiting for guests. "I found the basement. Now, all I have to do is figure out a way to get Mac down there."

"Easy peasy." Donal winked at her. "Ask the cats to help. Then, he'll have to go find them."

CHAPTER FOUR

After dinner, Mac cleaned the kitchen. He barely finished loading the dishwasher when the calico arrived, winding through his legs and meowing plaintively. She wanted something, but he didn't know what. Her dishes in the pantry were still full but he didn't see her kittens anywhere. He followed her into the hallway, and she led him to a partially open door.

He pushed it wider and glanced inside, finding two sets of stairs. The cat rubbed against his leg before she headed down one flight and he went after her, using the flashlight on his phone. He brushed away the cobwebs that sprouted from the walls, draped along the bannisters and seemed too close to his face. When they reached the bottom of the stairs, he spotted little pawprints on the dusty tile floor. More cobwebs hung from the ceiling and in the corners. Mentally, he made a note to either clean the basement himself or arrange for his cousin, Linda, to do it.

He glanced around, finding a bank of light switches and flipped them on, although not all of the overhead lights worked. The basement was cold, and he saw a thermostat on the wall. It read sixty-eight degrees, but he didn't believe it. He'd contact the utility company tomorrow and have the heat pump checked. Dominique had said it was a new one, so why wasn't it working?

Plus, he needed to change a few fluorescent bulbs. He'd pick up new ones at the hardware store tomorrow. For an instant, he thought he glimpsed the shadowy figure of a woman watching him. He shook his head, and the vision faded in the dim light. Sometimes, his imagination ran away with him. He and the cat proceeded to explore the staff area. Next, he found a small theater, another room with two pool tables as well as three arcade game machines and two pinball ones as well as a gym where they discovered the kittens romping and playing with other cats of varying sizes and colors.

More cold winter air brushed his face, and he tracked the breeze to an open window. That must be how his four-legged visitors found their way inside. He closed the window and called them. The calico and her babies trailed behind him when he headed for the stairs. The rest were more wary, and he hoped they'd realize he didn't intend to hurt them.

On the way to the main floor, he noticed two elevators, one that must have been for human guests and the other for hotel employees, but he opted not to try them. He'd wait until they were inspected, and he knew how reliable they were. He wasn't getting stuck in a small metal cage between floors. Just the idea of being trapped in a metallic box made him shudder. Back upstairs, he left the door to the basement slightly ajar.

He didn't want any of the feline contingent confined down there, especially since he'd closed the window that they apparently used for entrance and egress. He topped off the food and water dishes, then found another, larger bowl and filled it with dry kibble. He eyed the original cat. "I don't want you, your family or friends going hungry."

She purred a response. Then, she and her kids followed him through the kitchen to the living-room in the manager's apartment. He contemplated turning on a movie, before deciding to work on his new manuscript instead. He still hadn't heard back from his mother, so he sent another text. If all else failed, he'd ask his questions when he called on Thanksgiving.

Lilly curled up on the couch and watched Mac type away on his laptop. It surprised her that he hadn't unpacked the new desktop computer, but he'd probably do it tomorrow. She smiled when the cats joined her. She wished she could truly pet them, feel the softness of their fur against her fingers, but that wasn't possible. Her hand floated above the mother's hair and the older female stretched and purred.

The kittens climbed on Lilly's ghostly lap and snuggled down for a nap. She knew if Mac looked at them, he wouldn't see her. He'd think they slept on the couch cushions. When they were in the basement, she thought he'd seen her accompanying him. He hadn't said anything, and she decided he didn't know he wasn't alone.

"This place feels like the home I never had before," she told the cats.

She had more new places to explore. Tomorrow afternoon, she'd meet Florence MacGillicudy. The other ghost had promised to show her the rest of the hotel and Lilly couldn't wait to see the guestrooms. There were supposed to be two historic, luxurious honeymoon suites and a terrific view from the rotunda on the second and third floors.

"I just wish you'd come with us," she told Mac.

He didn't pay attention, his gaze focused on the computer screen in front of him. By the intent look on his face, he had an issue with something in the book. He muttered a swear word when he wasn't able to reach the Internet and verify some obscure facts.

Well, she'd read the story later and correct whatever was wrong. It wouldn't be the first time. That was her job, and she loved it.

Monday morning while Mac drank his first cup of coffee, he watched the sunrise through the large kitchen windows. Streaks of red, orange and yellow light painted the snowcapped mountains in the distance. Four pickup trucks pulled into the hotel parking lot, one towing a wood-chipper on a trailer. Wondering what was happening, he went outside to greet his guests, a cluster of young men, most of them in their twenties. A big blond appeared to be the leader of the group.

He waved at Mac, strolling toward him. "Morning. I'm Jack Madison. Did Veronika text you about the trees on the driveway?"

"Didn't hear from her." Mac pulled his phone out of his pocket and eyed the screen. "No signal."

"No worries." A brown-haired, bearded man wearing a toolbelt around his narrow waist spoke. "I'm Ted Fenwick. Once I update your phone lines, add a new modem and install high-speed Internet, you should get all your messages. Meantime, Ronnie ran the pool table on us a few times last night at Pop's. For once, she didn't want money. She sent us instead."

"The logging company we work for is closed this week because of the holiday." Jack gestured to some of the men in rugged clothes. "She thought if we cleared the driveway, you'd split the timber with us, and we could sell our share of the firewood, make up for lost wages. Dray's boss let him borrow the chipper so we can clean up the branches."

"I'm Dray MacGillicudy." The youngest guy, a lanky teenager, waved at Mac. Black hair curled down to his shoulders. He had distinctive angled eyebrows and electric blue eyes. "You met my mom, Linda yesterday. She said to tell you that she'll be here to clean today with her full-time people and the part-timers will be here when they get out of school."

"What part-timers?" Jack grinned. "Aren't they leaving for Thanksgiving?"

"Not until Wednesday morning." Dray must be accustomed to explaining family dynamics because he glanced past his friend to Mac. "I'm adopted. My bio-mom lives outside of town and her step-daughters, and my cousin work part-time for my mom."

"Amazing everybody gets along so well." Mac pointed toward the kitchen. "I found a big urn in the pantry, so I'll put on the coffee. When you're ready for something hot, come inside."

"Sounds like a winner." Ted carried a duffle bag in one hand and a toolbox in the other. He nodded to his friends. "I'm the lucky one. I'll think of you guys while I'm upgrading the system inside. Dray, you said your boss is stopping by with a couple electricians. Do you know what time?"

"Not until Wednesday afternoon. He had to pick up a bunch of turkeys and hams in Lake Maynard first thing this morning for the food bank here. Then, he has projects down south to supervise."

The arrival of a half-dozen men ready to work was a shock. Mac hadn't seen a detail like this since his Army days. And he didn't have to pay them. They wanted half the fallen wood which was more than fair. And he owed his cousin for rounding them up. He'd have to take her out for dinner or buy her flowers.

"This is great. Thanks again." Mac eyed Ted Fenwick. "Glad you're here to do the Internet. Writing my books requires a lot of research because they're set in the 1940s. I couldn't do it last night, but I was still able to draft two chapters."

"Hey, any luck at all, I'll have you up and running tonight." Ted shrugged. "If I'm wrong, it will be tomorrow or the next day."

Lilly followed a bearded young man in jeans and a purple sweatshirt from the kitchen to the study where he put down his bag and toolbox. As usual, Mac didn't sleep a lot, so he spent hours on his laptop last night, writing the latest book. Now, the stranger dropped to his knees and analyzed the phone jack. In moments, he'd removed the cover and began inspecting the wires.

None of the visitors could see her or knew she'd listened to their conversation with Mac and now this one, Ted Fenwick, was working away on connecting them to the outside world. She was grateful. It meant she could watch TV tonight and stream the latest *Bridgerton* episode. She glanced at the wall when Donal drifted into the room.

"Why do we have company?" He studied the young man, then nodded. "Has to be a Fenwick. They've always worked in communications. I hired them to install more phones in the hotel when we re-opened it after our kids grew up and left home."

"Have they lived in Baker City for a long time? I don't remember meeting any at the café yesterday."

"Might not have been there yet. They tend to show up at the end of the day." Donal shrugged a thin, ghostly shoulder. "The Fenwicks come in on the Sweeney side and the O'Sullivan founding families. The first Sweeney hated being tied down and living in town, so he headed into the hills with his Native American wife. That didn't stop their kids from marrying into other families or bringing their new husbands and wives here. Everybody's related somehow, but nobody's too fond of some of the folks in my clan."

"Why not?" Lilly folded her arms. "Mac is a good guy and your great-granddaughters seem decent."

"They're not like my grandson, their father. Herman is a chip off my father's block. He won the hotel in a crooked card game. I inherited it when he was murdered." Donal sighed and shook his head. "Folks weren't very friendly when Florence and I moved here. Didn't have much choice because this place was all we had. Couldn't make a living on our farm outside of town. Gave it to one of my cousins who was single at the time. Once it was a paying proposition, he married, and his kin kept it for years. Meanwhile, this place provided a home for us and our six children."

"Mac's mother lives out of state. Are the rest of them still here?"

"Some are, like Pop and his family who have the café. Mindy, one of our granddaughters had a riding stable outside of town. She sold it and retired. She lives at the dude ranch now with Cat O'Leary."

"I already met her and the twins." Lilly watched Ted who hummed while he tested wires. "It really surprised me when I arrived and discovered there were more ghosts around, not just me."

"And you've only been here two days." Donal chuckled. "I can't wait to hear what you think when you've been in Baker City for a week."

It was Lilly's turn to smile and nod. For the next two hours, she and Donal floated around behind Ted, observing the phone tech's work. Then, a brown-haired, sturdy woman in jeans and a flowered shirt, accompanied by two other women and an older man showed up. They unloaded various cleaning supplies and came in the kitchen door. After Mac greeted them, three of them started vacuuming, dusting and washing windows on the ground floor.

Meanwhile, Lilly returned to the kitchen and popped up on a stool at the island in the middle of the room so she could listen to the conversation between Mac and Linda. The two had apparently met the day before when Lilly was in the cocktail lounge because Linda mentioned not asking about his plans for Thanksgiving.

"Dad and I put on a big meal at the café. Most of the people in town show up and pay what they can." Linda nodded her thanks when Mac handed her a mug of coffee. "You should come and meet more of the Baker City folks."

"Only if you let me help with either the food or the service." Mac leaned against the counter, eyeing her over his cup. "I started working in fast food restaurants when I was a teenager. I wanted to study hotel and restaurant management in college, but that was a no-go. Ended up enlisting instead."

"Did you cook when you were in the Army?"

"For a while. I'd volunteered for Ranger School, but I had to wait for an opening." Mac shrugged. "Then, our country was in a war, the longest since Vietnam."

"Exactly." Linda focused on her coffee for a moment. "I'd appreciate having help in the kitchen on Thursday. Dad always ends up serving and Dray handles the cleaning. It's a family affair and we'll love including you in our menagerie."

Lilly saw sudden shock appear on Mac's face, but only for an instant. Then, all emotion faded. He'd learned to compartmentalize his feelings long before he joined the military and went to war. She'd learned why when they visited his mother and stepfather last year. They were polite to Mac, but made it clear he was little more than a stranger. He stayed less than an hour, and they didn't even offer him a glass of water or cup of coffee.

When she heard his token relatives admit they didn't read his books and his stepsister say she'd donated the copies he sent to the local thrift store, Lilly had struggled not to unleash her anger. She longed to teach them to suck eggs as the saying went. It was all she could do to keep from knocking on walls and doors, throwing objects at them, moving the furniture, playing with the thermostat, banging around the house, and making the lights flicker.

Mac received more attention, hugs, kisses and small gifts from the various owners of different bookstores. When they asked if they should set up chairs for his family, Mac had said they were too busy to attend his readings or book signings. Luckily, that hadn't made the local papers or TV interviews or podcasts, so he wasn't embarrassed in public by their behavior.

If he could hear her, Lilly would have told him that she was happy he'd found a place with real people, not shallow, narcissistic megalomaniacs. Oh well, she thought. *Maybe, I'll include that next time he's describing someone like them in a book. There's more than one way to get his attention.*

He'd only been in Baker City, Washington for a day and it seemed so different, Mac thought. Everyone he'd met was very friendly and made him feel welcome. He and his cousin, Linda spent most of the morning and part of the afternoon checking out the hotel and developing a plan for her company to clean it. She'd agreed to take charge while he went to the hardware store for light bulbs, so she'd be able to start on the basement that afternoon.

For the first time, Mac wondered what it'd have been like if he grew up here. Would he have received letters and packages from family the way other soldiers had when they were overseas? He never showed how envious he was of the connections they had with their relatives. He couldn't. It made him less of a man.

He parked in front of the cedar shake building in the middle of the block and walked inside. He smiled at the sight of the old, narrow boards that made up the ancient wooden floor that creaked under his boots. He crossed to the counter and the cashier, a scrawny twenty-something in baggy jeans and a black T-shirt, pointed out the aisle with electrical supplies. Halfway down it, a rugged, older man with silvered red hair approached, a smile on his weathered features. "Hello. I'm Aiden O'Leary, the owner. Are you finding everything okay?"

"Mac MacGillicudy." He held out his hand. "I need some tube lights for the basement at the hotel."

"This way." Aiden turned. "Welcome home, Mac. We're glad you're here."

"I am too."

Before they reached the end of the aisle and the selection of fluorescent bulbs, three young girls about nine years old wearing jeans and sweatshirts hurried toward them. One of the girls, a redhead flashed a bright smile at Mac. "Hi, I'm Sophie. This is my twin sister, Samantha, and our friend, Penny Sinclair. Where's Miss Lilly?"

"What?" Mac choked, staring at the trio. "Who is Miss Lilly?"

"You're her friend, aren't you?" Samantha twined a strand of long strawberry blonde hair around one finger. "Mister MacGillicudy? She came with you. So, where is she?"

"We're 'sposed to ask her to visit our old teacher at the school." Sophie tilted her head to one side. "She has to come 'make her manners' with Mrs. O'Sullivan."

"What does that mean?" Penny, the young blonde girl asked. "I never heard it before."

"It's an expression that means to perform a polite or expected social courtesy." Aiden gestured toward the front of the store. "The twins are saying Miss Lilly needs to introduce herself to the first teacher in Baker City. Now, if Miss Lilly isn't here, then she's probably at the hotel. Each of you can get one of those stick candies from Lyle and ask him to walk you over there."

"Thank you for the candy, Uncle Aiden, but we'll ask Daddy to take us," Samantha said. "He brought us with him 'cause he needs more nails for the new fence he's building."

"That works." Aiden waited until the girls walked away. Amusement filled his face, and his eyes crinkled when he chuckled. "You look like you haven't seen a ghost, Mac, or have you?"

"I don't believe in them." The truth escaped before he could stop it.

Aiden laughed. "Oh, you've only been here two days. I'll give you a week before I ask again. In Baker City, ghosts are real, and my niece, Cat, is the town medium. She has the *O'Leary Gift* of being able to talk to them, but her responsibilities don't stop there. She controls them too."

"And her daughters also claim to see them?"

"Cat says they did even before they moved here." Aiden shrugged. "My younger brother is their grandfather, but it's easier for the twins to call me, Uncle Aiden like their mom does and it works for us."

CHAPTER FIVE

So far, Lilly had enjoyed a highly entertaining day. First, she and Donal continued observing Ted Fenwick upgrading the communications system on the main floor of the hotel. She peered over his shoulder, watching graphs appear on what he called a 'tablet' and listening to him comment on the speed and signal strength when he talked to his supervisor at the phone company.

She explained to Donal that things certainly had changed. Back in their day, a tablet would be a pad of paper, and they'd write on it with a pen or pencil. Once the Internet worked, she streamed three episodes of *Call the Midwife* on the flat-screen in the manager's apartment. When two of the cleaners interrupted her binge-watching, she left them to tidy the suite.

She headed off to find Florence. The two of them floated through the left and then the right wings of the hotel. Lilly didn't say the various bedrooms all looked alike with the white and beige color schemes. Maybe she could figure out a way to let Mac know the rooms needed some individuality. Since the cats patrolled the place, she didn't see any signs of mice or rats.

After she and Florence finished their inspection of the two wings, they went upstairs to the rooms in the older part of the structure. On the second floor, the rotunda, a long, inside balcony that encircled a round room caught Lilly's attention. A domed skylight lit the area and when she glanced down, she saw the lobby and Donal back in his usual spot behind the reception desk. The painted ceiling with images of wild horses was beautiful and she knew guests would enjoy the classic Victorian style architecture.

Then, she and Florence moseyed toward two luxurious, matching honeymoon suites on either side of a spacious hallway. At least the rooms on the second and third floors weren't as dull as the others in the newer section of the hotel, Lilly thought. Instead, there were common vintage colors from the 1950s that included pastel hues, shades of browns and oranges, with bright pinks, forest greens, golden yellows and bold blues as accents in different areas.

When they finished the tour, Lilly headed down to the basement to check on the progress there. She found Mac installing light bulbs while his cousin, Linda supervised her crew. Two teens chattered away while they cleaned the media room assisted by the Hendrickson twins. Meanwhile the adults worked on other sections of the recreational area.

"Hi, Miss Lilly." Samantha stopped wiping down one of the chairs and waved in greeting. "We came to see you 'cause you weren't at the hardware store with Mister Mac."

"I was checking out the rest of the hotel." Lilly drifted closer. "Why were you looking for me?"

"You need to visit the school and meet Mrs. O'Sullivan," Sophie announced. "She decided she wanted to be the principal when we started going there. She likes meeting new people."

"And the guys say it's kind of creepy if you get sent to her office." A slender teenager in jeans and a snug tank top under a long-sleeved flannel shirt stopped mopping the floor. She had long curly black hair around a lovely golden face, high cheekbones, big electric blue eyes framed by long dark lashes. She stared toward Lilly, then shrugged and returned to work. "It's real quiet and if they don't start filling out the discipline forms right away, the lights start flickering and the door slams again and again."

"That's Araceli Taggart. Her aunt owns the riding stable outside of town." Samantha pointed toward the older girl who scrubbed the counter in the corner of the room. "And that's Vangie Sinclair. They can't see you, but they believe us when we tell them about ghosts who live here."

"And the horses talk to you too." Vangie popped her gum. She was older, and wore fashionably torn, faded jeans, a tight pink, shrunken t-shirt, and flip-flops. She had shoulder-length, ebony curls. "And the dogs."

"What about the cats?" Lilly asked. "Can you convince them to go see the veterinarian?"

"Sometimes, but most of them are really scared so we just do 'picture talk' with them until they agree to make friends with Dray."

"We'll work on it." Lilly glanced over her shoulder at the sound of footsteps.

A young girl with ash-blonde hair about the same age as the twins came into the room. "Hey, your dad is ready to go. He sent me to find you. Did you find your friend?"

"Yes." Samantha put the rag on the chair. "We'll help more next time."

"No worries." Vangie smacked her gum again. "We've got this. We're being paid and you're not. We'll see you at home, Penny."

"Okay. I'll walk your dog when I get there."

"Good luck with that. Bonzer and Shasta hang with Ramsey when we're at school, so they probably need snacks more than walks."

"I can handle that." Penny and the twins headed out the door.

Lilly followed them, coming to a halt when she saw the girls stop by a tall, muscular man with the same typical 'high and tight' military style haircut that Mac had. The stranger advanced toward her.

Since they were indoors, he didn't salute but still raised his right hand. "Afternoon, ma'am. I'm Rob Hendrickson. You already met my daughters, and they told me—"

"I'm First Lieutenant Lilly Bryce." She gestured toward the twins. "And they've made sure I feel welcome here. I met your wife too. She's very kind."

Rob grinned. "She is until I annoy her. Don't do that."

"I wouldn't be so rude." Lilly smiled back at him. "And I will pop in and visit the school soon. The mayor didn't say anything about it when I talked to him yesterday."

"He probably hadn't thought of it yet." Rob glanced over his broad shoulder when Mac and Linda approached. "We'll stop interrupting and let you two get back to work. Nice meeting you, ma'am. I'll look forward to seeing you at church or the café."

"That sounds nice. And please call me, Lilly."

"All right. Enjoy your stay in Baker City, Lilly."

"Oh, I am!"

Mac eyed Linda who didn't seem too surprised by the other man's attitude and words before he left. "I don't get it. What's in the water or the food around here? Am I the only sane person in Baker City?"

Linda laughed, shaking her head. "Is this when you repeat you don't believe in ghosts?" She looked past him toward the media room. "I can't see them either, but then again, I'm not an O'Leary. I still don't want things going bump around me because then I'd have to clean up the various messes."

"Well, I'll leave you to it. I'm going to check on the driveway and the trees the guys are cutting."

"Grab one of the mauls and work out some of your aggression splitting firewood."

"Not a bad idea."

He spent the next two hours attacking chunks of cedar and hemlock with a maul and breaking them into smaller pieces. Jack and one of his friends stacked firewood beside the driveway while Dray fed branches into the wood-chipper. They didn't finish clearing all the fallen trees, but they made a good start. At the end of the afternoon, Mac helped the other men finish loading the last pickup truck.

"We still have a ways to go." Jack wiped his forehead with a bandanna. "We'll be back tomorrow to finish up. Of course, it may take us until Wednesday. Does that work for you?"

Mac nodded, drinking the last of his bottled water. "Yeah. After this, do you know someone who has a dozer. I want the driveway graded and a couple loads of gravel until we can afford to have it paved."

"I'll text my boss and ask if we can handle it," Dray said. "He said it's okay if I leave the chipper here as long as you're good with it."

"Lock it in the machine shed behind the hotel and it will be fine," Mac said. "We don't want it stolen and I'm not sure the Baker City ghosts will watch it."

The comment sparked laughter from the half-dozen men. Jack shook his head. "Don't tease them. Wait until next October to see what they do at the Haunted Town. They send the tourists running."

"Yeah, but they always come back with their wallets and lots of money," one of his friends pointed out.

More laughter as they headed for the hotel. Halfway there, Mac's phone vibrated, and he drew it out of his pocket to answer. He recognized his mother's number. "Hey, I'm glad you called. Did you get my message?"

"Yes, but I don't understand it. Why are you in Baker City?"

"Because I inherited the hotel." Mac frowned at the smart-phone. "I told you when I visited last spring."

"I must have forgotten." She heaved a sigh. "Well, aren't you going to sell it?"

"I haven't decided." He walked toward the hotel and the wrap-around porch. He sat down in one of the new wooden Adirondack chairs and switched over to the video-conference app so he could see her face.

Donna MacGillicudy-Galsworthy didn't look much like her cousin, Linda, although both of them were brunettes. His mom was barely five feet, six. He remembered her as being wiry and strong enough to muscle around her huge equine patients back in the day. But since she retired, she'd traded in her coveralls for dresses and spike heels.

"As the saying goes, Baker City isn't the end of the world, but you can see it from there," Donna pursed her lips, brown eyes worried. "You don't really intend to stay in such a small town, do you?"

"I haven't decided yet," Mac repeated. "I've barely explored two floors of the hotel. And I have a book to finish so I'll stick around a while."

"Nobody's beating down your door for those stories of yours, are they?"

"Only my agent, my publisher, and my readers." Mac leaned back in the chair. "So, I'll be here a while. What do you remember about Baker City?"

"Not my kind of place," Donna said. "If my mother hadn't thrown fits, I wouldn't have visited on college breaks. Thank heavens, my sisters started having babies when I was in my senior year so I could call it quits then."

Mac frowned, rubbing his jaw with his free hand. It didn't sound like she'd be receptive to sharing any so-called ghost stories or telling him about her childhood. He changed the subject and asked how her husband was. That led to news of his stepbrothers and stepsisters. He ended the call with a promise to check in on Thanksgiving. Maybe she'd be willing to share more details of her own family and eventually that might lead to stories about his biological father. She'd always refused to discuss the man, saying he was only a short-term hookup when she was in college.

If not, I can play detective and ask what people in town remember. When I help with the holiday meal at the café on Thursday, I'll certainly be meeting more of my relatives. I'll ask Pop to introduce me.

He arrived in the kitchen in time to make his farewells to Linda and her crew of cleaners along with Jack Madison and his buddies. The guys told him they'd return the next day. Linda repeated she'd see Mac at the café bright and early on Thanksgiving.

After dinner, the calico and her kittens accompanied him to the manager's suite. In the glow from the TV, he saw someone sitting in the recliner, a woman in a distinctive Women's Army Corps uniform from World War Two watching *Bridgerton* on the flat-screen. Barely any makeup highlighted the hazel eyes, and her light auburn hair was coiled in a bun.

He stopped, froze in the doorway. "What the hell?"

She whipped her head around and looked at him.

They stared at each other for another moment. He switched on the overhead light, and she was gone.

Sure, people had told him there were ghosts in Baker City. *But I don't believe in them.* He'd stopped drinking five plus years ago, so it wasn't something conjured up from a bottle of whisky. He clenched his fists. If he wasn't an Army Ranger, he'd swear his knees were shaking.

Nope, he controlled his emotions. He'd really seen someone or something. It wasn't his imagination. He'd been through the wars, too many times in combat, but he'd never seen anything or anyone like that. He'd learned to control his emotions, not to allow them to control him when he was a kid. It was how he survived, first in his stepfather's house, then as a teenager working in one restaurant after another and finally as a soldier.

"Okay, I'll deal with it but not now. Gonna lock it down for later."

He crossed to his desk and powered up the laptop. *What the hell is wrong with me? I haven't fallen off the wagon. Am I coming down with something? What the hell?*

He kept looking around the room while he answered emails and tried to work on the next chapter in his book. He didn't see her again. He still couldn't focus on the story. Finally, he gave up and decided to enjoy *Bosch*, one of his favorite action-adventure cop shows instead. He picked up the remote and scrolled through the various options. For the first time he wondered if his strange guest was the reason why so many different historical dramas like *Downtown Abbey* or *Call the Midwife* were suggested whenever he turned on the TV.

Her real estate office kept Dominique so busy Monday, she didn't have time to go to the hotel and check on Mac. Her younger sister had texted and said she sent a crew to clear the driveway. That was a surprise. Dominique hadn't expected any support from Veronika who made it plain she wanted to sell the hotel and see it destroyed. So, what was her agenda? Why was she helping?

No answer came to mind while Dominique stuck a frozen dinner in the microwave. Normally, she'd have created a main dish salad, but she was too tired to make the effort. She poured a glass of white wine while she waited. Tomorrow afternoon, she'd go to the hotel and check on Mac. By then, he'd have inspected the place and have some ideas what it needed.

She'd reviewed different websites already. Much of the furniture was still useable but most of the beds needed new box-springs, and mattresses. Of course, they also had to buy pillows, linens, blankets and comforters. New carpets, window treatments, flat-screen TVs for each room — the list went on and on. There was so much they needed to do to restore the place before they could even consider opening it for guests.

Well, I'm not giving up. Maybe my father didn't live there when he was growing up, but my grandfather did with his brothers, his sisters and his parents. It's our home and I'm keeping it!

Veronika strolled into the cocktail lounge looking for what her older sister would call her scout troop, but she didn't see Jack Madison or Ted Fenwick anywhere. Most of the tables appeared to be empty, not an unusual sight in Baker City. The corner booth had a cord across the end and a 'Reserved' sign hung from it. Pop MacGillicudy, the owner had said his grandfather always held the place for the mayor and his cronies, all of whom had died years ago. In this town, ghosts were real and treated with respect. Or else!

Pop's daughter and her cousin, Linda MacGillicudy, a plump, brown-haired woman in a flowered shirt and black slacks approached. She wiped the bar with a damp towel and smiled. "Ready for a drink?"

"You know it." Veronika hitched onto a stool. "I need a beer after staying forever at the church to finish up the holiday baskets."

"Well, it means you made a start on those community service hours." Linda picked up a mug that looked like an old-style jar and moved to the taps. "Did you have dinner there or shall I have Dad make you a burger? The kitchen is still open."

"Sounds great." Veronika heaved a sigh. "So, where are the guys? I know it's Monday night, but they're not working this week. Shouldn't they be hanging out here?"

"I think they wore themselves out cutting firewood over at the hotel." Linda put down a paper coaster, then set the icy glass on top of it. "I had my crew there too. We refreshed the main floor and then Mac had us clean the basement. I'd forgotten all the amenities that were downstairs for the guests and the work areas."

"Like what?"

"Oh, a media center, a gym, game room, staff area, laundry and storerooms." Linda's smile widened. "Wait until you see the pool tables. Mac says he's going to rehab the arcade game machines rather than getting rid of them."

"Wow, he has a lot of different skills."

"Yes, he does." Linda laughed. "He made these giant chocolate chip cookies, and they were definitely a hit with everyone."

"I hope they left some for me."

"No guarantees. I'll call Dad to throw on your burger." Linda walked to the phone at the end of the bar and used the intercom to pass on the order. "Remember you're going to the church first thing tomorrow. You'll have to visit Mac afterwards."

"I know." Veronika grimaced and drank more beer. "I hate it, but I'm doing it."

"Well, be responsible. Don't drink and drive."

"Funny thing for a bartender to say."

Linda shrugged. "I'm a responsible bartender. I don't let my customers get wasted and if someone's impaired, I call Chief O'Connell."

Veronika stared after her cousin when she walked to the far end of the bar. *I'm not asking if that's why he came after me. Did she rat me out? What a bitch! And there goes her tip!*

CHAPTER SIX

He looked right at me. Did he really see me? Lilly stood still, staring at Mac. He hadn't spoken to her again. Instead, he opened his laptop and started answering emails. *What am I going to do? Is this real?*

She didn't know. Granted, she'd been seen occasionally by little children, usually those under five at the library in Seattle and then on book tours with Mac. She'd never expected to meet a medium or her daughters in Baker City. *I need advice. It's time to go to the cocktail lounge and find another ghost to advise me.*

This time when she arrived, she discovered the place wasn't as busy as it'd been on Sunday afternoon. Yes, the mayor and his buddy sat in their favorite booth. Lilly recognized the blonde at the bar as one of the women who'd showed Mac around the hotel.

Tonight, she wore a light blue, knee-length, vintage floral dress, darker blue tights and stilettos that matched her stockings. Very conservative, Lilly thought, remembering the jeans and low-cut tops the woman wore before. What was the occasion? Mac's other cousin, Linda, was behind the bar, chatting away to the few living customers who still remained in the room.

Lilly bypassed them and went toward Bridget and her friends in their booth, two men and Raven Barlow. "Hello. May I join you?"

"Of course." Raven gestured to their companions. "Lilly, this is Zeke Garvey and Moises Pride. Lilly arrived a couple days ago. Zeke died in Afghanistan too and Moises—"

"Didn't make it back alive from a covert op in South America." Moises was a young, African-American with close-cropped black hair. He wore camouflage fatigues, combat boots and had a beret stuffed in one pants' pocket. "Nice to meet you, ma'am. Bridget told us you passed in World War Two."

Lilly nodded, then glanced at Zeke whose attention was on the blonde at the bar. She waited until the bartender was distracted before she stalked out the door to the street. "What's wrong?"

The dark-haired soldier in camo fatigues shook his head. "I must have seen her 'Dine and Dash' at least a dozen times since I've been back in Baker City, and she just did it again. Surprises me that Linda and Pop haven't 'eighty-sixed' her from the café like my wife has from her bakery."

"I'm not sure what that means," Moises said.

"When I was growing up, it was slang at soda counters when something was sold out," Lilly told him. "Now, it means someone is refused service at a bar or restaurant." She turned her attention to Zeke. "I haven't been to the bakery yet. Tell me more about it."

"Twila and I met in high school, and we went everywhere when I was in the Army. She trained as a pastry chef. We planned to move back home to Baker City when I retired from the Army." Zeke shrugged a broad ghostly shoulder. "She brought the kids and came home to be close to my family after I died. She opened a bakery to support herself and our kids. I visit almost every day."

"I'll have to check it out and I'm not the only one. Mac bakes a lot. It's how he deals with his memories of combat."

"We all have our strategies," Bridget said. "Most of us hang out here and talk to the other vets. Our wars are different but most of our experiences are the same."

"Good point." Lilly hesitated, then decided to throw her question out to the group. "So, do any of the living see you? And I'm not talking about Cat O'Leary or her daughters."

"What do you mean? Sometimes, I think Twila knows I'm there, but she's never said so." Zeke frowned thoughtfully, his dark brown eyes narrowing.

It was Raven's turn. "My husband, Kord is a trucker. He knows when I go with him on long hauls or climb in bed with him. He even told my BFF's fiancé that he hadn't slept alone since I died. His new age therapist, Estelle offered to have one of her daughters cleanse our house in some sort of weird-ass ceremony to get rid of my spirit and Kord refused. He says I'll move on when I'm ready and I'm not. Does that help?"

"The munchkin at the feedstore sees me." Moises chuckled. "She's about two years old. She throws a stuffed toy dog at me. If her mom isn't looking, I toss it back. Lots of giggles before she hurls it at me again. Is that what you mean?"

Lilly shook her head. "Not really. I was watching TV tonight when Mac came into the manager's apartment. He saw me. I've been haunting him for three plus years, and he never has before."

"Well, that's intriguing." Bridget propped her chin on her fist. "So, did you talk to him?"

"No. I was so shocked, I just vanished when he asked who I was."

"Wake up and smell the coffee, girl." Bridget grinned appreciatively. "I'll bet he has some O'Leary blood in his veins. His talent might not be as strong as the town medium's, but it doesn't mean he's impervious to you."

Lilly tilted her head to one side. "How could I learn if that's true?"

"Let's talk to the mayor. He and Newt O'Leary would know for sure." Bridget rose to her feet. "Come on."

Lilly followed her new friend across the room to the corner booth where the two older men sat. As usual, they stood up politely. Once she and Bridget were seated, the other woman explained the situation.

"Is Mac MacGillicudy related to the O'Leary family?" Bridget asked. "Is that why he might have the gift of sight?"

Newt rubbed his grizzled jaw. "I don't know. I had seven young'uns, four boys and three girls. One of them was the last

O'Leary, Cat's grandma. And she had seven of her own. The youngest was Liam. He had her gift, but he didn't become the next town medium because he's an embarrassment. I suggested we wait for his daughter, Cat to grow up and the responsibility passed onto her and the twins."

"We don't know if her youngest will be able to see us or not." Mayor O'Connell chuckled. "I won't be surprised if she does, not when both her parents see and talk to us."

"Makes sense to me." Newt nodded. "My wife used to keep track of all our kin in the family Bible."

"Did Donna MacGillicudy know any of them?" Lilly asked. "She's Mac's mother. She left here to go to college and didn't come back after she graduated."

"I'll ask around and find out more about her," Mayor O'Connell promised. "My great-grandson, the police chief, can hear me just fine in his dreams, especially after he's had a beer or two. I'll ask him to stop by and talk with your writer."

"Thank you." Lilly took a deep breath. "Am I allowed to try and talk to Mac? I don't want to break any of the rules."

"There's nothing against that." Mayor O'Connell studied Bridget for a moment. "You remember Rob Williams, don't you?"

"Yes. Some of the younger, newer ghosts don't realize he was one of us for years. He died at Hamburger Hill in Vietnam. Things changed when the new O'Leary won the Williams' place in an essay contest." Bridget raised a ghostly hand. "This is something we haven't truly shared with everyone, Lilly."

"I won't say a word." Lilly frowned, remembering the man she'd met at the hotel earlier that day. "How did he get a second chance? Did the medium arrange it?"

"No, it's not part of her gift." Bridget lowered her voice. "When her first husband died, he wanted to move on to the next world. He gave his body to Rob."

"That rarely happens. Most of the time the living use up their bodies when they're ready to die. They don't sacrifice them to one of us." The mayor collected his fedora. "Well, I'm off to visit my relatives. Newt, why don't you see if you can find that Bible?"

"It's probably at Aiden's house. His wife adds the names to the family tree now."

On her way out of the cocktail lounge, Lilly drifted close enough to the bar to hear Linda and her father talking about the blonde woman who'd left without paying for her dinner.

He pointed out it wasn't the first time she'd done it. "A lot of restaurant owners would make the waitress pay for the meal."

"It's not your style or mine, Dad. If she's hungry enough to steal, we can let it go this time."

"You say that each and every time." Pop patted her shoulder. "We oughta report it to Dick O'Connell. Then, he could track her down and take it out of her hide or her daddy, Herman's."

"You know we won't do it." Linda kissed his wrinkled cheek. "Dick has issues when you don't let homeless folks dumpster dive here. You always give meals to them, and they're not related. Ronnie's part of the family."

"Well, if she shows up on Thursday for the holiday dinner, you make her help Dray wash the dishes. I can't send her to 'hunt snipe' in the alley behind the café. The last two guys we fed swept up all the cigarette butts and litter. There's nothing left until more crap gets thrown down by lazy people."

"I'll keep that in mind, Dad."

He didn't sleep much anymore. Too many bad dreams, Mac thought. After he finished working on the book, he left the cats dozing on the couch and went to his new office. He began unpacking the new desktop computer. He turned on the pole lamp, not bothering with the overhead light. Then, he lifted the printer out of its carton and set it up on top of the two-drawer, file cabinet next to his rolltop desk.

A cool breeze brushed his face. He frowned and looked toward the pair of double-paned windows that faced the side yard. He crossed to them to check the latches. No problem. Both were securely locked. He closed the blinds, then the drapes over top of them.

It didn't make a difference. He felt a second cold wind. "What the—"

"It's me," A low, feminine voice announced. "Do you hear me, Mister MacGillicudy?"

He swung around and saw her. The same woman who'd been watching TV earlier. She stood in the doorway. She'd added a garrison cap over her auburn hair. That made sense. Army regulations required a hat if she went outdoors.

That was a stupid idea. Why was he recalling the regs when there was a beautiful woman talking to him? He stared at her, slowly realizing he could see through her. "Is this some kind of joke? A film? A video? Computer generated? You're not solid, not real."

"Because I'm dead, Mister MacGillicudy." She sighed, walked to the rocking chair and sat down, putting her purse neatly beside her on the table, before she peeled off the black dress gloves. The hat followed those onto the end table. "Honestly. I thought you were smarter than this. I've been haunting you over three years now."

"Haunting me?" He repeated, feeling as if he'd stepped into an insane asylum, not a paneled office in a vintage, family hotel. "I don't understand."

"Seriously?" She arched a dark red-brown eyebrow. "You invited me to join you when you left Seattle for your first book tour. Are you saying you don't remember, Mister MacGillicudy?"

"Mac. Call me, Mac." He took two steps closer to the chair. He could see the faded, flowered material of the cushions through her. "Who are you?"

"Isn't the proper way to say it is, who was I?" She smiled, her hazel eyes almost green in the dim room. "First Lieutenant, Lilly Bryce."

"You're dead." He gaped at her, feeling as if his jaw hit the floor. "I saw your obituary."

"And you read it at least a dozen times before you printed it out." Her smile widened and she laughed, a soft throaty sound. "Oh, my goodness, are you going to faint?"

"Pass out. Women faint. Guys pass out." He stumbled over to the chair at the desk, sat down, still staring at her. "I don't believe in ghosts."

"Well, it's a good thing I believe in you, or we'd be in trouble, Mister MacGillicudy."

"What are you doing here? You must have a reason. Shouldn't there have been a door or something when you died? Why didn't you go to Heaven if there is such a place?"

"I told you already. I'm haunting you." She shook a scolding finger at him. "Now, if you didn't want me to come along and join your adventures, you never should have suggested it."

"I didn't know you were real."

She clicked her tongue against her teeth. "That lack of imagination is appalling when you're such an amazing author."

The praise sent warmth rocketing through him. "You've read my books?"

"Of course, I have. How else could I help fix them?" She gathered up her purse, hat, and gloves. "Well, that's enough chit-chat for tonight. I have work to do and if I stay much longer, you'll never get our new computer put together."

"Wait a minute." He vaulted to his feet. "What are you talking about? How do you 'fix' my books? I don't need another editor. I already have one. And my agent, Gwen is an absolute—"

"Angel. You should send her flowers for Thanksgiving." Another soft laugh. "Whoops, I already did."

"How could you?" He stalked after the barely visible woman drifting out the door. "You're dead."

"You already knew that. You always take your wallet out of your pants when you go to bed. It's not any trouble to find a credit card and use it for you. It was good manners to send a holiday bouquet to your editor, a gift basket to the art department that does your book covers and one to the publicity folks at your publishing house, so I did."

She was gone. Well, at least he didn't see her any longer. He turned around and went back to the office. She hadn't answered his questions. Why was she here? Wasn't there a white light or a door or something? Shouldn't she be in Heaven? Or Hell?

Wait a minute. Other than being a bit sarcastic, which wasn't a sin in his mind, she didn't deserve to suffer. A ghost. She said she'd been with him at least three years. Why hadn't he seen her before? The young girls who visited today said they'd met her yesterday. And their father, Rob Hendrickson, had told him there were a lot of ghosts in Baker City. Was the town some sort of spiritual nexus? Did it provide Lillian with more energy or power to appear?

Since she apparently took it upon herself to show what she believed were "good manners," it answered a lot of questions about his professional relationship with his publishing firm. The people there always went the extra mile for him and now he knew why they claimed he appreciated all their efforts. He prided himself on being courteous whenever he contacted them, but he hadn't known someone else, the woman who haunted him was exhibiting what his mother always called "old-school" etiquette.

Humming softly, Lilly headed for the manager's apartment where she'd find the laptop and be able to read through the chapters Mac completed. Halfway there, Florence appeared. Lilly nodded to the older woman. "Good evening. How are you?"

"Donal and I heard you and Mac talking." Florence glanced at the door to the study. "We couldn't believe it. Did he really hear you? How?"

"I don't know, but after he found me watching TV, I went to the cocktail lounge to get some advice." As they floated in the direction of the suite, Lilly shared what she'd learned from the other ghosts and the fact that the mayor approved of her experiment to try a conversation with Mac. "When I returned, I decided to try talking to him. He saw and heard me."

"Donal and I have a lot of ideas for how to restore the hotel. Do you think he'd hear us?"

"I don't know," Lilly repeated. "It's certainly worth a try, but I have to be honest. I've been haunting the man for three years and this is the first time he's ever interacted with me." She paused. "Well, I have made quite a few changes to his books during that time, but he seems to think he's done that."

"What kind of changes?" Amusement crept across Florence's pale features. "Did you make them spicy? When I was alive, I got quite a few unmentionable ideas from the novels I checked out of the town library. Donal certainly appreciated them and it's undoubtedly why we had so many children. Some of the ladies who come here joined my book club."

"The best times of my life and to be honest after my death were at the downtown Seattle library. I read constantly, everything from Shakespeare to Jane Austen to Charlotte Bronte to Louisa May Alcott. Who are your favorite authors?"

"Oh, I always wanted to be entertained so I read popular fiction, books by Georgette Heyer and Frank Yerby." Florence flushed slightly, an odd sight in a ghost of her age. "Some of my favorite old-time authors were Elinor Glyn and E.M. Hull and Ethel Dell."

"I never heard of them."

"Of course not, my dear. They wrote to pay their bills, to support themselves and their families. Doireann O'Sullivan, the school-teacher here, used to quote the critics who called those stories "Domestic Fiction.' They said it was novels written by women, for women, and for the most part, featuring a woman as the main character."

"That's not a bad thing."

Florence smiled. "Well, Doireann told me that actually more people in our day actually read the kind of books I did, not the ones that are taught in school like *The Scarlet Letter* or *Moby Dick*."

"I've read those too." Lilly lowered her voice. "What was a best-seller back in your day?"

"Well, I really liked *The Hidden Hand* by Mrs. E.D.E.N. South-worth. I read it so many times that Donal actually bought a copy for me."

"What was it about?"

Florence's description of a young orphan girl's adventures in pre-Civil War America took several minutes. Capitola Black wasn't a typical innocent heroine. She dressed like a boy to find employment. After she was 'rescued' by an elderly relative, her trials and tribulations didn't end, although Florence refused to give away the culmination of the story.

Totally intrigued, Lilly demanded to know where to look for the book. "Is it still here?"

"Oh no. After I died, my boys got rid of my 'trashy' tales when they cleared out my belongings." Florence sighed. "I suppose you could go to the Baker City library and see what remains. The last librarian isn't around anymore so you can't ask him."

"I'm new here. Will you go with me? Tomorrow?"

"I'd love to." Florence smiled, clasping ghostly hands. "I'll ask Doireann to join us. She loves a good literary frolic too."

"Wonderful. The O'Leary twins said I should meet her, and this will be a terrific opportunity."

CHAPTER SEVEN

Tuesday morning after he showered and dressed, Mac paused to look at the laptop on his desk before heading to the kitchen for coffee. He'd shut down the computer when he finished writing the previous day, but the screen revealed his latest book. He sat down and read through the document. He usually made notes in the margin when he needed to check historical details and then continued with the story.

Someone had included the answers in the narrative and developed the setting even more. Had he ever truly believed that he'd made these additions to earlier books in the series? He grimaced. *Wow, I was so arrogant. Come on, Mac. Why would you think you literally had a ghost writer haunting your sorry butt?*

Coffee! He required caffeine and he'd get to work. In the kitchen, he brewed a cup and watched the sunrise over Mount Carmody. More snow had fallen on the peaks, and he wondered how much normally landed in Baker City. He'd have to ask the locals. Later today, he'd visit the hardware store and see if Aiden O'Leary sold small appliances.

It'd be handy to have a smaller coffee machine in the manager's quarters and then he wouldn't be distracted by the quest for his favorite beverage. The cat arrived and he went into the pantry to top her dish. The other felines didn't visit as much as she and her kittens did, but they certainly helped eat the food.

When he returned to the kitchen, Lillian sat on one of the stools at the center island. In her blouse and skirt, she looked like a professional businesswoman if he discounted the fact that he could see through her to the far wall.

"Good morning." Mac paused in the doorway. "Thanks for doing that research. I appreciate it. Now I can focus on the dead trucker in the alley."

"The secretary should find him, not Titus." Lillian swung a ghostly leg back and forth, the low heel of her brown oxford shoe striking the stool although it didn't make a sound. "You don't give her enough dirty jobs to do."

"She's a woman," Mac protested. "And back then, it was a man's job to do the heavy lifting."

Lillian laughed, shaking her head. "Don't be such a chauvinist. You already told your readers that my namesake is a veteran. Show that, instead of simply saying it."

"Have you been reading Gwen's emails? She keeps repeating that same litany." Mac finished his coffee and went to brew a second cup. "Would you like a 'cup of Joe'?"

"I'd love one but it's impossible. I'm a ghost, remember? I can't drink it anymore." She heaved a sigh. "I always had it with cream and two lumps of sugar. Those were rationed during the war. So was coffee."

"Okay, I'll remember that." He put the mug on the machine tray, placed a fresh pod in the basket and turned to face her. "As far as the books go, I'm the author and I make the final decisions."

"Sure, you do!" Lillian narrowed her hazel eyes. "Here's the deal, Mister MacGillicudy. More than 350,000 American women joined the United States Armed Forces during World War II. They were nurses, pilots, clerks, mechanics, drivers, instructors, air traffic controllers, postal workers, translators—"

"Lillian Burroughs is a fictional character in my books. She's not an actual human being."

"You're an idiot!" Lillian jumped off the stool to her feet. "She's real to me, your agent, your editor and your readers. Give her some depth. Stop making her a cardboard cut-out who placates your moronic, misogynistic detective!"

"He isn't—"

The coffee cup sailed at his head. He flung up his hand and caught it in mid-flight. "Damn it, Lillian!"

He spun around. She was gone. Well, she was invisible. He couldn't see her, but he knew she'd be back. She had to come back!

———

Fury rising, Lilly stormed toward the reception area and the front doors of the hotel. Despite serving with women in combat in Afghanistan, Mac didn't have a clue they followed in the footsteps of their grandmothers. He seemed to buy into today's rhetoric that in the late 1940s, females were happy domestic servants, and they never wanted their own identities. Even after helping on the homefront and risking their lives in the war, they loved the opportunity to return to their homes and look after their husbands and children.

It's not true. It never was true. We didn't have the same rights as men. We couldn't own property or have credit cards or even bank accounts in our own names once we married. We're not second-class citizens who love to bow and scrape to our masters.

As a nurse, I was one of the so-called, lucky ones, not like other women who died, and their units paid for their funerals. The Army paid for mine, but I was buried in Italy. And since I was an orphan, my bones are still there. I didn't have any relatives to pay to bring me back to the U.S.

"Are you a poltergeist?" Donal flagged her down from his post at the reception desk. "Or a decent ghost looking for a home?"

"I'm sorry." Lilly gulped back a sob. "I died for my country, and I don't get any respect. If I lived to come home, I wouldn't have been called a veteran."

"I'd have said you were one, but I know my granddaughter, Mindy was treated like dirt when she came back after she served in Vietnam. Didn't agree with it then and I don't agree with it now. If you fight for this country, you're a soldier regardless of your sex." Donal leaned an elbow on the counter. "I know some of the jackasses in this town thought I should tell Florence how to vote in elections once we moved here. She got mad when I threw one of the worst idiots through that plate glass window."

"Because our insurance didn't cover the cost to replace it." Florence hugged Lilly quickly. "I heard what you told Mac. He doesn't understand what you're trying to tell him. Perhaps, you should show him."

"How?" Lilly sniffled. "I've been haunting him three years and he's so stubborn."

"Well, you're the one who works on a computer, and I saw you watching his TV. As the saying goes, 'a picture is worth a thousand words.' Couldn't you find some of those?"

Lilly considered the suggestion. "I've seen some appropriate postings on social media and there's quite a few documentaries he should see. You're right. I can adjust the settings on the computers and the flatscreen."

"All right." Florence beamed at her. "While you do that, I'll pop into *The O'Leary's* house and ask her to send Mindy over to visit him. She helps at the veteran's center in town and a big part of her job is what she calls, 'validating' issues for women. She'd call this a 'teachable' moment."

"So, you gals will teach him what he needs to know." Donal chuckled. "I'll enjoy the show."

She hadn't returned by the time Mac cleaned the kitchen after breakfast. Ted Fenwick arrived to continue updating the phone system. When Mac opened the door to greet him, he heard the sound of multiple chainsaws and the wood-chipper from the driveway.

He liked to write until lunch. Back in the manager's quarters, he sat down at the desk. He clicked the monitor, and a new screensaver appeared, a picture of Supreme Court Justice, Ruth Bader Ginsberg with a famous quote. It read, "I ask no favor for my sex. All I ask of our brethren is that they take their feet off our necks."

Okay, so Lillian was still around even if he didn't see her. And she was still pissed at him. Mac answered the latest batch of emails before he opened the file that held his manuscript. Instead, he saw a women's history meme. It contained significant dates in the 1960s and 1970s, ranging from when employers couldn't refuse to hire them because of their gender to when they could have their own bank accounts to when they couldn't be fired because they were pregnant.

"All right, Lillian. I get it."

"Not yet," her disembodied voice announced. "You will."

"Are you talking to me, Mister MacGillicudy?" Ted Fenwick stopped in the doorway. "I was on my way to get a cup of coffee. What's up?"

"My laptop is being weird." Mac swiveled his chair to gaze at the younger man. "This is my writing time, and I haven't been able to open the document I want." He shrugged. "I tend to talk to myself when I'm working."

"No worries. It happens a lot in Baker City. Most of us talk to people who aren't there even if they don't answer us." Ted started away, then paused. "Try apologizing to whoever you offended and see if that does the trick."

"Apologize for what?"

"You're the one who annoyed a ghost, not me. It's a good idea to make amends. They can do more than leave sarcastic posts."

Mac glared at the younger man. "I didn't do anything wrong."

"Hey, I'm not the one you have to convince."

On Tuesday afternoon, Rogan Murphy, one of the agents arrived to do her floor time at the real estate office. Once the petite brunette was comfortable answering the landline phone, Dominique left to complete a few errands. She started by visiting the hotel where she found Jack Madison and his crew of logging buddies clearing the trees off the old entrance driveway.

She praised their job and agreed with Dray that the chipped wood should be used for mulch on the muddy paths around the flowerbeds and garden area. Then, she headed for the parking lot behind the hotel. When she entered the lobby, she discovered Ted Fenwick working on the phone system at the reception desk. "Where's Mac?"

"He went to the hardware store." Ted grinned at her, mischief shining on his youthful features. "He's ticked off somebody and can't get past a series of women's history memes on either of his computers."

"Can't you fix it? You're the town techno-guru."

"Oh, it doesn't do it to me." Ted connected another cable. "I suggested he grovel to whichever ghost is pissed, but he hasn't gotten the idea yet that things are different in Baker City."

"That's surprising since he already had a chat with Rob Hendrickson on Sunday at the café."

"Linda told me he stopped by yesterday with the twins. The girls wanted to talk to the ghost that's haunting Mac."

"What ghost?" Dominique wondered if she'd have to scrape her jaw off the floor. "This is news to me."

"A U.S. Army officer who died in World War Two. According to Rob and the girls, she's been accepted by the rest of the haunts who live here. And it's not against the rules for her to mess with Mac's electronics."

"Or for you to laugh at him." Shaking her head, Dominique strolled toward the kitchen exit.

It didn't take long to drive to the hardware store where she spotted Mac's SUV. She parked and went inside. She found her cousin studying the selection of small appliances. "Hey, just the guy I wanted to see."

Mac glanced over a broad shoulder. "Well, you found me. What's up?"

"I wanted to talk to you about painting holiday scenes on the windows facing the main drag." Dominique pulled out her phone and brought up pics from last spring. "This is what I did for Easter. I thought we could do something with Santa and his sleigh—"

"And eight tiny reindeer," Mac teased.

"Nine if we include Rudolph."

"Well, we can't leave out him." Mac chose a box containing an electric percolator. "Next question. Do you put up garlands and lights on the outside of the hotel?"

"That's a big project." Dominique tilted her head to one side. "I don't know what's in the attic storerooms, but I remember Pop telling me stories about the big parties his parents and grandparents had. He said they always decked out the place."

"One of my buddies is coming to visit. He'll be here from Thanksgiving until New Year's. We'll search for the classic decorations and begin putting them up around the hotel." Mac turned and started toward the cashier. "I'm glad to see you. It saves me a trip to your office. I wanted to ask where I get mail."

"At the mercantile." Dominique nodded to Lyle O'Leary. The scrawny college student wore baggy jeans and a black sweatshirt. "I'm here to pay for my paint. Did your dad decide what he wants on the windows?"

"You'll have to ask him." Lyle jerked his head in the direction of the stairs leading to the loft. "He's tracking down water pipe for Rob Hendrickson. He's repairing two or three more cabins out at their place. His wife plans to rent them as soon as they're ready."

"Interesting. Is it someone who may want to buy a house eventually?"

"Possibly." Lyle rang up the sale for Mac. "If I hear that, I'll send them your way."

"Sounds great." Dominique flashed her brightest smile at Lyle. "Could you drop off the paint at the realty for me? I'd like to get started on the windows this Friday afternoon when it warms up."

He nodded. "Sure. I'll do it as soon as my sister gets here to take over the register."

"Fantastic. You're a doll!"

If Lyle had been a puppy, he'd have wagged all over. Since he wasn't, he just grinned back at her. Outside, Dominique suggested Mac follow her to the large cedar-shake building that held the mercantile. It was across from the feedstore, and she'd take him there next. He needed to meet a few more of his new neighbors and other business owners.

What would have been a general store in the past was a combination of a grocery store and the nearest deli. Before Aiden reopened the hardware last year, it'd also been where the locals picked up a few needed supplies for repairs. Maxine Garvey, a tall, distinguished woman with silver hair stood behind the hot food case, boxing up an order of fried chicken.

Dominique inclined her head in greeting and waited while Maxine finished with the customer and the woman left after a lingering, admiring look at Mac. "This is my cousin, Mac MacGillicudy. He needs a mailbox."

"Of course, he does." Maxine smiled and gestured toward the far wall. "Go take a look and see what size suits you, Mac. There's a couple cardboard boxes waiting in the back for you too."

"Good. Hopefully, one of them is my new coffee grinder." Mac looked around. "Do you have organic beans?"

Dominique could have sworn the older woman rolled her eyes and hastily answered. "Mac, you're in the boonies here. The closest place you'll find those is in Lake Maynard at a bigger store with more selection."

"Didn't you say one of the local farmers had organic produce, meat and eggs?"

"Yes, that's the Murphy clan. I'll take you there tomorrow." Dominique waved to the rows of shelves filled with various groceries. "For now, see what you can find here."

Once he was out of earshot, she whispered. "Sorry, Maxine. I thought he was a big, tough Army Ranger. I didn't realize he was a gourmet."

"Not your fault." Maxine laughed. "It shocked me for a moment, but I'm happy to do special orders. Tell your cousin to make a list."

"I will."

The bell jangled over the door and a tall, older man entered the store. Broad shoulders filled out his blue uniform shirt tucked neatly into dark blue slacks. A belt around his waist held all the paraphernalia that a law enforcement officer needed. Short black hair liberally sprinkled with white was barely visible under his western hat, modeled after the Canadian Mounties' version. "Saw your rig, Dominique, and wanted to touch base with you."

"Is something wrong with one of my listings, Dick?" Dominique frowned, concern mounting when the police chief shook his head. "Has a property been vandalized?"

"No, it's Veronika." Dick folded muscular arms. "She isn't hurt. Didn't crash her car or anything. I stopped over at the church, but she darted into the restroom and wouldn't come out when I was there."

"What's she done now, Dick?" Maxine rearranged an assortment of candy bars on the counter. "She hasn't been in here since I kicked her out a couple weeks ago for bouncing another check on me. Told her I was going to include her in my 'bad paper' club and hang those on the wall to embarrass her daddy again."

Heat swamped Dominique's cheeks. She saw understanding mixed with pity on Dick's rugged features. She repeated the question. "What's she done?"

"Dined and dashed at Pop's last night and she still owes for everything she's drank and eaten there during the past two months. He's not pressing charges. He wants her to do dishes with Dray at the holiday dinner on Thanksgiving. Will you see to it?"

Dominique clenched her fists, tears burning, nails biting into her palms. She longed to scream that it wasn't fair. She had plans for the day. She wanted to be with her friends in Seattle, not have to babysit her younger, bratty sister. For God's sake, the woman was thirty-two. When would she grow up?

Things never changed in Baker City, Dominique thought. "Sure, Dick. I'll make it happen."

"Or I will." Mac advanced on them, holding out his free hand to shake Dick's. "Hello. Mac MacGillicudy. Linda's already enlisted me to help cook, so it's no problem to give Veronika a ride to the café. Plus, I owe her for sending the guys to clear the driveway and Ted Fenwick to get me connected to the world. Do you want to text her and let her know I'm coming, Dominique?"

"No. I'll let you surprise her. Whenever I touch base with her about something like this, she disappears."

Dick chuckled. "I'll meet you at Veronika's on Thursday morning, Mac. She can either go with you to work at the café or I'll arrest her, and she can spend the holiday weekend in jail."

CHAPTER EIGHT

Throughout the day, Veronika pasted on a polite smile and struggled not to be her snarky, nasty self when several poor, pathetic losers lined up in the church parking lot outside the community room. Holding a clipboard, Reverend Tommy Thompson greeted the needy parishioners at the door. They signed in and then came to the tables where his wife, Virginia and her crew waited to dole out the appropriate holiday baskets.

Well, they weren't actually baskets. They were cardboard boxes and large paper sacks filled with assorted food items including bags of russet and sweet potatoes, celery, onions and apples from the Murphy farm. Nighthawke Security had once again donated turkeys, hams and prime rib roasts. It didn't surprise Veronika that turkeys were the most popular choice. Families received bigger birds while single person households had smaller ones or leg quarters.

When dusk fell, Reverend Tommy locked the doors. The silver-haired elderly man came toward the table and remaining baskets. As always, he didn't wear the traditional dark suit associated with most preachers, but a plaid, flannel shirt tucked into faded jeans and battered cowboy boots. "Great job, everyone."

"I'm so glad nobody in town will go hungry this year." Virginia, a stately woman with silver-streaked dark hair began to pass out the last of the baskets to the volunteers. "We couldn't have done it without all of you. Thanks again for the help."

Like I had a choice, Veronika thought bitterly. She didn't say that. Instead, she went to the coat rack and collected her fake leopard-skin jacket. She swung it around her shoulders. "See you later."

"Don't forget your Thanksgiving dinner." Virginia's friendly smile didn't fade. "You're so helpful, Veronika. I know we can count on you for the food drive next week."

Veronika nearly told the older woman to choose a different sacrificial lamb. *No way! I'm not coming back here and sucking up for one more crapfest.* She stopped, recalling the time-sheet kept in the church office. She had to complete a hundred hours of community service and Virginia had only signed off on sixteen. *That means I have to do another eighty-four hours before the end of December and so far, Jack's father hasn't approved any of those I did at the library. He seems to think being President of the Baker City Business Association makes him in charge of the world. Not mine!*

"Here you go, Ronnie." Reverend Tommy brought over the last box. "See you on Sunday."

"I don't do church." Veronika reluctantly accepted the food. "I'll be here Monday."

She walked out the back door before the older couple continued the conversation. She was done talking to them. Her father had ignored all the texts she sent him during the last two days, so she'd been stuck working here. He couldn't avoid her forever. She'd go to the bank he managed in Lake Maynard tomorrow and raise hell until he arranged for his lawyer to step up and get her out of helping with the food drive. Enough was enough!

She put the box on the passenger seat of her Subaru before she walked around to the driver's side. She wanted a beer, but she couldn't go to Pop's Café, after the old man sent the police chief to find her. She grimaced. Why had she been such an idiot yesterday? If she hadn't bailed after dinner and refused to pay her bill or her bar tab from the past month, then she could go to the cocktail lounge.

Now, she'd have to settle for the Baker City Saloon and Happy Hour appetizers. The owner, Steve Garvey wouldn't let her run a tab, not even for the night. She'd have to pay for her beers as soon as he delivered them. For a moment, she contemplated going home to her apartment upstairs in the old library, but that meant preparing her own supper. Nope, not happening. The bar would have to do.

Luckily, there was an on-street parking spot in front of the tavern. She glanced at the holiday basket on the other seat. Steve's partner, Jasmine Shaw, would undoubtedly know someone who needed it and probably wouldn't let the minister, or his do-gooder wife know what Veronika actually did with it.

Wednesday afternoon, Lilly joined Florence, and they left for the town library. Because school ended early today, Doireann O'Sullivan, the original Baker City teacher, would meet them there. Lilly froze when she glimpsed the distinctive brick building with two white columns across from the decrepit post office and the marquee of a once grand movie theater.

Lilly climbed up the stairs of the old structure, staring at the words engraved above the doors and the windows on either side of them. "It's a Carnegie library. I don't believe it. How did the town ever manage to get one?"

"By meeting Andrew Carnegie's requirements. He was a rich industrialist who made his fortune in steel. At the end of his life, he decided to use some of his wealth to promote literacy and build free libraries all around the world." A woman conservatively attired in a white blouse and long black skirt, beautiful red hair pinned up in a loose bun on her head joined them. Her voice still held a musical lilt, straight from Ireland. "I helped the first Baker City town council draft our proposal."

"What did that include, Doireann?" Florence asked.

"We had to demonstrate the need for a public library, provide the building site, agree to pay staff and maintain the library, draw from public funds to run the library—not just private donations, provide ten percent of the cost of the library's construction to support its operation and give free service to everyone in town."

"You did a wonderful job." Lilly glanced at the other ghost. "It's beautiful. I'm Lilly Bryce. I just arrived last Sunday."

"Doireann O'Sullivan. I was the first teacher here." She led the way through the doors, and they floated into a beautiful entry that opened into a large room filled with empty bookshelves. "After my husband died, I returned to teaching and remained at the school until I died when several avalanches wiped out part of the town."

"I'm so sorry," Lilly said.

"Oh, it happened more than a hundred years ago. This is my home now." Doireann smiled and tucked her arm in Florence's, hugging her. "I love it here and I have so many friends, especially since Cat O'Leary-McTavish and her girls came."

Lilly listened to stories about the town as they explored the different rooms in the building. Most of the remaining books were carefully packed in boxes and kept in a storeroom in the back. "Why aren't they out where people can enjoy them?"

"Because the Baker City Business Association has arranged for Veronika MacGillicudy to live here and refurbish the place. So far, all she's done is put away the remaining books that were still on the shelves." Florence gestured to the fading paint on the walls. "New paint, new carpet, new desks and computers are on order, but she isn't ready for those yet."

"Heaven knows when she will be." Doireann heaved a sigh. "The last time I was here, she was trying to convince Frank Madison, the president of the group that he should persuade his people to sell it to her father. Frank told her to scrub down the place and get it ready for his crew to paint it, but she told him to send a cleaning service because she wasn't a maid."

Florence shuddered in horror. "If Herman buys it, he'll just tear it down for his gravel pit. He wants to destroy the town."

"It's been his plan for years." Doireann led the way upstairs,

82

floating through the ceiling. "We have to stop him. It's why most of us are still here."

"Sign me up to help." Lilly drifted around the one-bedroom apartment, checking out the architectural features from the large bay windows to the old-fashioned, eat-in kitchen. "The downtown library in Seattle was my sanctuary when I was a child. After I died, I went back there and stayed until I met Mac. When he invited me to join him on his book tour, I did, and we've been together the last three years."

"And now he can see and hear you." Florence turned to face Doireann. "We haven't learned why, at least not yet."

"Is he an O'Leary?" Doireann tilted her head to one side, sky-blue eyes curious. "Newt O'Leary says his kin have enough O'Leary blood in them that they can see us if their minds are open and the MacGillicudys are like the rest of the families here. We're all related if you go back far enough."

"His mother hasn't told Mac about his other relatives, and I don't know if he's an O'Leary or not." Lilly explored the kitchen, admiring the china in the glass-fronted cabinets. "He doesn't know either."

"Talk to him and find out," Doireann suggested. "I'll be asking around town and learning what happened with his kith and kin."

"That means I'll have to stop co-opting his computers and TV for a few days," Lilly said. "I've been streaming women's history documentaries and making him watch them for the past two days."

"Why?"

"Because he talked when he should have listened," Florence announced. "The three of us have enough energy that we could drop a book or two beside his bed. Let's find a copy of the *Handmaid's Tale* for him. If he reads that, he may learn we don't want to live it."

"Sure, and there are other tales to teach him we want equality and respect." Doireann pointed at the small, dusty bookcase near the windows. "We may find some there."

On Wednesday, Mac reconned the entire main floor of the hotel but didn't find Lillian anywhere. He knew she had to be somewhere in the building because she was still messing with his computers. When he went to the café for lunch, he took his laptop but couldn't get past the memes to his manuscript.

Dray came in from the lounge to tell his grandfather that customers were complaining about the women's suffrage documentary on TV. It didn't matter how often he changed channels. The show kept popping up regardless. "What do you want me to do?"

"Tell them to stop annoying the ghosts." Coffee pot in hand, Pop strolled around the room topping off cups. "It's better than the late-night John Wayne war movie marathons."

Mac waited until the teenager left. "Are you serious? Do you think your place is haunted?"

"Pretty much it's the cocktail lounge." Pop lingered by the corner table. "It's not actually open yet but I have a few loggers who like to play pool in the morning. It won't hurt them to learn some American history."

"True enough." Mac focused on finishing his cheeseburger. He wouldn't tell the old man he'd already seen that particular show or two others about women who served in the military during World War Two or a real-life film about life in the late 1940s.

The bell jangled over the door, and he saw Dominique, accompanied by a tall, blonde man in cowboy gear – jeans, a flannel shirt and boots. He kissed her cheek, then sauntered toward the lounge.

She waved at Mac and came to join him. Instead of a clinging dress and stilettos, she wore slacks, a blue sweater and low-heeled boots. "Ready to go to the Murphy's? I'd have introduced you to my older brother, but he has friends waiting for him at the bar."

Pop arrived with a pot of tea and a ceramic mug for her. "I don't know how long he'll stay because the local spirits are watching educational shows."

"It'd do him good to learn some sensitivity." Dominique laughed and sat down. "He always makes piecrust promises, easily made, and easily broken. He's such a commitment-phobe and breaks hearts everywhere. I'm tired of apologizing for him to the single women in town."

"Well, he'd better watch his step, or the ghosts of Baker City will decide to teach him a lesson in manners." Pop walked away before Dominique answered.

"So much for sympathy or male solidarity." Mac drank his coffee. "I made a list of the vegetables I want."

"Shouldn't be a problem." Dominique sipped her peppermint tea. "At this time of year, Lock has a great selection in the greenhouses." She paused. "Quick FYI. His older brother was my high school sweetheart. I went off to college and he enlisted in the Army. No broken hearts on either side, but sometimes old news is new again."

"Especially in small towns."

"Exactly."

Outside of town, it only took a few minutes to reach the Murphy home. After they crossed a narrow, arching private bridge over the river, Mac saw black Angus cattle grazing in pastures that lined the evergreen-shrouded driveway. Frost glittered on the trees and rimmed the grass. The gravel drive swirled around and eventually, Dominique stopped in front of a three-story house with a tower, balconies, and even a wraparound porch. She'd no sooner parked when the back door opened and a short, silver-haired woman in jeans and a flowered top hurried across the porch toward them.

Smiling, she greeted Dominique with a quick hug and a kiss on her cheek before turning to Mac. "I'm Bronwyn Murphy. Welcome to my home."

"Mac MacGillicudy." He held out his hand to shake hers. "I'm Dominique's cousin and she said this was the place to find organic produce."

"That's perfect." Bronwyn beamed at him. "You two timed it just right. As soon as the girls get home from school, we're going to visit

Sully and my grandbabies. On Wednesdays, we always jump in and help around her house."

"Aren't mothers-in-law supposed to be mean?" Dominique teased. "It doesn't sound like you're doing a good job."

"Such a sassy girl." Brownyn tucked her arm through Dominique's and led the way to the gravel paths behind the house. "Be nice to me or I'll fix you up with one of my single sons. What about you, Mac? Do I need to matchmake for you too? After our brood grew up, Joe and I started doing foster care, so we have several single daughters."

"Oh, I'm good, Mrs. Murphy." Mac laughed. "I just arrived on Sunday. Let me be here for at least a week before you find me a wife."

That earned him a long, steady look from Bronwyn's blue-gray eyes before she nodded. "I couldn't believe you called about veggies, Dominique. I didn't know you cooked."

It was the glamor queen's turn to laugh. "Not hardly. It's Mac's thing, definitely not mine. If we decide to open the hotel again, he'll have to supervise the cooks and the kitchen. He prefers 'real' food and that's why I brought him here."

Bronwyn guided them to the first of the greenhouses. It was a high tunnel design, an unheated, plastic-covered structure with an arched frame. "We use this one to extend the growing season and protect plants from harsh weather."

"That makes perfect sense." Mac walked down the aisle, spotting root vegetables like carrots, beets, and various types of potatoes in the raised beds.

Further down, he saw leafy greens – spinach, lettuces and kale. At the far end, there was winter squash and pumpkins. When he headed up the next row, there were other vegetables, onions, leeks, Brussel sprouts and even some cabbage.

"Wow, this is impressive." Mac glanced at Bronwyn. "Do you have a CSA program? I'd like to join it."

"What's that?" Dominique asked. "I never heard of it."

Bronwyn gave an approving smile at Mac before she answered the question. "My son, Lock started our Community Supported Agriculture programs when he came home from the Marines." She glanced at Dominique. "It's the system where people invest in a farm's harvest at the beginning of the year before we actually start planting. They receive a share of the crops throughout the growing season, depending on what we have."

"I know a lot of people around here get their eggs, milk, cheese and meat from you too."

"We're pretty self-sustaining." Bronwyn pointed to a smaller bed filled with dirt. "I'll have fresh garlic next summer."

"Oh, I definitely need some of that."

After he chose what he wanted in the hoop house, Bronwyn took them to the heated greenhouse so he could select tomatoes, cucumbers and bell peppers. They finished off with a trip to the building where Lock kept the frozen meat. His mother explained that they didn't butcher on the farm but arranged for the animals to go to a local slaughterhouse. The beef, pork, lamb and poultry came back in neatly wrapped paper packages which were sold to their customers.

After they loaded his purchases in the back of the Jeep, Bronwyn lingered by the passenger door for a moment. "I think I may have gone to school with your mom, Mac. What's her name?"

"Donna MacGillicudy." Mac opened the door. "She's a veterinarian and specialized in horses before she retired."

"Then I do know her." Bronwyn patted Mac's arm. "It always surprised me that she didn't come back to Baker City. Tell her that I said, 'hello,' next time you talk."

"I will." Mac hesitated, then deliberately added, "Next time I come, maybe you could tell me more about the two of you growing up in Baker City. It's the first time I've been here, and I'd love to know everything."

"Oh, honey, I'm not the one to ask." Bronwyn smiled, shaking her head. "I grew up in Lake Maynard. I didn't come to Baker City until I finished college and married Joe. Talk to Aiden O'Leary. He's always lived here, and he and your mom were an item in high school."

CHAPTER NINE

Mac left two pumpkins on the back porch, but everything else went into the refrigerator and freezer. He found a note from Ted Fenwick on the counter by the coffee urn saying that the phones and Internet were good to go on the main floor. He'd be back on Friday to work on the rest of the system.

After he cleaned the litter boxes, Mac headed down the driveway to check on that project. A tall, brown-haired man about his age stood watching the loggers work. Under a long, black overcoat, he wore a dark three-piece suit, a white shirt, black tie, and despite the mud, highly polished dress shoes. In his right hand, he held a thickly carved wooden cane. A fedora covered part of his short, salt and pepper hair.

Jack Madison lowered the splitting maul and gestured to the stranger. "Hey, Mac. This is Jeff Ransom, the manager of Hawke Construction. He finally had a chance to get here to talk to you about the elevators and the electricity at the hotel."

"The job they're on took too long so the electricians will be here on Friday. Did Dominique tell you that we have a painting crew?" Jeff limped forward to shake Mac's hand. He spoke in a deep, gravelly voice. "Because of the winter weather, things will quiet down, and I can send a few of them here to start before Christmas."

"It will take at least a couple months to do the renovations." Mac glanced toward the huge building behind them. "And we'll want to paint the exterior in May or June unless it's warm enough in March or April."

"Let's go look inside and see where you want to start."

"Works for me." Mac slowed his pace, so Jeff didn't have to hurry although he barely seemed to need the cane. They strolled up the driveway.

Mac gestured toward the cane. "If it's none of my business, say so. Was it a car accident?"

"No. I flew choppers for the Army till the last one went down. Spent two years as a prisoner in Colombia until I was rescued by some mercs from Nighthawke Security."

"I had a few offers from them when I left the Army." Mac led the way through the main doors. "What about you? Did you ever want to be an independent contractor? Fly for them?"

"I've served my time. I'm happy running the construction company with my wife for Durango Hawke. He has a lot on his plate between it and the local office of Nighthawke at the dude ranch outside of town." Jeff nodded at the reception desk. "Hello."

Mac followed his gaze but didn't see anyone. Was Lillian skulking around? "Who's here?"

"I'm not a medium like Cat O'Leary-McTavish," Jeff said. "Sometimes, I catch a hint of those who've been here before. According to what I've heard, the hotel has been here since the late 1940s, so I'm sure we'll see the previous inhabitants once in a while."

"The last two wings were added in the 1970s." Mac pointed to the elevators. "I don't want to use those until they've been checked out."

"Makes sense to me. I'll have it done Friday." Jeff paused. "Guess I should tell you that a few of our crew haven't been back that long from Afghanistan. They need time and space to decompress. Painting rehabs them."

"Works for me." Mac eyed the other man. "Let's start with the parlor, the dining rooms, and bathrooms on the main floor. The kitchen, pantry and manager's apartment are already updated. I want to keep the wood paneling in the library and my office. My cousin, Linda MacGillicudy had her crew wash and oil those walls."

"Fair enough." Jeff adjusted his hat. "We already painted the bathrooms and put down new floor tile on this level. It won't take long to install the new toilets, mirrors and sinks."

"Good to know," Mac said.

They spent the next two hours deciding what needed to be done on the main floor and then in the basement. Mac's phone buzzed before they could go any further. When he checked it, he found a text from Linda asking if he could come to the café and help Pop prep for the holiday meal. They'd start serving at noon on Thursday. Hawke Construction donated a dozen large turkeys, plus hams and prime rib roasts, but they needed to be cooked. Of course, they also needed to deal with the usual dinner crowd today.

Mac sent a message that he'd be there soon. He saw Jeff out, took care of the cats and then headed for his Jeep Wrangler-Sahara. The note from Linda reminded Mac that he'd promised to bring Veronika with him for KP the next day. He texted Dominique and asked where her sister lived. On his way to the café, he made a point of driving past the small, brick building that housed the town library. He recognized the distinctive architecture, even before he saw the lettering that proclaimed it was a Carnegie library. He'd have to ask Veronika for a tour.

———

Moises Pride drifted through the cocktail lounge at Pop's Café in Baker City, Washington. It wasn't super busy on the Wednesday night before Thanksgiving. Most people had other commitments, shopping, cooking, visiting their relatives, but he wasn't one of them, not anymore.

That's because I'm dead, dead, dead! Sorry, Momma. Another year of missing the family reunion, all the relatives and your sweet potato pie.

He spotted a few of the other ghosts hanging out, watching the action between the living patrons. An old-time holiday movie played on the big-screen TV in the corner of the room. He floated toward the booth where Mayor O'Connell, a middle-aged fellow in a black suit sat talking to Zeke Garvey and Raven Driscoll-Barlow, two former soldiers who'd died in ambushes in Afghanistan. Their war might not be his, but it didn't mean they didn't have a lot in common when it came to paying the ultimate price for serving their country.

Nodding respectfully, Moises waited to join the conversation. Raven, a thin, dark-haired wraith in camouflage fatigues and combat boots, gestured at two of the people sitting at the bar, focused on their conversation and one another. "You have something to do with that, Pride? Are you following Garvey's example and playing Cupid the way he did with Ann Barrett and Harry Colter?"

"I just gave them a little nudge." Moises followed her gaze toward the lovely ash-blonde woman in a red dress and the soldier next to her. Derek Waller was a solid, muscular man whose worn features looked as if he'd won more fights than he'd lost in his thirty-plus years of military service. A 'high and tight' style for his receding salt and pepper black hair, dark brown, almost black eyes, he was all man.

"I've hung out at the barn for the past few months, and I've seen Kyra O'Neill busting her butt. She deserves someone decent, not that candy-assed horseshoer who bullies the animals when he's sure nobody's watching."

"These two were betting on how long she'd wait for some guy tonight." Raven frowned thoughtfully. "Is that him?"

"Not the Sergeant-Major," Moises said. "I already told you. She's hung up on Nick MacGillicudy and I'd like to do something about the jerk."

Mayor O'Connell rubbed his jaw. "What do you have in mind, Pride?"

"Oh, let's get in the holiday spirit." Moises pointed at the TV. "We could do our own *Christmas Carol* to Nick MacGillicudy and teach him what he needs to know."

"He might even move on and leave town," Zeke agreed. "I never liked the guy when we were in high school. Do I get to be the *Ghost of Christmas Past*?"

"You're not the only one who has issues with Herman MacGillicudy and his son," Mayor O'Connell said. "That banker has been running Baker City into the ground for years. He tries to get his grown kids to help him rip off our kin."

"He won't be happy until he levels the place and turns it into one of his gravel pits," Zeke said. "His daughter, Dominique, the realtor may say she's on the same page, but that isn't true, not when she finds buyers for the houses and businesses here. She helped my wife purchase the bakery after I died. "

"She restores the places that need it before she sells them," Raven pointed out. "I like Dominique. She did right by my bestie and her hubby. They love the home she found for them. I visited a lot before Sully had the twins and now I check in on the babies too."

The mayor nodded. "Dominique takes after her momma, one of the O'Leary women." He paused, obviously considering Moises' suggestion. "Most of our folks will be here tomorrow when Pop sets up his holiday meal. Let's get everyone involved. Things have been downright dull since the haunted town festival last month and the Veteran's Day Parade a couple weeks ago. We need something to do now."

It'd taken energy from all three of them to bring books from the library to the bedroom in the manager's apartment at the hotel. Lilly chose It's *Up to The Women* by First Lady, Eleanor Roosevelt, a book of advice to women of all ages on every aspect of life during the Great Depression. Florence insisted that Mac needed to read *A Handmaid's Tale* by Margaret Atwood and suggested Lilly stream the TV series for him.

Doireann picked a newer release about Hemingway's third wife. *Yours, for Probably Always: Martha Gellhorn's Letters of Love and War*

1930-1949. She was a novelist, journalist, and intrepid war correspon-
dent who didn't hesitate to express her views about what she saw
and heard. She was often annoyed and exasperated by the fact that
her short time as "Mrs. Hemingway" from 1940 to 1945 invariably
eclipsed her writing and, consequently, she never received her
full due.

"Hopefully, this will open Mac's eyes, and he'll realize we're real
people with dreams of our own." Lilly smiled at the two older ghosts.
"If we were still alive, I'd offer you some sort of refreshments."

"Well, that's why we often go to the café," Florence explained.
"We can smell whatever Pop is cooking."

"Let's go to the bakery instead." Doireann turned from where she
petted the kittens who nestled on the king-size bed. "Sure, and Twila
Garvey will be making pies and rolls for Pop's feast tomorrow. She
has those lovely cheesecakes too."

"Perfect." Lilly started for the door. "I haven't been there yet, and I
want to see everything in Baker City."

After a half-dozen combat tours, Mac didn't sleep much anymore.
Too damned many nightmares and flashbacks. It was after two in the
morning when he returned to the hotel. He'd chopped onions, and
celery, then combined them with day-old breadcrumbs, butter and
herbs. Pop added dried cranberries, eggs and chicken stock. Once the
stuffing was ready, it went into the birds. Since he had three commercial ovens, he could roast three turkeys at a time, and they put the first
batch in before Mac left.

Linda and Dray said they'd cook the hams at their house and
bring those back with them in the early morning when they traded
shifts with Pop. Mac promised to pick up Veronika and be there by
nine to meet Twila Garvey. The bakery owner was preparing desserts
and several varieties of rolls ranging from the traditional crescent
ones to cloverleaf to Parker House ones. It seemed like everyone
around town jumped in to help make the holiday dinner special,

either by supplying food or assisting in other ways. Mac found himself looking forward to the experience.

He stopped in the bedroom and eyed the three hardcovers on the nightstand. Obviously, Lillian had been there, but how did she manage to bring books here, especially since he hadn't found any in the hotel yet? She was a ghost. Yes, she could move objects. She certainly caused a coffee cup to fly at him. But, books were much heavier than a mug, especially three of them.

How on earth had she done it? Well, he couldn't ask when she was ignoring him and playing least in sight. As soon as she turned up again, he'd try to find out. Meanwhile, he had to decide how to approach Aiden O'Leary and see if he remembered Mac's mother. Too many unanswered questions, he thought. He'd only been in Baker City four days. No wonder, he didn't know enough about what was happening in town. He'd see what he learned when he made his duty call to his mom later today.

Lillian still didn't seem to be around when he left a few hours later. If she was, she didn't appear in person, or at least in an insubstantial form. It only took a few minutes to drive to the library. He parked behind Veronika's Subaru. He wasn't the first one to arrive. Dick O'Connell climbed out of his cruiser and led the way to the rear of the brick building.

They climbed the stairs and Dick knocked on the back door. He waited and then pounded again like a cop on TV. "Come on, Veronika. We have places to go."

When the door opened, she stood there in a short, red robe over a flimsy nightgown with cute bunny slippers on her feet. Confusion filled her stunning face. "What are you doing here?"

"Giving you two choices." Dick folded muscular arms. "Get dressed and go with Mac to help with the holiday meal at the café."

"Why should I?" She lifted her chin, danger glinting in the big blue eyes. "I'm going to my dad's."

"Not today. You owe Pop some major bucks for a bar tab and your meals. Go with Mac or I'll arrest you. You'll spend the weekend in the county jail."

"You can't do that!"

"Don't push your luck, kid. You're thirty-two. Grow up!"

She scowled at the police chief and then at Mac. "I'll call Daddy. He'll pay whatever Pop wants."

"And until he does, you're on dish duty." Dick jerked his head toward the inside of the apartment. "You have five minutes. Get dressed or you'll go in your jammies."

Muttering swear words, Veronika spun around and stormed away. "I'm telling my lawyer to sue you."

"Good luck with that."

Mac waited until she was out of earshot. "Do you think her dad will show up at the café and raise a ruckus?"

"He never has before." Dick shifted so he could watch the interior of the one-bedroom apartment. "Now, if it was her momma, then I'd be scared. However, she moved to Liberty Valley when Veronika left for college. We probably won't see Jenny O'Leary before Christmas."

"O'Leary? Is she related to Aiden?"

"One of his cousins." Dick grinned. "He wouldn't allow his younger sisters to date Herman MacGillicudy, Veronika's dad."

They heard footsteps and she stomped across the loft-style apartment toward them. She wore a plain white long-sleeved shirt over a blue tank-top, her favorite slashed jeans, and running shoes. Amazingly, she'd had time to put on makeup, a spritz of cologne and French braid her hair.

Mac glanced quickly at his watch and realized Dick had actually given her twelve minutes rather than five. They waited while she locked the door and then headed for the vehicles. "I'd love a tour of the library."

"Why?" Veronika shot a glare at him. "There isn't anything to see."

"How is the restoration coming?" Dick asked. "Frank Madison says you're supposed to open in January and start literacy classes for kids. Aren't you and his daughter, Ann Barrett working together on those?"

"She's a pain in the butt and I'm not doing it." Veronika heaved a dramatic sigh. "She always wants to know why I got a teaching certificate when I didn't plan to use it."

"Why did you?" Mac asked.

"Because it was easier than the other degrees and it kept Daddy off my back when he had fits about me majoring in parties and jumping cute guys."

"Fair enough. Sounds like you enjoyed the college experience." Mac opened the passenger door for her. "Let's go."

"I'll be in and out of the café today checking on you." Dick stood close by while she slid into the Jeep. "You'd better stay there and work until Pop says you're done, Ronnie. If I have to track you down, you know where I'll take you."

"All right. You already said that." She yanked the seatbelt into place. "And I'm not going back to the Gray-Bar Hotel. It sucked the last time."

Pity stirred within Mac. He walked around to the driver's side. When they were alone, he asked, "Why were you in the hoosegow?"

"It wasn't my fault." She lifted her chin, still glaring. "Linda ratted me out for driving home when I had a couple drinks. And Dick was being a major jerk. He didn't have to embarrass me by making me do stupid things like putting my finger on my nose or giving me a breathalyzer test. Then, he freaking arrested me."

"Driving under the influence risks your life and everybody else's on the road."

"Save the lecture for someone who cares, Mac. I get enough of that crap from my relatives. Even Daddy said I was lucky to end up with community service."

"What about ninety meetings in ninety days? Did you do those?"

"Not yet." She shrugged. "My lawyer said to do the other stuff first. It's why I'm stuck at the library doing community service for Frank Madison. I have to get rid of the old books so there will be room for the new ones that Ann is ordering. Jack is coming Friday to take most of them to the dump."

"No!" Mac's hands tightened on the steering wheel. "I'll take them for the library at the hotel."

CHAPTER TEN

That afternoon Mac stood at the steam table. He filled three plates with servings of mashed potatoes and gravy, candied yams, slices of turkey, stuffing, and green bean casserole. Near a counter adjacent to the walk-in cooler, Linda completed the order with dishes of ambrosia fruit salad and Thanksgiving slaw.

Dray came through the swinging doors from the dining room. He began to fill the baskets on his tray with an assortment of warm rolls from the oven. "Jimmy Penrose is here looking for you, Mac. I told him you'd be out in a few minutes."

"Thanks." Mac picked up the full plates and followed Dray. Once he served them to the waiting guests, he headed toward his buddy who sat on a stool at the counter. Jimmy had dressed down for the occasion in jeans, a purple University of Washington sweatshirt and boots.

"Hey, glad you made it."

"Told you I would when you texted me." Jimmy grinned, shaking his head. "Should have known you'd find a kitchen somewhere to work. What's good?" He paused. "Well, since you're cooking, probably everything is."

"I'm just the sous-chef here." Mac chuckled. "My cousin, Linda and her father are actually in charge."

"And if he believes that, I'll sell him a bridge in Arizona." Pop strolled over and held out his hand to shake Jimmy's. "Pop MacGillicudy. Now, why don't you and Mac grab some food and go eat in the lounge."

"We can stay out here." Jimmy immediately took charge. "I've closed my pub for the few weeks. I'm not interested in a busman's holiday."

"Not offering one. The lounge is closed today, which makes it a perfect place for you two to have some privacy to catch up. It's where the rest of the volunteers eat supper." Pop eyed Mac. "Don't think you've been there yet."

"No, I've only been here for a few days, and I really enjoy your kitchen."

"Take a load off." Pop walked behind the counter and called Linda's name. "Make up a couple meals for Mac and his friend, please. Dray can take them to the lounge." He turned back. "Plenty of places to sit in there except for the mayor's booth. Leave it unless he invites you to join him and his cronies."

"Sounds fair. Thanks, Pop." Mac led the way through the smaller dining room, bypassed the larger one and they eventually ended up in the empty cocktail lounge. Booths with vinyl seats lined two walls. Tables and chairs took up the center of the room with two pool tables nearer to the stage.

Sure enough, one of the booths had a gold rope, similar to that in a theater, cordoning it off from visitors. A placard on the table read, 'Reserved for Mayor O'Connell.'

Jimmy jerked his head toward that special booth. "Have you met him yet?"

"Nobody has in forever." Dray came in behind them, carrying a basket of bread rolls, a pitcher of ice water and two glasses. "He died seventy some years ago. He used to run the town from here once his office closed for the day. The story goes that he wanted to hear from the loggers and other folks who couldn't make it there to see him so he could solve their problems. My grandfather says he still does."

"Right." Jimmy walked over to an empty table, pulled out a chair. "And if I have an issue, I just tell him."

"Well, it's Baker City." Dray put the basket on the table, filled the glasses and left the pitcher. "You'd do better to ask *The O'Leary* to run interference when she's in town unless you're a medium like her who can talk to the dead and hear them answer."

Jimmy waited until the teenager left before he turned his attention to Mac. "So, is this when I hum the theme song from the *Twilight Zone*?"

"I wouldn't." Lillian Bryce sauntered closer. "You won't like the outcome."

Mac drew out the other chair and sat down, staring at her. Her Army uniform was perfect, including the hat and gloves she wore, her leather shoulder bag hanging precisely in place. "I thought you were pissed at me."

"I am, but I have high hopes you'll start to listen to me." She gestured to Jimmy. "Now, you better tell him that I'm here or he'll think you're totally bonkers."

Mac glanced at his long-time friend. "Okay, I haven't totally lost my mind, but we're not alone in here."

"Really?" Jimmy arched a dark brown eyebrow. "Is the mayor here?"

"I have no idea, but First Lieutenant Lillian Bryce is."

Jimmy blinked, looked around the room. "Okay, hate to break it to you, Sergeant-Major, but we're alone. Have you fallen off the wagon? Do you need to call your sponsor? Have you contacted him since you're back in Washington State?"

"I'm sober. And I know how crazy this sounds, but I've been seeing things since I got here." Mac shook his head. "Okay, not things. A ghost. One ghost. A woman who claims to have been haunting me for three years."

"And she's here now?" Jimmy shook his head. "I don't believe it. If you don't call your sponsor, I will."

"My goodness, he's nearly as stubborn as you are." Lillian gestured and a third chair moved away from the table. She sat down across from them. She beckoned again and the glass of ice water in front of Mac slid over to her. "Those crescent rolls smell divine. I think I'll try one."

Jimmy gaped at the basket when one of the buttery rolls floated in mid-air, then landed on a saucer and it moved to what appeared to be an empty place at the table. "Are you seeing this? Maybe, I'm the one who needs to talk to your sponsor or see about getting one of my own."

Mac sighed. "Welcome to my world. Lillian, that's enough. How can you eat a roll when you're dead?"

"I can't." Lillian admitted. "I'm just having fun here. And now that he's opening his mind and not threatening you, I'll leave you boys to enjoy yourselves. The mayor called a meeting and since everyone else is here, I'll go see what he wants."

Mac reached for the glass and saucer. "She's left. Now, let's have dinner."

Since it was Thanksgiving Day, the cocktail lounge was closed. Well, to everyone alive, that was, but Moises hadn't seen this large of a crowd of ghosts in months, not since his arrival last summer. Some wore various military uniforms, which went well back before World War Two. He looked around, spotting women in pioneer dresses, a few in flapper attire from the 1920s, and more in what he considered regular civilian clothes. He saw guys dressed as loggers and miners.

Wearing his usual dark suit, a black fedora shading his face, the mayor circulated among the group. A gray-haired man in a red plaid shirt that jarred with the orange suspenders holding up the cut-off, logging jeans joined the mayor on his rounds, and the two approached Moises.

"This is Newt O'Leary, Moises." Mayor O'Connell nodded a greeting. "He wants a part in the little melodrama you're directing for Christmas, and I promised we'd talk to you about it."

The notion of being the director rather than a participant was a pleasant idea. "I'll need some help, Mayor. I'm new here and I don't know everyone like you do."

"That's his job," Newt announced. "Get on with it, young fella. Tell the folks what we're doing this year. I wanna be *The Ghost of Christmas Present*. That no-good Nick always steals from my hardware store and my kin are tired of dealing with him. Causes holy hell with his family when they hear from the cops. I'll give him the kinda lesson he deserves."

His booming voice attracted attention, and the rest of the ghosts drifted closer. Moises glanced around and saw interest rather than disapproval. He hesitantly outlined his idea of reforming Nick MacGillicudy for the holidays.

That caused a snort of disgust from one of the women dressed more flamboyantly than the others. She twirled a red feather boa. "Honey, if that man came to my place back in the day, I'd have shown him the door. I had no room for a lounge lizard who wouldn't pay his shot or tried to take advantage of my gals."

"Faith and bejabbers." This time it was a woman more conservatively attired in a white blouse and long black skirt, beautiful red hair pinned up in a loose bun on her head. "Sure, and you'd have taken pity on the lad if you'd seen how his pa came after him more than oncet and lathered him with a belt in front of half the town."

"We can't all be as kindly minded as you are, Doireann O'Sullivan." Zeke Garvey drawled, standing next to Raven Driscoll-Barlow, a troop of soldiers behind them, including First Lieutenant Lilly Bryce and Bridget McElroy. "It's what makes folks recall the lessons you taught them even now. You're right. I remember when Nick won the toy semi-truck at the church Christmas bazaar. Before he could even drive it around the parking lot or give us rides in it, Herman took it away and sold it."

Moises saw some of the others nod in agreement. "I haven't been in Baker City that long and I don't know all the people around here like you do. However, I've seen Nick MacGillicudy in action out at Miracle Stable when he went after one of the horses and the new owner fired him. He's not much good as a horseshoer."

"Scuttlebutt is he only does it to try and get folks with large tracts of land to sell them to his dad and his cronies," Newt said. "Like we need more gravel pits around here. We don't. We need our town back. That's what Cat O'Leary-McTavish and the folks in the Baker City Business Association are trying to do, and it's why we're helping them."

"Nick should learn nothing he does will be good enough for his pa and quit trying." Florence MacGillicudy, a plump, gray-haired woman in a pioneer dress, spoke up. "When my granddaughter was a counselor at the high school twenty years ago, Mindy tried telling him that, but the boy never listened."

"It does sound like she made a good choice for someone to follow in her bootsteps out at the stable when she retired and sold Miracle," Mayor O'Connell commented. "And I understand what you folks are saying, but we've all seen that fellow scamming drinks from young ladies here at Pop's."

"The apple doesn't fall far from his daddy's tree." This time it was a different, older man who spoke. Moises had often seen him standing behind the bar giving directions to Linda MacGillicudy or Pop, but they didn't seem to notice the one-time bartender in his light shirt and dark slacks, garters on his sleeves. "I don't remember the number of times Herman claimed to have lost or forgotten his wallet and when I 86'd him back in my day, his pa would raise hell and put props under it."

"Well, let's vote on the proposal Moises Pride has suggested," the mayor said. "When I call for it, all those in favor of using a Baker City version of *A Christmas Carol* to redeem Nick MacGillicudy, say Aye. Those opposed will say, 'Nay.' Anybody undecided?"

"Just another question." A police officer in full regalia waved his hand. "What's to be the final result for young Nick? We can't harm him, or we'll answer to *The O'Leary*."

"Sure, and he either shapes up or he ships out of our town. No harm, no foul play." Doireann O'Sullivan folded her ghostly arms and nodded sternly. "It fair breaks my heart to see that girl, Kyra O'Neill a-weeping and a-wailing over the wastrel day after day, month after month, year after year. She deserves better than a lay-about."

"We couldn't agree more," Raven told her. "It's why Moises already fixed her up with one of Harry Colter's friends, Sergeant-Major Waller. He reminds me of that tough-guy, Canadian actor on TV, the one who sizzled even if he played a villain. When my husband was on the road, I used to stream that old series where he fought aliens who'd come to destroy Earth and eat all the humans."

"I'd like to see that." The former madam twirled her boa again. "I do enjoy a man who is one, even if I can only look nowadays."

The comment earned laughter from many of the other women, but before Raven could start the TV show, the mayor held up his hand. "We're voting now. All those in favor—"

Lilly abstained from the voting because unlike the other ghosts, she didn't know enough about the various participants. While it sounded like Nick MacGillicudy was the proverbial 'street gentleman and house-dog', she hated judging someone she hadn't met. Since they had the same last name, she wondered how Nick was related to Mac. Well, next time she talked to Mac, she'd ask. For now, she'd learned something new about the man she haunted.

She'd admired the fact that he didn't spend off-duty hours in bars when they traveled across America during his book tours. If he spent time with his old Army buddies, he didn't drink with them during their interminable poker games. At hotels, he preferred visiting various kitchens and talking to chefs. He never opened the liquor cabinets in the rooms but spent his free time working on the next book in his series or occasionally watching TV.

She didn't know where he'd gone when he explored different parts of the cities, but now she suspected he'd been attending AA meetings, not just tracking down somewhere to buy his favorite potato chips and Mexican Coca-Cola. She was a ghost. It didn't mean she haunted him day and night. Besides, she always had work to do on his manuscripts.

When Mac and his friend finished eating, they cleared their table. Taking the dishes with them, they went back to the kitchen to help serve holiday meals to latecomers. She liked that too. They didn't leave messes for others to clean. She drifted after them, through the hallway and past the large dining room to the smaller one closer to the kitchen. Mac helped his cousin dish up more holiday meals.

Jimmy jumped in to rinse empty plates and then pass them to the grumpy blonde woman who loaded the dishwasher. He ignored her complaints about Pop taking advantage of her good nature. Frankly, Lilly didn't think she had one.

I've never liked goldbrickers, someone who shirks responsibility or performs duties without proper effort or care. I already heard Pop say she's here because she owes him serious money.

"Are you sticking around here?" Raven floated closer. "Or coming back to the lounge with us? I have to give a sitrep to everyone."

"About what?"

Raven pointed a ghostly hand toward a tall, blond man talking to Dray. "Nick. He's refusing to give Pop a donation for the meal and bitching because the café doesn't provide leftovers."

"If he wants a second meal, he can pay for it." Lilly joined the other soldier and the two of them headed back toward the cocktail lounge. "Is he related to the gal doing the dishes?"

"That's his younger sister and as we already heard today, the 'apple doesn't fall far from the tree.' If I sponged off people, my family would totally freak out. What about yours?"

"I have no idea. I never met any of my parents' relatives. Of course, I always did chores in my foster homes and at the orphanages. None of us girls wanted to listen to the lectures the nuns gave us and they never 'spared the rod' if we were sassy or lazy." When Lilly brushed by the two men near the register, the older one flinched. He must be aware he wasn't alone, even if he didn't say so.

Later that night when she and Florence returned to the hotel, Lilly found Mac giving Jimmy a tour of the place. She decided to follow them through the basement although she'd heard most of their stories before. They usually talked about boot camp, military schools, stateside adventures, and rarely about what happened in combat.

"Thanks for helping Veronika with the dishes, Penrose. I know she wasn't thrilled with the idea, but it beat the alternatives."

"What were they?" Jimmy scooped up the orange kitten winding through his legs. "She kept bitching about Pop, Linda and Dray. They seemed decent enough to me."

"They are. Veronika's an alcoholic, but she doesn't seem to know it yet." Mac frowned. "Well, maybe she knows but she's not in touch with it. She doesn't admit it to anyone, much less herself. She doesn't pay her bar tab or for her meals at the café. She's a MacGillicudy so Pop won't press charges."

"He's not doing her any favors." Jimmy opened the door to the theater and glanced inside at the huge screen on the wall. "She needs to take responsibility for her actions, not take advantage of people in her family."

"I know, but she hasn't hit bottom yet." Mac leaned a broad shoulder against the doorframe. "She spent the morning complaining because Linda called the cops when Veronika was driving under the influence. She doesn't seem to understand that Linda didn't have a choice any more than you do if somebody's incapacitated."

"I always remind my bartenders to do the same thing when someone is too drunk to drive." Jimmy clicked on the light switch. "Washington State has a "dram shop law." Establishments and servers can be held liable if they serve alcohol to visibly intoxicated individuals who then cause harm or injury to themselves or others."

Mac stood watching Jimmy check out the theater. "Her older sister, Dominique, hasn't said anything about why Veronika self-medicates with booze."

"She may not know." Jimmy swung around. "You don't share all your traumas. Neither do a lot of other vets."

"I do with my sponsor, Jared. He's served. Written his share of letters when his soldiers couldn't come home." Mac shrugged. "And you've survived a few ambushes of your own. You don't need to hear me describe mine."

"True enough. Let's see what else there is to see here."

CHAPTER ELEVEN

At oh-two-hundred hours, Jimmy headed off to sleep in Mac's bedroom. Since he wasn't tired, Mac turned on his laptop to see if he could write or if Lillian still intended to block his efforts. Sure enough, a new screensaver appeared, a quote by Shirley Chisholm, the first African-American woman in Congress. "If they don't give you a seat at the table, bring a folding chair."

He rubbed his bearded jaw and glanced around the room. He didn't see Lillian anywhere, not even a wisp of her ghostly self. "Okay, you win. I'll quit treating the female characters like stereotypes. Now, will you please let me work?"

"All you had to do was ask nicely, Mister MacGillicudy." She laughed, the sound hanging in the air. The display on the computer changed, showing several small icons on the monitor. "Did you see the email from Gwen? She agrees the secretary should do more than make coffee, take shorthand and type."

"I saw it," Mac grumbled. "I should have realized the two of you were in cahoots. Thank heaven, my editor was off for the holiday or I'm sure she'd have agreed with the pair of you."

"I told you I sent them flowers."

This time when he glanced across the room, he glimpsed Lillian sitting on the couch. The cat and kittens curled up beside her. His mother must have been busy with her family and didn't pick up when he called to wish her a happy Thanksgiving. He'd ended up sending a holiday text to her and figured he'd touch base on the weekend.

"Are you going to tell me you sent a bouquet to my mother too?"

"No. I don't like her. She didn't read our books."

"Is that how you judge people?" Mac chuckled. "Lillian, some people don't like mysteries."

"It wouldn't matter if you wrote the next Pulitzer prizewinner. Your mother still wouldn't read it." Lillian flicked a glance at the TV. "Do you mind if I watch the next episode of *Call The Midwife*? Or will it bother you?"

"Nothing bothers me when I'm writing. You should know by now I'm not a diva."

"Good point, but in Italian, it's *divo*."

"Whatever." Mac shrugged and clicked on the icon he wanted.

The flat-screen came alive, and her favorite drama started. In moments, the show totally engrossed her, and she didn't speak to him again.

As usual, he had different files for his work in progress. One held the full story, and he read the first forty pages to the point where there was a dead man in the alley. He'd decided to humor his resident ghost and let her namesake find the corpse, but he hadn't expected it to be the detective's latest client. Well, that was a twist and a half.

He started a new document. The words flowed as he typed the next chapter. Dialogue snapped and sizzled between the secretary, her boss and then she stalked off when the local police officers arrived. Nobody seemed to understand why a man who wanted his runaway wife found would end up with his head bashed to bloody pieces.

Once the cops finished talking to him, Titus went into his second-story office where he discovered his secretary, Lillian, drinking coffee and rescheduling appointments. When he asked why, she pointed out nobody would want to see him while the police were investigating a crime close by. She suggested he track down the missing wife and see if she was still alive or find her remains if she wasn't. Her deceased husband might have killed her, disposed of the body and then hired a detective to cover his tracks.

That idea prompted an argument between the investigator and his wanta-be partner. Determined to prove her wrong, Titus decided to visit the house and next of kin. They needed to know about the death and then they'd undoubtedly hire him to continue solving the case. Mac frowned thoughtfully at the screen. The story was changing before his eyes, and it meant the original plot would have to evolve too.

He glanced over his shoulder at the woman engrossed in the show she streamed. "So, what do you think happened to the client's wife? Why did she leave him?"

"Well, if he didn't kill her this time, then she escaped before he beat her and the kids to death."

"Domestic violence wasn't that prevalent back then —"

A heavy silence fell before Lillian sighed, shaking her head. "Congress didn't pass the Violence Against Women act until 1994 and there have always been men who are family annihilators." She pointed at the laptop. "Time for you to do some research, Mister MacGillicudy."

A new tab on the screen opened and he saw an article detailing spousal abuse in the 1940s. For a moment, he considered telling her that he wrote to entertain his readers but then the statistics snagged his attention. He began to read the details in front of him.

About oh-five-hundred hours after Lillian faded away, he crashed on the couch. He woke to the smell of coffee four hours later. When he stumbled out to the kitchen, he found Jimmy making buckwheat pancakes. His buddy promptly handed over a mug of strong, black coffee.

Mac sat on a stool at the center island and took a hefty swallow. "Thanks. I needed this."

"Thought you might." Jimmy spooned batter onto the griddle. "I heard you talking last night but I wasn't sure if it was to yourself, the computer or the TV. Why were you watching some girly show?"

"I wasn't." Mac chuckled. "Lillian really likes *Call the Midwife*. And I don't mind listening to the TV or to music when I write. Besides, she lived during the 1940s, so it helps when I have questions about the setting of one of my books."

Jimmy scowled at the pancakes, then flipped them. "Okay, this is going to be totally weird but tell me more about your dead girlfriend."

"Not my girlfriend." Mac stared into the depths of his coffee for a moment, wondering if that was the truth. Maybe, he hadn't bothered looking at other women because he fantasized about the one who died so many years ago. "First Lieutenant Lillian Bryce was an Army nurse in World War Two and she didn't make it home. I didn't realize she haunted me until I arrived in Baker City."

"Good story. Stick to it." Jimmy stacked four pancakes onto a plate, two strips of bacon beside them and slid the dish across the counter. "Dude, you've been hung up on her since you wrote your first book. Otherwise, you wouldn't have named your heroine after her."

"Don't call me dude." Mac slapped butter on the hotcakes, drowned them in maple syrup. "And I thought she was a fictional character. I knew she was."

"Rangers don't lie to each other." Jimmy greased the skillet, ladled out more batter. "Or to themselves. Wake up and smell that coffee you're drinking, dude. You've got a thing for a ghost, man."

She'd had a great time hanging out with her friends in Seattle on Thanksgiving, but it was time to start her holiday painting, so Dominique loaded the containers of paint and her other supplies in the back of her Jeep and headed for the hotel. She'd paint Santa's sleigh and the reindeer on the hotel windows first. Sometimes, it took a while for her to regain the artist's skill she barely used in the real estate office.

Granted, she'd painted signs for the dude ranch and Heather

McElroy's place, plus she had an order for a new one at the riding stable, but those were different than the ones she did every year on the windows in Baker City. She spotted Jack Madison's pickup and pulled in beside it, wondering why he was here.

Did Mac want him to harvest more trees? Why? She'd noticed the driveway was cleared when she drove past it. Before they ordered in gravel, they just needed to get it graded and leveled to be rid of the potholes that were deep enough to sink an Army truck. She walked to the kitchen door, tapped on the glass before she entered.

She recognized Jack and her cousin, Mac. The guy in jeans and a plaid, flannel shirt with them was a stranger. Nice, she thought, taking time to study the handsome face. His golden-brown hair had specks of silver, and she guessed he had to be in his late thirties. She met his dark blue gaze and smiled. "Hi. I'm Mac's cousin, Dominique MacGillicudy."

"Jim Penrose." He gestured to the coffee maker. "Shall I make you a cup?"

"Please." She hitched up onto a stool at the center island, next to Mac and eyed him. "Tell me you're somewhat civilized and still have cream from the Murphy's place."

"In the fridge." He looked over his cup at her. "So, what's the occasion? Shouldn't you be doing a girly shopping spree on Black Friday?"

Dominique laughed and elbowed him. "I love shopping as much as the next woman, but my sorority sisters and I always do a big extravaganza. We check into a fancy downtown hotel in Seattle, shop all day, go to upscale, gourmet restaurants for dinner and take in a few shows. Meantime, I have windows to paint all over town first."

Jim put a cup of coffee in front of her and followed it with the container of cream. "Painting windows? What's that about?"

"Dominique is our resident artist." Jack leaned against the counter, flashing his most charming smile. "You should have noticed the signs at the Cedar Creek Guest Ranch and Hawke's Horse Heaven on the way into town. She painted those. Aren't you doing one for Debbie Ramsey, the new owner of Miracle Riding Stable?"

"As soon as we agree on the design." Dominique glanced at Mac. "Last time, I used the heated shop behind the hotel, next to the machine shed because it's big enough for me to work. I've stored supplies there for the renovations. Do you mind if I do my big projects there?"

"Not at all." Mac drank more of his coffee. "Let me know if you need me to move sheets of plywood or something." He stared across the room for a moment, then lifted one shoulder. "Okay, so I'm acting like a chauvinist when I offer to do the heavy lifting for a woman. I still think males are physically stronger than females. It's my macho thing. Deal with it."

"Where is that coming from?" Dominique demanded. "I didn't say anything that rude. Last time, Lyle O'Leary helped me when he delivered my order of wood."

Faint red crept along Mac's cheeks, but he didn't answer, and she frowned. "Anybody have a clue?"

Jim opened a container and proceeded to place a half-dozen large chocolate chip cookies on a plate. "I'd say somebody got his tail chewed by his girlfriend when he overstepped the bounds."

"Really?" Dominique watched the color deepen on Mac's face. "Oh, I definitely want to hear more. I didn't know you had a significant other. Will she be visiting at Christmas?"

"Not discussing her. Penrose talks too much. He should focus on his own love life and stay the hell out of mine." Mac drained his coffee, stood and headed to the sink. He rinsed his cup before he placed it in the dishwasher. "Come on, Madison. Let's get those boxes of books into the library before they turn into dust."

"Wow." Dominique flicked a glance at Jim, who grinned back at her. "I guess it was my turn to overstep. What's she like?"

"Have you read his books? She's the secretary in them." He winked at her. "And I really don't have anyone significant in my life right now. What about you?"

"Not at the moment!" Dominique picked up a cookie. Anyway, Lillian Burroughs kicks ass. I really like her, but I gotta say I can't believe how unaware Titus is sometimes. He totally doesn't realize how much he depends on her or how she feeds him some of the answers to whatever crimes they're solving or how she's crazy about him."

"You're preaching to the choir, sweetheart." Jim brewed a fresh cup of coffee for himself, then turned back from the counter. He leaned toward her, hands on the center island. "Now, tell me all about your project. I'll be on Mac's shit list for a while, so I'd better help you instead of him. Plus, I don't read literature and I'm sure it's what's in those boxes since they came from the town library."

Lilly lingered a moment longer, wishing she could play matchmaker for Jimmy and the blonde woman sitting at the kitchen island, then decided it wasn't necessary. They seemed to be hitting it off and didn't require her assistance. She hadn't realized Mac's cousin had painted the signs at the businesses outside of town. Remembering the one at Hawke's Horse Heaven with the flying purple and pink ponies and little cherubs wearing cowgirl gear riding them, still made Lilly smile.

She floated out of the room and headed for the library where she found Donal and Florence. They weren't the only ghosts eagerly waiting for the delivery of books. Doireann O'Sullivan and Zeke Garvey stood nearby. "What's going on?"

"We want to see the books," Zeke told her. "When I was alive, I was a total booklover. I used to hang out at the high school library when I was a kid. I didn't care if the other jocks made fun of me. I always claimed it was a way to get girls, and most of the guys actually believed me. Some of them even started reading. Later, when I was home on leave from the Army, Twila and I always took our boys to the Lake Maynard library when they wanted new books to read."

"We went to the bakery a few days ago." Lilly smiled at the tall, dark-haired ghost in camouflage fatigues and combat boots. "The cheesecakes smelled and looked amazing. I wish I could have tried the turtle one. I love chocolate, caramel and pecans."

"That's always been one of Twila's favorites too." Zeke grinned. "I usually offered to sample the flavors when she was experimenting with new varieties."

"That was good of you," Donal teased. "For me, it was Florence's sugar cookies." He winked at his wife. "She made them all year round, so we didn't just eat them at Christmas."

"I used to find old cookbooks for Twila so she could try different recipes. And while she investigated those, I'd sit and read to our kids and any others who were at the library in an impromptu story hour. Twila and my best friend, Harry Colter would wait for hours until the library was about to close, and I was ready to go."

The hotel library had a half dozen tables of various sizes around the large room. Mac decided it'd be easier to use the biggest one to organize the books, so they left the boxes close to it. Someone had written the genres on a few of the cardboard cartons, but most weren't labeled. This would be an intense, time-consuming project.

"Well, I know what I'll be doing for the next few weeks when my book stumps me." Mac put the last box on the table.

He took a moment to glance around the room, wondering where Lillian had gone. He'd seen her earlier, but now she wasn't anywhere in sight. He was sure she'd arrive soon. She wouldn't miss the opportunity to investigate, not when she loved a good story as much as he did. "Veronika said you were taking these to the dump, and I couldn't let that happen."

Jack chuckled, shaking his head. "Yeah, I thought my sister, Ann, was going to have a fit and fall into it when Ronnie dropped that bombshell. I texted Ann and she's rounding up the other teachers to come here tomorrow and help you out with them."

"Why tomorrow?"

"Because it's girl time for them." Jack ran a hand over his blond hair, narrowing spring green eyes. "They'll leave their kids home and have a couple hours away. Two of the gals are new moms. They're drinking tea not coffee, so you can't use that big urn for them."

"It gives me an excuse to make cookies for them." Mac led the way back to the kitchen where they found Jimmy and Dominique discussing the renovations to one of the new wings. "What's happening? The painting crew is coming today, and I thought we'd finish the main floor."

"Jim needs a room of his own." Dominique drank the last of her coffee, rinsed the cup and put it in the dishwasher. "Come on. Let's go find one for him. We can check out the furniture. Jack, do you have time to make a run to Lake Maynard for me and pick up a few things?"

"Sure. I know what happens when you hear the word, 'No.' You rat me out to my folks and they threaten to tell Santa I've been naughty."

Mac chuckled. "Sounds like you're the recreation director once again, Dominique. I haven't had time to inventory the gallons of paint out in the shop. What did you plan to use for the color schemes?"

"Cream on the ceilings to reflect light, antique white on three walls and a bright gold, red, green or blue on the last ones for accent colors." Dominique headed toward the main hallway and then veered off to the doors between the parlor and the adjacent dining room. "Jim says he can do plumbing repairs. Mac, do you want to help him? Not only does he need an ensuite, we have five bathrooms on the main floor that require attention."

"Do I have a choice now that Jack's given us a sitrep about you and Santa?" Mac grinned at his friend, both of them already knowing the answer. "Why do I think you've already ordered toilets, vanities and heated towel racks?"

"Because you're smarter than you look!"

CHAPTER TWELVE

It took all morning for Lilly and the rest of the ghosts to inspect the boxes of books. Doireann remembered the library closed after the previous librarian died ten years ago. Before his death, he'd marked each carton with its contents. Discovering her favorite novels were packed away in two of the boxes delighted Florence. She and Donal moved the containers closer to one of the smaller tables.

Lilly glanced around the room with its floor to ceiling shelves on two of the walls. More bookcases framed the far wall between a trio of large windows. The open blinds revealed an overcast day and late November rain soaking the side yard.

"I think there should be special shelves for these." Florence opened one of the boxes. "I just don't know where yet."

"Those would be perfect for the kids' books." Zeke pointed to the shelves beneath the paintings of Baker City on the wall by the door. "They could help themselves to whatever they wanted."

"And we'll have the older ones up high," Doireann suggested. "Sure, and then, we won't be a worrying over Florence's collections. Some of her books are more than a hundred years old."

"We should check with Mac and see what he thinks." Lilly waved her hands and managed to part the seal on the top of the box he'd left closest to the large table. She frowned at the dusty hardcovers inside. "Who packed them away like that?"

"I'll bet it was Veronika MacGillicudy." Annoyance filled Zeke's deep voice. "Nobody who respects the written word would do such a thing."

Lilly left the other ghosts contemplating vengeance for the neglected books and went to find Mac. She located him in one of the bathrooms. An employee from the construction company installed a new toilet that seemed a bit higher than a standard one. One woman held a large mirror in place while a younger man secured it.

"There are vanities and sinks out in the shop." Mac glanced quickly at Lilly, before gesturing toward the hallway that led to the back door of the hotel. "Are you comfortable bringing in those?"

"We got it," the woman told him. "You should check in on the electricians and see how they're doing with the elevators. After we finish this bathroom, do you want us to move onto the next one?"

"Yes. Jack Madison told me to expect his sister and her crew of teachers tomorrow, so we definitely need restrooms."

"Works for us. We'd rather install new potty fixtures than paint the guestrooms."

Mac followed Lilly from the bathroom and into the lobby where they wouldn't be overheard. "What are you doing today?"

"We're inspecting the books. We already have plans for how they should be arranged. Do you want to make some notes so you can share them?"

He chuckled, shaking his head. "And then I guess I'm supposed to believe I'm in charge of this place. All right. Let's go."

Back in the library, he muttered a string of obscenities when he saw the dirt-stained books in the first box. He opened three more cartons, finding more hardcover novels in the same condition. His jaw tightened. "How do we clean them?"

"You'll want a soft, dry cloth or brush to dust the covers and edges," Doireann told him. "Sure, and I saw Ann Barrett use a vacuum cleaning attachment on some of the ones at the school."

Lilly relayed the information and Mac pulled out his smart

phone. He sent off a text to Jack who agreed to pass the word to his sister. Next came the suggested plan for the placement of the books. She acted as an interpreter for the others because Mac could hear her. He wasn't ready to listen to more than one spirit at a time. He strolled around the room, making notes on his phone.

"I think the best solution is to arrange the books by publishing dates." He pointed to the shelves that were only accessible by the rolling ladder. "We'll put anything from the nineteenth century through the early 1920s up there."

That decision prompted ghostly applause from Florence and Donal. The four other ghosts followed Mac and Lilly as they worked their way around the room, deciding where the volumes from each decade would go.

"Mac, we need your input in the left wing." Dominique stood in the doorway. "Can't this wait until tomorrow? Or is it the writer in you? Do books always come first?"

"Definitely." Mac grinned at her. "My thought is to have a limited number of televisions in the various rooms and make people pay extra for those. We'll promote the 'get away from it all' motif for our guests. They'll be able to borrow books from the library and if they want to buy one, we'll charge 'beaucoup' bucks for it."

"Veronika said they're really old. Would anybody really pay anything for them?"

"First editions can be worth several thousand dollars." Mac frowned at the document, saved it and then put away his phone. "I'm going to need to do some research and make sure we protect those from thieves. We may need a display case or two. If anyone handles those, they'll need white, cotton gloves and I'll make sure there's indirect lighting. You'll have to shop for all that stuff."

"Sounds good." Dominique waited for Mac to join her. "So, I thought the focal point in the first bedroom would be a blue wall, then red in the next, followed by yellow in the third and finally green in the fourth. Then, we'd repeat the pattern."

"What are the painters doing?"

"They've finished the ceiling and are starting the other walls. Jim is painting the ensuite."

"You've totally got an artist's eye." Mac and his cousin left the library discussing what else might draw potential guests to Baker City.

"Who is Jim?" Donal inquired. "I don't remember anybody on the construction crew with that name."

"He's one of Mac's Army buddies." Lilly flicked a quick glance at the old owner of the hotel. "I think he and Dominique are interested in each other."

Zeke laughed. "Are you playing Cupid like me, Raven and Moises? We enjoy matchmaking for the living."

"I don't know about that." Lilly managed to smile, hoping it looked genuine. She didn't want anyone deciding to intervene in Mac's love life. During the last three years she hadn't seen him date a woman and with any luck at all, he'd remain single a while longer, at least until she found a way to move onto whatever came next, so she wouldn't have to see it.

Okay, so I'm selfish. I don't want to share him.

Jimmy and Dominique went to Pop's Café for dinner. When she mentioned there was live country music on Friday nights, he told Mac not to wait up for him. Mac agreed. He expected company the next day, so he intended to make an assortment of cookies for them. He'd use a tablespoon and butter knife to measure them onto the baking sheets, not the ice-cream scoop he chose for the large size ones.

When he was at the mercantile earlier in the week, he'd purchased a selection of decaffeinated teas. They came in handy when he wanted to write all night, but didn't want to overdose on caffeine. He dropped two cubes of butter into a large bowl, followed by cups of granulated and then brown sugar. While he started

JOSIE MALONE

creaming them together with a wooden spoon, Lillian floated into the room.

He nodded to her. "I've hardly seen you today."

"We certainly had a lot of company." She hitched up on a stool at the center island. "Florence and Donal were impressed by everything you accomplished."

"Who are they?" Mac kept stirring. "Friends of yours?"

"I didn't meet them until we moved in here. They inherited the hotel from Donal's father and have been here ever since."

"Okay, so is Donal's dad here too?"

"No. I'm pretty sure he broke the mayor's rules and got booted out of town." Lillian propped her chin on her fist. "He cheated at a poker game when he won the deed, and he was murdered. There seems to be a certain amount of what some would consider 'karma' around here."

"How so?" Mac broke the farm fresh egg into a cup first, although Bronwyn Murphy had assured him she candled all the ones she sold, and they never contained any baby chicks. Still better safe than sorry, he thought. "Define that for me."

"Well, good actions have good consequences and bad actions have bad consequences." Lillian thought for a moment. "Donal's dad apparently made bad decisions, and it eventually led to his demise. When we arrived, the mayor explained the rules for ghosts to me. The big one is not to scare children. No blood or gore. Newt O'Leary says, if you're one of those folks nobody liked when they were alive, they're not wanted around by the dead."

"That makes sense." Mac continued adding ingredients to what would become his favorite chocolate chip cookies. He enjoyed his conversations with Lillian, even when they didn't include the latest conundrums in his books. She told him more about what she and her friends found in the boxes from the town library.

He shared everything that had been done in the rest of the hotel. The electricians had inspected and made minor repairs to the elevators. They were functional now. The painting crew completed three rooms on the first floor in the left wing. After he finished painting the ensuite, Jimmy started on the flooring.

"I'll help him install the fixtures tomorrow afternoon." Mac began spooning batter onto the baking sheets. "Jack says his sister and her friends are only staying a few hours. They're teachers here in town."

"Wow, you're getting to know everyone."

Mac heard the amusement in her low voice and saw it sparkle in the hazel eyes. "You're making friends here too."

"Good point." She slid off the stool. "I'm going to work on the new book for a while before you get there. Anything in particular you want me to check?"

"Washington State had capital punishment in the 1940s. If my client's wife actually killed him, wouldn't she face that?"

"Well, first we'd have to make sure she gets away with it, but no women were executed then, or at any time in the state's history. All executions in Washington State have been of men."

"All right. If she's a victim of domestic violence, I want her to get away with killing him." He slid the tray into the oven and set the timer. "I don't know if we can make 'self-defense' a valid reason for her murdering him in the alley. It's not as if she were in imminent danger."

"True. Your detective hadn't located her or returned her like a lost pet to her husband yet."

"I don't know if he'd do that."

"Remember the story is set in the 1940s and your hero is a man of his time. If he won't do that, you'll have to make it believable when he goes against social norms."

She always made excellent points, Mac thought, as he started a batch of snickerdoodles. He still hadn't come up with a plausible explanation for that particular plot-hole. The radio began to play a selection of classic 1940s swing music. Obviously, Lillian decided he needed inspiration and entertainment while he prepared for his visitors. The living ones, that is.

Mid-morning, a convoy of vehicles, a pickup truck, SUVs and a classic pink Mustang pulled into the parking lot behind the hotel. Mac opened the door and strolled toward the truck in the lead, pausing when he saw an elderly white-haired woman in jeans, a cowgirl shirt, and lace-up riding boots.

She waved a greeting as she popped out of her rig. "Hello, I'm Mindy MacGillicudy, Pop's cousin and yours too. I heard about the books and came to help."

"Mac." He held out his hand to gently shake hers. "Welcome. I'm glad you're here."

"Not when I ask if that's your given name or a nickname." Mindy tilted her head to one side, looking like an inquisitive bird. "I think it's an occupational hazard because I'm the town therapist and work at the local veteran's center."

"I didn't know there was one of those, but I've only been here a week." Mac nodded at a younger woman coming toward them. Like Mindy, she wore jeans but opted for a black and red Washington State University sweatshirt. Her hair was the color of a sunrise, gold, red and bronze waves, yet her eyes were the same spring green as Jack Madison's. "You must be Ann."

"Yes." She flashed a brilliant smile at him. "You met Mindy. She sorts out all our issues, so we usually invite her to all our events. It's easier than bringing her up to speed when we have group therapy."

Mac blinked, slightly shocked. "Why do you have therapy?"

"My husband says it's because we brought the war home with us." Ann turned slightly, gesturing to a strawberry blonde woman coming their way. Like the others, she dressed casually. "This is my best friend, Margo Endicott. She's only staying until lunchtime because she has to get home to her son, Garrett."

"Same goes for Sully Murphy." Mindy beckoned to the red-haired woman exiting the Mustang Fastback. A flowered knee-length dress billowed in the winter breeze, and she edged carefully around a puddle to keep her feet dry in her sandals. "She has twins but thankfully, her husband is here this weekend."

"Where is he usually?"

"At Fort Clark." Ann signaled the youngest of their group, a dark-haired girl who hurried toward them. "This is Lisa Jensen. She's our newest teacher in Baker City."

"And it's Saturday so I get to smile." She grinned mischievously at Mac. "This is my first teaching position, and it isn't easy handling a blended classroom of kindergarten, first grade and a few second graders."

"Only because they haven't learned you're large and in charge." Ann put an arm around the younger woman's shoulders and hugged her. "Harry said I should remind you what Sergeant-Major Waller says about you."

"What's that?" Lisa beamed around the group. "He always offers to bring me coffee because he says the care and training of junior officers is—"

"Sergeant's business!" Ann and Sully chimed together. Then, both women laughed before Ann added, "Derek says you should remember that you're one tough officer. You kick butts and take no prisoners when we're at the fort, but then you're telling grownups what to do, not little kids."

Mac stared at the group of women, before he eyed Mindy again. "Are you a vet too?"

"Yup. Vietnam was my war, but it took years before I was acknowledged as a veteran. Don't get me started on gender bias and discrimination." Mindy winked at him. "Dray works as our receptionist at the center, and he told me that you made amazing cookies for him and his buddies. Do we get some too? Or do we have to start work first?"

"I wasn't sure what you'd like so there's oatmeal raisin, peanut butter, chocolate chip and snickerdoodles." Mac started for the porch, then recalled the text he received from Jack. "Did anyone bring a vacuum cleaner because some of the books require it? I'll get that for you."

"Oh, it's in my car." Ann pointed at her car. "And Mindy has a box of soft, dry cloths, brushes, and cheesecloth for my vacuum attachments too."

"Let's do it. Cookies first and we'll start work afterwards." Margo took charge and led the way inside.

"And that's why she's the commander of our Army Reserve unit," Ann said. "She knows what's important."

Lilly heard laughter and female voices in the kitchen. She floated into the room and saw several women clustered around the table. Two of them drank tea while they munched cookies and the other three had coffee. The oldest one, a petite silver-haired dynamo, seemed to be in charge of the conversation. Whenever it flagged, she had another question that initiated more discussion.

Mac walked past them, carrying a box of cleaning supplies. Lilly followed him to the library. "You look overwhelmed. Did somebody say something inappropriate?"

"No." He glanced over his shoulder, at the women and lowered his voice. "They're all vets."

"What?" Lilly gaped at him. "Seriously? Were they in the Army?"

He nodded. "They even have a veteran's center here in Baker City. We need to check that out. Maybe, you could join their group."

"I'm not waiting for an invitation. I'm going back to the kitchen now. Even if they can't see or hear me, I can see and hear them."

Luckily, the stools at the breakfast bar were empty so Lilly chose one of those. It was a perfect place to learn what was happening.

The older woman glanced around the table. "Okay, so Margo and I had Thanksgiving dinner at Ann's house. Sully, tell us about yours. At our last meeting, you mentioned going to your mother-in-law's home for the holiday. How was it?"

"Terrific." She tossed her head, and brilliant red hair bounced against her back. "Most of Tate's brothers showed up with their girl-friends. They oohed and aahed over our babies and helped his sisters take care of Raven and Reveille."

"What about your folks?" the youngest woman asked. "Did they come to Baker City too?"

"I didn't invite them, Lisa. I didn't want to hear my mother talk about how much she loved my BFF, Raven or be blamed again because she died when that IED took her out and I came home alive, and she didn't."

This time it was the silver-haired woman who asked a question. "Isn't she pleased that you named one of your daughters for Raven?"

"Yes, but World War Three continues because my mom said she was looking forward to being a grandma when Raven and my step-brother, Kord had a baby with her cheekbones and his thick, curly brown hair."

"Your twins are beautiful with their red hair and Tate's blue eyes." Lisa snapped. "And First Sergeant Raven Barlow would be the first to say so."

Knowing the other ghost, Lilly didn't doubt it for a second. Apparently, neither did two of the other former soldiers at the table who nodded agreement. The conversation continued, but it changed to plans for Christmas and the upcoming meeting at the veteran's center next week.

I'm definitely going there too, Lilly thought, *and when I'm at the cock-tail lounge tonight, I'll ask Raven to join me and them if she doesn't already. I wonder if she realizes how obnoxious Sully's mom is acting.*

CHAPTER THIRTEEN

On Sunday morning, Mac parked in the lot adjacent to the church. He and Jimmy walked toward the over-sized carved wooden doors where a silver-haired elderly man stood waiting. Of course, his buddy didn't see Lillian floating behind them. She'd said that some of the ghosts found the services entertaining and a few used the opportunity to connect with their living relatives.

The minister didn't wear the traditional dark suit associated with most preachers, but a plaid, flannel shirt tucked into faded jeans and well-worn cowboy boots. He nodded a greeting. "Good morning."

"Hello. I'm Mac MacGillicudy and this is Jimmy Penrose."

"I'm Reverend Tommy Thompson." He held out his hand to shake Mac's. "I've been hearing about you from your cousins. Veronika was a big help with the Thanksgiving baskets this year."

"And she also did dishes with me at the café last Thursday," Jimmy drawled. "Seems to be a real sweetheart."

"I don't know if I'd go that far." Reverend Tommy gazed at the lot as more vehicles pulled into it. "She has issues."

"Who doesn't?" Mac said in even tones. "I haven't had a chance to check out your bulletin board yet, but do you have self-help groups meet here at the church?"

"Like what?"

"I've been sober five years, seven months, two weeks, four days
—" Mac paused. "I could continue, but the only way I stay away
from alcohol is by going to meetings. I don't know why Veronika
self-medicates with booze, but she undoubtedly has her reasons
and—"

"She probably isn't the only one in Baker City, sir." Jimmy glanced
at the approaching group. "Marijuana is legal in Washington State,
but other drugs aren't. I'm sure your town could also use a Narcotics
Anonymous group and there are co-dependent folks around here as
well."

"You two are going to be a great addition to this town." Reverend
Tommy nodded at the family who neared them first. "I hadn't realized we needed to expand our outreach to the people here, but it's a
great idea. Let's talk about it after the service."

Mac recognized Ann Barrett who was accompanied by a tall,
dark-haired man and a small girl who clung to his hand. "Good
morning. Jimmy, I don't think you had an opportunity to meet Ann
Barrett. She was in charge of the library detail who came to clean the
books yesterday while you were working on the ensuite."

"Careful. I'll tell Margo you promoted me." Ann grinned at him,
then introduced her companions. "This is my husband, Harry Colter
and my daughter, Devon. Mac and his cousins, Dominique and
Veronika own the hotel and are rehabbing it."

"What happens when you finish?" Harry asked. "Are you
reopening or selling it?"

"We haven't decided yet." Mac eyed the other man who was about
his age, or maybe a year or two younger. Something about the way he
carried himself screamed prior service. It wasn't just a high and tight'
haircut. "Army or—"

"Rangers lead the way." Jimmy held out his hand to grip Harry's.
"We've met before. 06-07? Germany?"

"That's right."

Jimmy gazed toward the parking lot. "Garvey here too? You guys
were—"

"Ambush last year. I.E.D." Harry looked down at the child beside him. "His wife, Twila owns the bakery in Baker City."

"I'll check it out," Jimmy said.

Lillian gestured toward the church. "I don't know how you can tell him Zeke Garvey made it home. He was at the hotel yesterday and he'll join us as soon as his family arrives."

Mac nodded, but didn't answer her. He couldn't, not when there were so many people around. They'd undoubtedly think he was crazy if he admitted talking to a ghost. Worse would be if they accepted it as perfectly normal. He was in Baker City after all.

Nick MacGillicudy was exhausted after spending the last two nights with dead people who took him slogging through his hometown, overwhelming him with holiday nostalgia. The first had been his old classmate, Zeke Garvey who'd died in Afghanistan a year ago. Playing the *Ghost of Christmas Past*, he revealed the glory days of Baker City when everyone got together to make the holiday special.

Next, there was cantankerous Newt O'Leary who took him to see what people had planned for this year, from the baker with her 'gingerbread house' contest to the town cemetery with the tiny, decorated Christmas trees on the graves. Enough was enough, Nick thought. It was time to leave town and change things up if he didn't want the ghosts to continue harassing him.

Saturday morning, he left Baker City and headed south into Liberty Valley. He had choices and it was time to make better ones. The long drive through non-stop holiday traffic didn't help. Neither had the strong coffee he drank while he ate breakfast, lunch, and supper at chain restaurants near the freeway.

While he was in the area, he stopped by his mother's house and visited her. He didn't know his future plans so he couldn't share them but promised to call, email, text, and drop by more often. He agreed to tell his sisters to do the same. Instead of making it all the way back to Baker City Saturday night, he checked into a motel. Distantly, he remembered his grandparents telling him there were very few ghosts in Liberty Valley. The witches in the local covens didn't tolerate them.

He didn't know if it was true or not, but a good night's sleep couldn't hurt. He had plans for the next day. Nothing disturbed him and he slept deeply in short stretches on Saturday night. He still woke up when he heard semi-trucks roar on the highway. But thankfully, the dead remained where they belonged in Baker City.

Sunday morning, he hit the shower before he dressed. He was on the road before daylight. A quick stop for gas provided the chance to grab a huge coffee and he barely managed to gag down an awful sandwich while he drove north. He reached Baker City in time to stop at the café for a real breakfast prior to church services.

Pop gave him a long look when he sat at the counter instead of taking up space in a booth.

"Morning. May I please have coffee and a stack of pancakes? Bacon on the side."

Pop nodded, wrote down the order and passed it to his daughter, Linda, working in the kitchen. Silence ensued while he filled a mug and slid it onto the counter, along with silverware wrapped in a paper napkin. "Are you all right, Nick? You don't sound like yourself, and you don't look too good either."

"I'm better than I was the past couple of nights. At least I got some sleep."

Bells rattled over the main door when it opened, then closed.

Nobody entered the restaurant, and Pop glanced over his shoulder. "Stop that. The boy isn't doing any harm to me or mine. Let him have a meal in peace and quiet. The pancakes will be up in a minute. You want syrup or jam?"

"Maple syrup, please." In the middle of his meal, the door opened again, but this time a real, living woman entered the café, his youngest sister.

Nick glanced at the petite blonde, in a tight-fitting sequined tank-top that emphasized her full breasts, sans bra as usual, and faded, glued-on, slashed jeans tucked into spike heeled, bling-covered, western boots. Her bright red lipstick matched her fingernail polish, but the technician had added glitzy Christmas trees. "What's going on, Veronika?"

"That's my question." She hiked up on the stool next to him. "Daddy's been hunting for you. He wants your latest report on the horse places he can get for their gravel."

"I told him before I'm not into being his spy."

"Then you better find somewhere else to live. He didn't pay for you to go to shoeing school for free."

"He didn't pay at all." Nick finished off his pancakes and had a last swallow of coffee. "The only paychecks that ever bounced were the ones he wrote me. And it made my name mud all over town when I passed on the pain with my debit card. I'm done being embarrassed and kicked out of Baker City businesses. I quit."

"What?" Veronika widened big blue eyes, gaping at him. "You quit what?"

"I quit shoeing. I sold my equipment yesterday. I'll quit renting his place too. I'll get my stuff from the trailer later today. Most of the furniture is mine, so I'm taking it with me. I'll change the utilities tomorrow. And if you don't irritate me, I won't quit being your big bro. Call Mom. For some odd reason, she loves and misses you."

Nick stood. "Don't ask me for any more money. Get it from Dad. You're his favorite chick right now."

"Where are you going?"

"To church. There are people I need to see." Nick picked up the check and waved at Pop. "Let me pay you now before Veronika takes the money and runs again. I'm done cleaning up her messes too."

"About time." Pop said as he approached. "You're amazing me today, Nick. I'm glad to see you're not a chip off your father's block. Your mother has class. Most of the O'Learys do. Keep acting like them, not him."

Veronika gasped, then glared at Nick. "How dare you call me a thief?"

"Because you are one. I've seen you do it time and again, not only to me. Mom used to call you out for stealing the tips she left for waitresses when we were kids and Dad just laughed about it. But I won't be like the pair of you. I'm changing. I suggest you try it before your sins come back and bite you."

———

Veronika couldn't believe her older brother actually intended to go to church and watched him cross the street to the building where Reverend Tommy still waited outside to 'meet and greet' his parishioners. The minister greeted Nick with a quick hug before they shook hands. Still stunned, she waited until her brother went through the ornately carved doors. Wow, he really must have something new and different in mind. Their father needed to know about this.

It didn't take long to drive to the gated community in Lake Maynard. For once, she arrived before Liam O'Leary did. Veronika parked and hurried up the walk to the front porch. She didn't have a key, so she rang the bell and waited for her father to answer.

Herman opened the door and greeted her with a warm hug. "I missed you on Thanksgiving, baby girl. I got your text. I couldn't believe you wanted to stay in Baker City and help at Pop's Café."

"I didn't." She struggled to smile. "I told you. It was Dick O'Connell's idea so he wouldn't have to arrest me. I thought you promised to pay for my meals and bar tab at the cafe."

"I'm sorry, honey. I figured I'd do it tomorrow. Today's the first of December."

She stared into his ruddy features. "Did you pay Pop for September and October? Everybody in town treats me like a deadbeat."

"I'll have to check and see." Herman wrapped an arm around her shoulders. "Come inside and let's have coffee before we meet Liam for lunch."

"Do we have to?" Veronika grimaced. "He's not one of my favorite people, Daddy."

"Sorry to hear that. He wants you to work for him when you finish the library project, and I think it'd be a good idea. He'll pay well."

She shuddered. No way in hell, she thought. Liam was too touchy-feely, and working for him would mean tolerating him pawing her on a regular basis. *So, not my thing. I choose who I want to sleep with and it's not a guy as old as my father.*

She definitely wasn't saying that today, not to Herman MacGillicudy, not when she wanted him to cough up some major bucks and keep his promises. "Coffee sounds good. Then, I have to go back to Baker City. Mac and Dominique want me to help decorate the hotel for Christmas."

Herman frowned. "I really need to introduce myself to your new cousin. Is he planning to stay in Baker City or will he be reasonable and sell me the hotel?"

"I don't know. He seems to like living there and he hasn't shared his plans. He and Dommi get along great. The Hawke construction crew was back on Friday doing stuff." She didn't mention she sent the loggers to clear the driveway. Her father hadn't asked about that and as she'd heard Ann Barrett say more than once, he didn't have a 'need to know' some stuff.

"Oh, and you should talk to Nick. He says he's not shoeing horses anymore."

"Sounds like I need to go to Baker City this afternoon too."

The pews in the church filled before the service and Lilly sat next to Mac. Jimmy's eyes widened when he saw Dominique in a blue dress that clung to her curves and asked her to join them. There wasn't a Sunday School class for youngsters, at least not that day and most of the kids behaved very well. Lilly looked around and recognized the Hendrickson twins with their parents. The sermon was short, simple and the topic of loving one's neighbors seemed appropriate for the season.

Reverend Tommy exhorted the parishioners to do their best and be kind to each other throughout the next month, regardless of how stressful the holidays were. Afterwards, Lilly and Mac followed the rest of the congregation to a reception area for refreshments. The people he'd met during the past week greeted him. When Linda and Dray invited him to join them at their table, Mac did. A few minutes later, Jimmy and Dominique brought their doughnuts and coffee and sat down too.

"I can't stay long." Dominique glanced around the room. "I have potential clients here. One of them wants a house and is determined to open an auto repair shop. I have the keys to the old one in town so I can take him to look at it."

Linda laughed. "You're just like the rest of us, Dommi. As soon as we finish socializing, we're going to the café to help Pop. Otherwise, he'll be trying to cook, clean and do it all himself."

"I'll come and help too," Mac said. "We don't have any plans for the day, do we, Penrose?"

"Only laying carpet in the rooms that are ready for it, and we can do that after the café closes." Jim drank more coffee. "I'll do dishes while you're cooking, Mac."

"And I'll hang out in the lounge with my new friends," Lilly announced. "I want to hear what the mayor has in store for us this week."

"If you're helping us, I'll come to the hotel with you later." Dray tore off a chunk of his apple fritter, then glimpsed his mother's stern look. "It's cool, Mom. I already emailed my homework to the professors and read the assigned chapters. No worries. I won't make a late night of it."

"We won't let him, Linda." Mac leaned back in his chair. "Coming to church this morning means I skipped writing, and I want to get in a couple chapters tonight."

"Glad we're on the same page." Linda tilted her head to one side. "Tell me everything done at the hotel this past week. What rooms do you want my crew to focus on tomorrow?"

Since it was the last day of the holiday weekend, the café closed at 4:00 p.m. because Pop was ready for an early night. Mac, Jimmy and

Dray headed for the hotel. After coffee and cookies, they carried a roll of the dark blue carpet Dominique chose into Jimmy's prospective room. Once they had the rug in place, next came the furniture. By the time Dray left at nine, Jimmy was unpacking his clothes.

Mac's phone vibrated and he answered. "Hello, Mom. How was your Thanksgiving?"

"I'm sorry I missed your call, but all the kids were here with their families."

"Sounds like you had a good time." Mac waved in the direction of the lobby and mimed his departure.

Once he was out of Jimmy and Dominique's earshot, Mac listened to the rest of the news she wanted to share and the upcoming plans for Christmas. Finally, she asked about his day.

"I helped Pop at his café. He always serves a big meal."

"I'm sure he makes a lot of money. Most restaurants do on holidays because people don't want to cook."

"In Baker City, he asks for donations." Mac sat on the couch facing the fireplace. He switched to the video option so he could see her face. "He says he's one of your cousins."

"Oh, I have a lot of those. My great-grandparents had six kids. Each of them had big families too. You'll find MacGillicudys all over Baker City, Lake Maynard and down south in Liberty Valley. How long do you plan to stay there?"

"I haven't decided." Mac shrugged. "I've only been here a week, and I like it. Everyone's been very friendly."

"What are you going to do with the hotel?" Donna wrinkled her nose in disgust. "I couldn't believe it when I keep getting requests to contribute to the trust to save it. So, not my thing. I haven't sent a dime, and I won't. It's not as if I'm ever going to visit or stay there."

"You don't have to." Mac crossed one knee over the other. "It is the MacGillicudy ancestral home. Dominique tells me it's been in the family for almost eighty years. That's a legacy and a half."

"Definitely not for me." Donna shuddered. "It looks like something out of a horror movie."

"I'm waiting on a bid to have the exterior painted next year." Mac saw Lillian drift into the room. He didn't speak to her, just inclined his head when she floated into one of the rocking chairs. "I want Dominique's input, but I think we should go with something similar to what they do to the Victorian houses, the ones called 'Painted Ladies' in San Francisco. Have you seen those?"

"Don't bother. It's too much work." Donna paused. "I had a call from my cousin, Herman. He manages a bank in Lake Maynard. He wants to buy the hotel. Have you thought about selling it to him? If you do, you won't have to waste your time and energy on it. You'll be able to use the money and go wherever you like."

"Where's that?" Mac held her gaze with his. "You're busy with your family. It'll be fine if I visit on my next book tour in a year or so. I'll stick around Washington State for a while." He rubbed his jaw feeling beard stubble under his fingers. "Is now a good time to ask about my biological father? Will I find him here or where should I look?"

"I have no idea." Donna sighed. "I've told you for years." She shifted in her chair. "We've been through this too many times before. He was just a guy I met at a party in college. We were kids. Neither of us wanted a commitment. We went our separate ways."

"That's bogus," Lillian said, although only Mac heard her. "A woman who keeps her baby and raises him for almost eighteen years, even after she eventually married your stepdad, certainly hasn't turned her back on a commitment. I don't know why she's lying to you. Didn't you need a copy of your birth certificate to enlist in the Army?"

He glanced at her and shook his head, hoping she'd get the idea they'd discuss the situation later.

"What are you looking at?" Donna asked.

"Just thinking," Mac replied. "And wondering about my family history."

"I'm done with this conversation. We'll talk later when you've got something decent to say."

CHAPTER FOURTEEN

Lilly followed Mac into his office after he finished his conversation with his mother. He didn't fire up the desktop computer. Instead, he opened the bottom drawer on the rolltop desk and pulled out a folder. He opened it, flipped through some papers and removed a copy of one document.

"Damn it. That's what I thought."

She moved close enough to read the birth certificate. It stated Donna Marcia MacGillicudy had given birth to a baby boy, Horatio Virgil MacGillicudy in Pullman, Washington on May 7th, 1979. "Well, now I know your 'real' name. No wonder you prefer, Mac."

"Yes, but she didn't provide my biological father's name, and he obviously wasn't there at the time." Mac tucked away the form. "If she won't tell me, I'll have to find it somewhere else."

"You could go online and join one of those genealogy websites," Lilly said. "According to the commercials on TV, they'll track down your relatives."

"Yes, but there's a town full of MacGillicudy folks here." Mac ushered her toward the door. "Let's start there. I'll talk to the living ones. You interview the ghosts, and we'll share the results. Sound like a deal?"

She nodded. "And now, you need to get to work. You still haven't written your twenty pages today."

"You just want to know what happens next in the story." Mac walked through the lobby, heading for the kitchen. "I'm going to have a slice of that pumpkin and pecan cheesecake Pop sent home with us before I start. I'd offer you some, but—"

"I'm dead. I can't eat it." She smiled at him. "I'll settle for smelling it."

Monday, Jimmy took charge of the painting crew. Some worked on the bathrooms while the rest continued with the guestrooms in the left wing. Mac supervised the electricians and Ted Fenwick who had moved onto the second floor of the main building. When Dominique and Veronika came, they headed to the attic storage rooms to find Christmas decorations.

Lilly went with them. She'd said one of the original owners of the hotel had agreed to help. The two ghosts would be able to guide his cousins to the boxes they needed. Mac didn't ask how. Anybody who could bring books across town or move a coffee cup or turn on the radio so it streamed the music she liked certainly had more tricks up her sleeve.

Halfway through the morning, Mac headed to the kitchen to set up the large coffee urn and a tray of assorted cookies before Linda and her cleaning staff arrived. His inventory of treats was running low, and he'd have to make more tonight. It'd give him something meaningful to do. His phone chimed and he pulled it out of his pocket. A text message from his sponsor, Jared Williams showed on the screen.

Mac leaned against the counter to read it. An attorney, Jared had worked at a law firm in Seattle before his Army Reserve unit went to Afghanistan. Back home again, he had a position in the branch office in Everett, the county seat in Liberty Valley. He'd sent a list of various A.A. meetings down south.

'Anything closer to Baker City?' Mac texted. 'I'm restoring the hotel here.'

'Small world. My wife, Margo, rents a cabin at the dude ranch. I'll meet you for coffee at the bakery tonight. She wants cheesecake.'

Mac chuckled and asked if Margo was one of the women who'd helped with his library. Jared agreed and said she'd be back when he was home to look after their son. The teachers intended to carry on with their book project and planned to pop into the hotel for a few hours on Thursday afternoon after their veteran's meeting with Mindy.

Mac promised to give his sponsor a tour of the hotel before their call ended. He'd barely put away his phone when he saw a different vehicle, an unfamiliar late model white Cadillac coming to a stop in the parking lot. A stocky man in a three-piece suit climbed out of the car and headed toward him. Mixed rain and snow dusted his silver blond hair.

Opening the back door, Mac crossed the porch and went to greet his newest visitor. "Hello. Can I help you?"

"It's more the other way around." He held out his hand, a plastic smile appearing on his face. It didn't touch the pale blue eyes. "I'm Herman MacGillicudy. I have the First Federal Bank in Lake Maynard. My daughters are supposed to talk to you about selling this rundown firetrap to me."

"Insulting my inheritance won't make points with me." Mac shook hands with the older man. "And I'm pretty sure that Dominique plans to get the place listed on the Washington State historical register as well as the national one."

"No need for that." Herman gestured toward the building. "Shall we get out of the weather and talk about my offer."

Mac shook his head. "No. You're not staying, and I'm not interested in selling to you. I spoke to my mother last night and she said you want to demolish the hotel. It's been in the family for eighty years. This is our legacy."

"So, what are you going to do with it? Restore it?"

"Yes. Then, if the three of us decide to sell it, we'll find someone who wants to pay a hefty price for it and operate it as a hotel."

"That's crazy." Herman's jaw jutted forward. "Nobody comes to Baker City anymore."

"Things change."

Herman reached in his jacket pocket and drew out a business card. "If you change your mind—"

"I won't." Mac didn't take the card, folding his arms instead. "Thanks, but no thanks."

He watched Herman turn and hustle back to his car. Moments later, he was driving out of the parking lot. Mac swung around and went back inside. In the kitchen, he discovered Dominique and Veronika drinking coffee. Both of his cousins had dressed down for the day in jeans, casual tops and running shoes. They'd braided their hair and foregone makeup since they were going for an attic adventure followed by decorating for Christmas.

Mac filled his own cup from the large stainless-steel, commercial urn. "I just had the pleasure of meeting your father."

"I can't believe you're calling it a pleasure." Dominique selected a snickerdoodle from the tray. "When are you going to start making holiday cookies? You know what I mean. The frosted kind with sprinkles."

"I'll have to find a good recipe first." Mac stopped and stared at the antique, small wooden box sitting on the back of the counter between the farmhouse sink and the double ovens. "Where did that come from?"

"We found it in the attic." Veronika took a second chocolate chip cookie. "It was weird. We'd barely started looking and there were all these boxes full of strings of lights, garlands, and antique decorations for Christmas trees. It came out of nowhere and Dommi tripped over it. So, we brought it with us."

"Florence wants you to have it." Lillian appeared in the doorway to the pantry. "It's her recipe box. She made all the meals back in the day for the guests. And she always served high tea in the drawing room when there were guests. You should do it too. As for Christmas cookies, I want the variation of Peanut Butter Blossoms you make. It's so fun trying to unwrap the chocolate kisses."

"High tea?" Mac arched a brow, struggling to ignore the ghost. "Who'd come here for it?"

"Seriously?" Dominique gazed at him. "I'll bet most of the women in town would and if you did a 'Ploughman's Lunch', we'd get the guys too."

"What's that?" Veronika asked. "I never heard of it."

"It's a traditional British cold meal, typically served in pubs," Mac said. "It has bread, cheese, and things like pickled onions, chutney, and sometimes ham or other cold meats. When I was stationed in England and we went to the pubs, it was often served with beer or cider."

"I could definitely go for the beer." Veronika slid off the stool and went to refill her cup from the urn. "I think you should get some Bailey's Irish Cream too. You could keep it in the fridge, and I'll bet I'm not the only one who'd add it to her coffee."

"Not happening." Mac opened the box and began to examine the various cards. Each recipe was handwritten, listing enormous quantities. It amazed him that the ink hadn't faded. "I don't drink and we're not serving alcohol here. I'm meeting my sponsor later and I'm going to talk to him about starting support groups for alcoholics, addicts and co-dependent family members."

"Don't forget the teens." Dominique passed her mug to her sister who refilled it. "You'll want groups for them too. Alcoholism is the gift that keeps on giving. It's generational."

"How do you know that?" Veronika demanded with a toss of her blonde head. "Are you planning to lecture me too?"

"It may come as a shock, but the world doesn't revolve around you, little sister. We had a lot of problems with liquor when I was in college and a few students died of alcohol poisoning." Dominique snagged another snickerdoodle. The cinnamon dusted cookies were obviously her favorite. "I agree with Mac. Our hotel is going to be dry. If people want to drink, they can go to the two bars in town or the café or buy booze at the mercantile and drink it at home. If they try to drink it here, Mac will kick their sorry tails to the curb, and we won't refund what they paid for their rooms."

Lillian sauntered toward Mac, and he almost felt the cool brush of her hand. "It sounds like you're all in agreement. Well, I don't know about Veronika, but she should lay off the sauce, especially since she doesn't pay for her drinks."

Mac replaced the card that described how to make divinity back in the box. He'd do it later when he had all the ingredients. First, he'd have to make a shopping list and take a trip to a larger grocery store in Lake Maynard.

Dominique stopped and stared out the kitchen window. "Wow, Frank is here."

"What does he want?" Veronika hastily put her half-full cup by the sink, grabbed her purse and leopard-patterned jacket. "I'm out of here. I don't want to be bitched at about that stupid library. I still think he should agree to let Daddy bulldoze it for a gravel pit."

"It's a Carnegie library," Mac protested, but his younger cousin was gone. He turned to face Dominique. "It needs a plaque and signs. Plus, it should be on the historical register."

"I'm on it already." Dominique slid to her feet and went toward the door. "Frank Madison is the President for life of the Baker City Business Association and also has Majestyk Morgans, a premier horse-breeding operation. We always want to be on his good side since he has so much clout."

"I'll keep that in mind." Mac frowned. "Wait a second. Jack and Ann—"

"Are two of his kids. He also has two older daughters and lots of grandchildren." Dominique opened the back door and smiled at the man skirting the puddles. "Hey, Frank. How's it going? We haven't finished off the cookies yet so come join us."

"I didn't have a chance to meet your cousin on Sunday at church." Frank Madison was in his mid-sixties but didn't look it. He wore a green checked shirt with pearl snaps under a denim jacket, ironed blue jeans and polished cowboy boots. "Your brother and I were setting up his new job. He'll be along later to meet Mac. Have you had a chance to talk to him about the holiday events in town?"

"Not yet." Dominique closed the door. "Let me get you a cup of coffee and we'll bring Mac up to speed. Nick has accepted a position as city manager."

"Well, that should keep the rest of the ghosts off his back," Lillian commented, although only Mac could hear her. "They weren't happy about him being so mean to the horses when he was a farrier."

"I think it's going to work out well for everyone." Frank accepted the cup of black coffee from Dominique. "Nick explained his father, Liam O'Leary, and some of Senator Tex Hawke's other minions might go after members of a city council again if we held another election. However, he also pointed out that they couldn't get rid of an employee hired by the Baker City Business Association since none of them are members. He says he isn't afraid of them, and he'll stick and stay."

"I met Herman earlier," Mac said. "I don't know any of the others. Is Liam related to Aiden O'Leary, the owner of the hardware store?"

Frank nodded. "His younger brother. Liam is an investment broker, but he's not very ethical. He's the seventh son of a seventh daughter and should have been the medium for Baker City—"

"Except none of the ghosts like him," Lillian announced. "I heard that at the cocktail lounge. It's why his daughter, Cat O'Leary-McTavish took the position last year."

Mac struggled to focus on the conversation between his living guests and hoped they didn't realize they had company of the unearthly kind. "I haven't met Cat yet, but I did meet her daughters last week. They claim I'm haunted."

"Well, you're not the only one. We do live in Baker City, and it seems to be a nexus for spirits." Frank studied the platter, then helped himself to a peanut butter cookie. "I wanted to invite you to our next meeting. It's easiest to have them at the café right now, but when the hotel is ready, we'd love to come here."

"Shouldn't you ask the other members if that's okay?" Mac inquired.

"If they have issues, they can choose a different president." Frank bit into the cookie. "If I'm the bad guy, then everyone has to convince me, and they talk themselves through any self-doubts."

"I always knew there was a method to your madness," Dominique teased.

"Got that right." Frank glanced around the room. "Where's Veronika? I thought I saw her car when I got here. I wanted to ask about the town library."

"It needs a good scrubbing." Lillian floated across the room to stare out the window. "Linda's here. Maybe she has time to do it. I don't think Veronika will clean it because if she intended to do it, she would have already."

It was Mac's turn to top off his coffee. "I'm talking to my sponsor today and once he agrees to help me set up support groups, we'll visit Reverend Tommy. I don't know why Veronika self-medicates with alcohol. Do either of you?"

His cousin and Frank Madison stared at him. Dominique shook her head. "I never thought of it that way. I just assumed she was a spoiled brat, and I definitely didn't want to be my father's fave. The price is too high. When he was giving me a hard time last spring, I arranged for one of my sorority sisters to buy into the realty so I wouldn't have to answer to him. Then, I could keep doing my part to save Baker City."

"I don't like Herman either," Frank said. "I didn't before he arranged to have Cat O'Leary-McTavish harassed when she moved here, and I still don't. It's why most of the business owners in Baker City choose other banks in Lake Maynard to handle their financial matters."

Mac nodded and glanced at his cousin. "Do we need to be concerned about your father, Dominique?"

"Not since Dray MacGillicudy was almost killed when someone cut the brake line on Cat's truck last year. He and her husband, Rob, had gone to Lake Maynard for supplies. They went off the road on the 'S' curves outside of town."

Followed by her helpers, Linda entered in time to hear

Dominique. "It was touch and go for Rob. They thought they lost him more than once, but he'd insisted Dray wear a seatbelt. My son walked away with a bump on the head, a few bruises, a twisted ankle and a cracked rib. The hospital kept him overnight, but I took him home the next day."

"And you attacked my dad when he visited." Surprisingly, Dominique grinned. "If I've never told you that you're my hero, it's a 'whoops' moment."

Faint red crept into Linda's pretty, plump features and she looked slightly embarrassed. "I lost it. Your father was a grown man when I divorced my husband and came home to Baker City. Dray wasn't even a year old, and Herman went after my baby whenever he got the chance. He kept saying he 'didn't want a stranger's kid' in our family."

"What an asshat." Mac shook his head. "Please tell me the rest of the MacGillicudy clan weren't that shallow."

"They weren't. They've always treated Dray as if he was one of us and nobody ever said anything about him being adopted." Linda tilted her head to one side, her attention on Frank. "I heard through the grapevine you wanted us to clean the town library. Shall I add it to my schedule?"

"I guess you'd better. I'll let Veronika know so she'll be there."

That afternoon, Mac went to the bakery to meet Jared Williams. Jimmy had agreed to supervise the work at the hotel. Since the rain stopped and it'd begun to warm up, Dominique was working on the windows facing the main road. Soon, they'd feature Santa and a sleigh drawn by nine reindeer. While she painted, Jimmy intended to hang holiday lights with the assistance of one of the construction folks.

The bakery featured a small dining area off to the left and another two tables with chairs on the right. Straight ahead was a display case and counter. Mac glanced through the open window at the kitchen where someone rattled pots and pans. He dinged the little bell beside the register.

A dark-haired woman in her mid-thirties wearing an old-fashioned apron over a bright blue t-shirt and black slacks came out of the back. "Hello. I'm Twila Garvey. What would you like?"

"I'm Mac MacGillicudy. I'll go with coffee and a slice of the fudge cheesecake." He paused. "One of my Army buddies served with Zeke. Jimmy Penrose's covering for me at the hotel right now, but he'll be along in the next few days to pay his respects."

"Thanks for the heads-up." Twila filled a cup with strong black coffee. When the bell jangled over the door, she smiled at the new arrival. "Hello, Jared. How's Margo and Garrett?"

"Oh, they're great." A tall man built like a truck driver, Jared advanced toward Mac. "Good to see you. How was the book tour?"

Mac gripped the older man's hand, before they hugged, a quick manly embrace. "Excellent. I really enjoyed it."

"And your family?" Jared raked a hand through his prematurely white hair. "Were they everything you expected?"

"That's a good way to say it. I'm ready to give you a sitrep. Then, we need to arrange a time for you to visit the hotel, my new home."

CHAPTER FIFTEEN

In an expensive, three-piece, black suit, pinstriped blue shirt and navy tie, Liam O'Leary prided himself on his appearance. In order to convince potential clients to invest their funds with him, he needed to look like the epitome of a successful businessman. He glanced at his gold watch. Nobody would guess it was a 'knock-off', not the Rolex he claimed it was. It was nearly time to leave for his lunch appointment.

He'd decided to downsize to a smaller office in Lake Maynard to save money. He told anyone who asked that his former assistant had left for a higher paying job on the East Coast. Since she was estranged from her family, nobody would be looking for her or realize she'd vanished permanently. She'd forgotten the basic tenet he insisted on when he hired her, or perhaps she decided it no longer applied to her because she'd worked for him ten years. '*No woman ever tells me, no.*'

Meanwhile, he asked Veronika MacGillicudy to fill in until he found a replacement. He wasn't sure how her father arranged it because she definitely wasn't happy helping out until Christmas.

The phone on his desk buzzed and he picked up the receiver. "Yes, Veronika?"

"I'm going to lunch. Did you want me to bring back a sandwich for you?"

"Not today. I have several meetings this afternoon. Get your lunch and come back right away. I'll have your check ready."

"Okay, I'll be there in fifteen minutes."

She actually strolled into the room sooner than she'd said. She wore a scoop-necked black blouse tucked into blue jeans and open-toed black stilettos that revealed the brilliant red polish on her toes. Her hip-length sunshine blonde hair was neatly braided. She kept her makeup discreet, highlighting the blue eyes and long lashes. She'd opted for matching red polish on her artificial fingernails.

Liam smiled and held out the check, making her walk to the other side of his desk. At five feet three in her bare feet, she was a perfect pocket princess. A lovely face with high cheekbones, angled dark reddish-brown eyebrows, a pointed chin, full lips. He wanted her, but she usually managed to avoid his touch. Soon, he thought. He'd figure out a way to have her again. Soon.

"Take off early this afternoon and go shopping."

"For what?" She lifted her chin. "This is temporary. I'm outta here in two weeks."

"Get some business clothes. A suit or two." Liam snagged her wrist before he put the check in her hand. He stroked the tender skin and felt her shudder. "If you don't find anything today, I'll take you to my favorite designer next week."

Veronika wrenched free. "I'll think about it."

Liam grinned and watched her flee from the room. Did she remember going with him a half-dozen times in the last six years when he picked her up at the café in Baker City? He always offered to take her home after a night of drinking, playing the understanding older man who was a good friend of her father's. She was so naïve.

More than half drunk on those occasions, she thought it meant he'd drop her off wherever she happened to be living. It didn't. He took her to his place and had her until she passed out. He had her then too. He hadn't told her father, his good friend, Herman, what a great lay his daughter was. The banker admitted he'd had to resort to emotional blackmail to get Veronika to agree to provide Liam with what he needed at his business. Herman just didn't know exactly what that was.

My latest divorce was final in June. I like being married, especially to a hot, young thing. And Veronika won't be demanding children like my fifth wife. Our divorce damn near turned into an annulment when my bitch of a daughter told her that I'd had a vasectomy years ago. Luckily, I had enough money to pay her off. Now, what will it take to get a ring on Veronika's finger?

Writing his latest book, rehabbing the hotel, putting away the newly cleaned books in the library, decorating for the holidays, socializing with new friends, investigating who could be his biological father and starting the support groups at the church kept Mac busy for the next ten days. Between editing the book and hanging out with ghostly friends, Lillian did her part to solve the mystery of his parentage. The two of them met in the kitchen during his late-night cooking sessions and shared their discoveries.

Veronika finally texted Mac on Wednesday afternoon, agreeing to show him the Carnegie library. Of course, Lillian insisted on coming along. They walked through the soft winter mist. Rain in Washington State always made Mac think of the joke his mom told about there being so many synonyms for precipitation, the list went on and on— drizzle, sprinkle, cloudburst, soaker, deluge, squall, and the newest term, 'atmospheric river'.

He made a point of walking between Lillian and the street. She'd said it was common practice in the 1940s and explained men walked closest to the street because they'd been taught it was the polite thing to do, along with opening car doors for women, holding their coats when they put them on, and carrying any packages or books they might have.

Lillian reminded Mac that Linda and her crew had cleaned the downstairs from stem to stern. The painters would arrive as soon as the Baker City Business Association agreed on the colors.

"Have you decided what they should be?" Mac kept his voice low so people wouldn't realize he was talking to a woman nobody else saw. "I researched it and traditionally it's supposed to be deep blue or dark green or maroon. That seems too dark for me."

"Maybe, they could do what Dominique suggests. Most of the walls could remain cream or eggshell and then have different sections that are focal points. I like maroon."

"I'll bring it up tomorrow at the B.C. lunch meeting." Mac didn't see Veronika on the front porch by the columns. The front door was locked. He checked his phone, but didn't have a text or call from her. "Let's go around back."

"I'll look inside." Lillian vanished and reappeared moments later on the porch. "No, she's not on the main floor."

"She has an apartment upstairs." Mac led the way around the building.

Halfway there, he saw Veronika's crumpled form at the foot of the stairs. He ran to her. His boots slipped on the damp grass. "Call 9-1-1!"

"I would but they can't hear me." Lillian reached his cousin first. She dropped to her knees beside the other woman and tried to feel a pulse. "Oh, for heaven's sake. I forgot. I'm dead."

Mac knelt beside Lillian. He pulled out his phone, pressed buttons. The call went to the police station. "It's Mac MacGillicudy. I'm at the library. Veronika's hurt. She—"

He pressed two fingers against her throat, felt nothing. He lowered his head, smelled whisky on her sweatshirt. "She's not dead. She can't be—"

———

Lilly felt someone watching and turned to see the shadowy form of Veronika MacGillicudy standing in the alley near her car. "Where do you think you're going? You can't drive without a body. Take my word for it. I've been dead for years. It doesn't work."

"Hmm, I never thought of that." Veronika came a little nearer, gasping when Mac started CPR, doing chest compressions on her body, then followed that, by blowing breaths into her mouth. "Tell him to stop that. I'm not going back in there."

"Why not? As Raven Barlow would tell you, being dead sucks." Lilly beckoned to the blonde. "Come on. Nothing is as final as death. Let's go. You need to live."

"I'm done." Veronika folded her arms, lifting her pointed chin and narrowing the big, blue eyes. "If you think living is so hot, you do it. I'm outta here. Where do the ghosts hang out in Baker City?"

"In the cocktail lounge at Pop's." Lilly heard sirens and saw an ambulance arrive, followed by Dick O'Connell's squad car. As if that was the signal she needed, Veronika faded away.

"That girl." Lilly sighed and shook her head. "What is wrong with her? There was so much I didn't get to do, so much I lost when I died. I'd give anything to have another chance—"

"What happened?" Dick O'Connell was the first to reach Mac.

"I don't know. I was supposed to meet her, and she'd show me the library." Mac stood and backed up a step when the paramedics arrived. "This is how I found her."

"All right." Dick stepped around Veronika's unconscious form and started toward the stairs. "I'm going to see what I find in her place."

Mac followed him. "I didn't see anybody else. There wasn't another car."

"Doesn't mean someone wasn't here. She hasn't been around for a few days. Dominique said their dad had a special project for her. She didn't know what." Dick grimaced. "I'm going to have to contact Herman."

Behind them, one of the medics shouted, "We've got a pulse."

Mac spun on his heel. She coughed, lifted a weak hand toward the oxygen mask. He hurried toward her. "Veronika!"

She managed to push away the mask. "Sorry, Mister—"

She struggled to sit up, fell back, and tried again.

Dick stopped her from a third attempt. "Stay put, honey. You took a bad fall. We'll take you to the hospital in Lake Maynard."

She shook her head. "No. I'm all right."

"We want a second opinion." Mac took her hand. "I'll go with you."

"The hotel." She closed her eyes for a moment. "You need—"

"I'll text Penrose and he'll handle it."

"Your meeting."

"Jared and Reverend Tommy are always in charge. I'll hit the one on Friday night." Mac gestured for the medics to put her on the gurney. She was still arguing when they carried the stretcher to the ambulance. "Can I ride with her?"

"Not enough room," a young woman told him. "Uncle Dick will bring you."

———

The waiting room was crowded with family and friends from Baker City filling the chairs and couches. Hands shaking, Dominique accepted the cup of strong black coffee Mac handed her from the vending machine. She blinked hard and looked around the room done up in antiseptic white and beige tones. Large windows over-looked the parking lot. Magazines dotted a few of the tables—not that anyone bothered to read right now. Instead, everyone had come to hold a vigil for her little sister, the family troublemaker.

Her older brother, Nick put his arm around Dominique's shoulders. "What the hell happened to her?"

"I don't know." Mac sat on the chair next to hers. "She said she'd be back in town this afternoon and she'd give me a tour of the library. I wanted to see it before the BC Business Association meeting tomorrow."

"Was that the only reason?" Dominique saw faint red edge Mac's cheekbones. "You had an ulterior motive. What was it?"

"I hoped to convince her to come to the meeting tonight. She must have a reason for drinking so much and I thought if she heard other people talk about their baggage, she might be willing to share some of hers."

Dominique nodded and lifted the cup to her lips. "I should call my dad, but we do best when we're stay no or low contact."

"And your mom?"

"I texted her. She's on the way."

The buzz of conversation continued with stories about the mischief Veronika caused. A sudden hush fell, and Dominique saw her father hurrying in their direction from the elevator. Her hand clenched on the paper cup, and she hastily put it on the table beside her.

"Why didn't you call me?" Herman demanded as he reached her. "Why did I have to hear from Dick O'Connell that your sister is badly hurt?"

"Because he and Mac found her." Dominique struggled to control her shaky voice. "We still don't know what happened. She hasn't been able to tell us."

"It looks like she fell coming down the stairs from her apartment." Mac stood. "It also depends on how much she had to drink. She may have blacked out."

"What the hell are you saying?" Herman glared at him. "My baby girl—"

"Is a drunk. We all know it." Nick glanced around the waiting room. "Maybe nobody else will tell you that, but I will. Mac will. Hell, Pop will. And Dick certainly will. He's pulled her over enough times when she's driving under the influence. If you gave a rat's ass about Ronnie, you'd tell her that she can't drown her troubles—"

"Damn things swim too well," Mac agreed.

A physician in light blue scrubs headed their way, a white mask on a string around her neck. "Who is Ms. MacGillicudy's family?"

"We all are." Pop said, looking at the doctor, a dark-haired woman in her early thirties. "But her sister, brother and dad are over here. Her mom's on the way."

"First things first. She's going to be fine. She bumped her head, had some bruises, a twisted ankle and cracked ribs. She can go home on Friday. I want to keep her overnight and possibly another day or two because I'm concerned about a possible concussion. The CT scan isn't showing anything abnormal, but I want to run more tests."

Dominique heaved a sigh of relief. "Thank God. Thank you. My brother and I want to see her."

The doctor smiled. "That will be just fine. She's been asking for Mac."

"He's here too." Dominique stood. "Come on, boys. Let's go see our girl."

"I'm coming too." Herman said. "I'm her father."

"We'll see how she feels after she has the visitors she wants."

She lay in the hospital bed, drawing one shallow breath after another. Her ribs hurt and Lilly wished doctors today would do what the ones in her hospital had. They bandaged them, but the nurse had explained the doctor wouldn't prescribe compression wraps, because they could restrict breathing, leading to pneumonia, or even a partial lung collapse.

All Lilly supposedly needed was rest, ice and breathing exercises. That was the same treatment for the rest of her injuries too. She heard quick footsteps and saw Dominique coming through the door with the doctor followed by a big blond man she recognized as the new city manager, Nick MacGillicudy. Oh yes, he was Dominique's older brother and now, he'd be Lilly's too. Mac brought up the rear of the parade.

"How are you?" Dominique hurried across the room. "You scared me half to death."

"I'm sorry." Lilly reached for the woman's hand. "Don't worry. I'm fine. Well, I will be fine. Hey, aren't you supposed to bring me flowers and candy?"

That prompted a chuckle from the blond man. He leaned down

to kiss her forehead. "I didn't know you liked candy. You always tell me to bring you a bottle of whisky."

"Not with the meds I'm taking." Lilly saw the doctor's nod of approval. "Chocolate. I require imported chocolate, not the cheap stuff."

"Well, she told you, Nicky." Dominique sat in the chair beside the bed, continuing to hold Lilly's hand. "Mom's on the way, Ronnie. Dad's already here. Do you want to see him?"

Lilly closed her eyes for a moment, remembering the man who'd visited the hotel regularly in the last few days. He insisted Mac consider an offer to buy the place, refusing to accept 'No' for an answer. She gave a faint shake of her head. "No. It's his fault."

Nick stiffened, a fierce scowl replacing his initial smile. "What did he make you do?"

"Not talking about it. Not seeing him. Send him away, Nicky."

"I will." He kissed her cheek. "I'm going to the gift shop for your chocolate. What kind of flowers do you want?"

"None. I was teasing. I don't like watching them die."

"All right." Nick strode to the door, pausing by the doctor to meet the young woman's gaze. "You heard her. My father abuses her. This is the first time she's admitted it. Please keep him away until I get a lawyer here to protect her."

"Who are you going to call?" Mac asked. "I've got one on speed dial."

"Bree Hawke. She handles a lot of domestic violence cases, protects victims, and she has history with my dad and his cronies. She'll kick their butts from here to Tacoma."

Lilly squeezed Dominique's hand gently. "I do like your big brother. He's being so nice."

"Being a city manager agrees with him. And he's your big bro too."

"Oh yeah." Lilly yawned. "I forgot."

"Really?" Mac sat in the chair on the other side of the bed. "Sounds like you whacked your head harder than we thought. You may have that concussion the doctor mentioned."

"I'm fine, Mister MacGillicudy. Takes more than a little tumble to slow me down." She winked at him. "You're going to have to wait for me to edit the chapters you wrote today."

"I didn't know you even read his books," Dominique eyed them. "You always sigh, yawn and walk off when I try to talk about them."

"It's boring when you keep repeating the books word for word. Try telling me what you think about them." Lilly lifted one shoulder. "I'd rather hear that. And when you go to the gift shop, you should find a nightgown that covers my derriere. You'll have to bring me clothes when they let me go home. They cut off my jeans, shirt and underwear."

CHAPTER SIXTEEN

It was after midnight when Nick dropped Mac at the hotel. When Jenny O'Leary-MacGillicudy arrived at the hospital shortly after eight p.m., she hugged and thanked him for saving her youngest daughter. He'd almost told her that he wasn't sure he had, then decided to keep that to himself. Something strange was happening with Veronika. He hadn't corrected her when she claimed to edit his books, but he knew damned well she hadn't read his work in progress.

Nobody did, well nobody but Lillian. And where had she gone? She disappeared when they were at the library in town. He hadn't seen her at the hospital. Okay, was he going nuts? Was it really Veronika in that hospital bed or was it Lillian Bryce? How could a ghost take the place of a living woman?

He brewed a cup of coffee and helped himself to two large chocolate chip cookies before he hitched up on a stool at the center island. He glanced over his shoulder, at the doorway when Jimmy entered, followed by the calico cat. "Hey there. How did everything go?"

"It's coming together." Jimmy went to the counter, put a pod in the brewer. "How's Veronika? Dominique texted me a couple times. Said she was staying with her mom and little sis. What happened?"

"I don't know. A weird shitstorm." Mac stared into the dark depths of the mug. "I found her at the bottom of a flight of stairs. It looked like she'd fallen—"

"But?" Jimmy snagged two peanut butter cookies and joined him. "Something bugs you, Sarge. What?"

"No pulse. I checked. She was dead. I couldn't let it go, couldn't leave her."

"What did you do?"

"Called 9-1-1. Started CPR. Chest compressions, rescue breaths—" Mac paused and met his friend's gaze. "I smelled alcohol on her clothes, but I didn't taste it on her lips. Dick found a broken whisky bottle on the landing outside the door to her place."

"We've both seen dead people before." Jimmy drank some coffee. "Too damned many of them. What's on your mind?"

"She was gone," Mac repeated. "The medics brought her back. Shouldn't have been possible. It wasn't possible. She didn't want to go to the hospital."

"People don't make good decisions when they're hurt." Jimmy picked up his cookie. "So, you were wrong. Wasn't the first time." He shrugged. "Bound to happen again. You're human, not infallible. She's alive and safe. You did good, Sarge."

"I don't know."

"What's burning your butt? Besides the proverbial flame three foot high?"

"She called me, Mister MacGillicudy." Mac stared into the pantry, wondering why the door was open. Had it been closed when he came into the kitchen? For a moment, he thought he saw the insubstantial figure of a woman in a housedress standing there, then dismissed it. "Lillian never says, Mac, but Veronika does."

"Where is your ghostly girlfriend? Ask her what's happening."

"Good idea." Mac took a deep breath, then reached for a cookie. "I'll do that. Now, give me a sitrep about the left wing. How many rooms are left to paint?"

The next afternoon, Mac pulled into the driveway at Cedar Creek Guest Ranch, heading past the row of cabins toward the corral and the barn behind it. He parked in the lot in front of the barn, then sat in the driver's seat, debating the decision to talk to Rob Hendrickson. This ranked as one of the stupidest things he'd ever done, Mac thought. It was either that or it had to be one of the craziest.

What was he supposed to say? How could he tell a man he barely knew the ghost haunting him had stolen the body of a living person? Was Veronika MacGillicudy still alive or somewhere in Baker City? And how was Mac supposed to fix this cosmic error?

When he walked into the barn, he spotted Rob Hendrickson pushing a wheelbarrow down the barn aisle and parceling out hay to the horses. "Got a minute? I need to talk to you."

"About what?" Rob dropped a flake of hay into the next stall to an eager buckskin. "How's the hotel? Lieutenant Lilly?"

"That's the issue." Mac hesitated, then rubbed his jaw. "I think she's— This is too weird. Lillian's a good person. She really is."

"Who are you trying to convince? Me or yourself?" Rob fed the next horse, a big black one. "What's happened?"

"I thought about talking to Cat after the BC Business Association meeting today, but I don't really know her. I know you and she was busy in the cocktail lounge. I couldn't believe she took a baby in there."

"Oh, the spirits like seeing Claire and they won't hurt her." Rob paused. "So, if you didn't bring it up to Cat, why are you seeing me? What's Lilly done?"

"He's trying to screw up the courage to tell you that First Lieutenant Lilly Bryce accepted a second chance at life." Cat O'Leary, a curvaceous redhead sauntered into the barn, holding a sleeping infant. "And there's a new ghost in Baker City. We had a nice little chat, and I promised to send you to the hospital with Mac to visit Lilly, Rob."

"Who's the ghost?" Rob continued feeding lunch to the rest of the horses. "Do I know her?"

"Veronika MacGillicudy." Cat waited near the entry. "I do hope you have a box of cookies in your Jeep, Mac. I understand it's your stock in trade and Lilly loves the smell of them."

Heat slipped into his face, and he nodded. "I searched the entire hotel last night and she wasn't there. So, I made my version of Peanut Butter Blossoms this morning."

"I know exactly how you feel." Cat cuddled the baby closer. "I went through that when my husband died last year and—"

"Wait a second." Mac held up his hand and pointed at Rob coming toward them. "He's right there. I heard he was in an accident."

"Not me. I died at Hamburger Hill back in '69 during the height of the Vietnam Conflict." Rob pushed the empty wheelbarrow past them. "I bought the farm with my blood. Well, actually my parents used the money from my military insurance to pay off the last of the mortgage on their home. I had no intention of passing on to what was considered a 'better place,' so I came here."

"And proceeded to haunt me until my soon-to-be, ex-husband passed away after that truck wreck last year." Cat waited while he parked the wheelbarrow in the hay-room. "Let's go have a quick sandwich while we bring Mac up to speed and then you two can head into Lake Maynard. Rob had to adjust to being human after an almost fifty-year hiatus and Lilly has been dead a lot longer."

"So, you believe she absconded with Veronika's body?"

"Hold up there." Cat shook her head. "You don't understand. Frazer wanted to leave and see what came next. My grandmother explained to me that he moved on to as peaceful an end as he could want. He may not have lived well, but he made up for it at the end."

"By saving Linda's boy, Dray." Rob joined them. "Dray wore a seatbelt and Frazer managed to drive so he took the brunt of the damage when the brakes failed, and the truck went off the road and hit a tree."

"And he stepped aside so Rob could love me and our daughters. It took honor and grace for Frazer to give his body to Rob, just like Veronika gave hers to Lilly."

"Why does Rob still see other ghosts around here?" Mac asked. "Shouldn't he have lost that ability when he took over for Frazer?"

"I didn't lose the power to see the unseen." Rob lifted the diaper bag off Cat's shoulder to carry it for her. "Lilly is probably blocking it while she's in the hospital. If she isn't, I'll tell her that she should when I get there. Otherwise, everybody will think she's bonkers when she starts talking to folks nobody else sees."

The two men left after lunch. Cat checked on the baby who slept soundly in her crib in the master bedroom and then went to start a load of laundry. She hadn't shared everything she heard from Veronika MacGillicudy. The rest of the story could wait until Rob returned from the hospital in Lake Maynard.

He had his own experiences with her father back in the day and seen what Liam was capable of long before Cat shared her history. Rob wouldn't be surprised to hear what the other woman said happened. *And neither am I*, Cat thought. *I'll talk about it with him when he gets home. I didn't tell her or the rest of the ghosts that Veronika wasn't the first woman he pushed down a flight of stairs.*

Cat shuddered and let the memory of a long ago visit to her grandmother's home flow through her mind.

A teenage girl that Cat recognized as a younger version of herself stood in an old-style kitchen decked out with red-checked curtains at the windows and a matching tablecloth on the small round table. A refrigerator hummed in one corner and a golden collie sat nearby, tail wagging as it waited politely for the dog treat in Cat's hand.

Her newly dead grandmother sat at the table, a plate of Oreos and glass of ice-cold milk in front of where Cat had obviously been sitting across from her before she went after a doggie snack.

Thirteen-year-old Cat handed the treat to the dog that crunched the bone-shaped cookie in less than a moment. Petting the collie, she asked, "So, what if I find a mean ghost, Grandma? How do I get rid of it?"

The back door slammed open, striking the wall and her father stormed inside. "How many times have I told you not to tell lies, Catriona O'Leary? How dare you tell Aidan that our mother is still here?"

"She had things to say to me," Cat said, glaring back at him. "And I don't care what you say. You're the liar. I know she's real."

"Oh God no!" Enmeshed in her vision, the grown Cat watched Liam *backhand the teenage girl. He knocked her into the basement door which flew open. The dog rushed forward, barking.*

It lunged for Liam, teeth sinking into his arm. He kicked it in the ribs. The blow sent the collie spiraling into the basement and Cat heard it howling in pain when it crashed onto the concrete floor a story below.

Teenage Cat scrambled to her feet, reeling, one hand pressed to a swelling cheek. She spat curse words at him. Then, she turned toward the basement and the stairs, obviously intending to go to the injured dog.

"Watch out!" Cat yelled at her younger self, even though she knew the *girl wouldn't hear, wouldn't be able to save herself. Liam shoved the teenager from behind, sent her tumbling down into darkness.*

Cat shook her head, forcing away the vision of the accident that nearly killed her and had slain her first beloved dog. When she originally remembered the assault a year ago, she'd gone to her uncle's hardware store. Aiden shared he was the one who found her in an abandoned gravel pit. It surprised him because she'd never been there before.

I thought I'd be safe if I watched out for him, but I never expected him to go after someone else. Now, he's hurt Veronika MacGillicudy. It makes me wonder how many other women he's hurt. Does my mother know? Would she tell me if she did?

It felt odd to sleep in a bed like a living human after all this time. Lilly opened her eyes and saw Veronika's mother dozing in a chair nearby. Jenny O'Leary-MacGillicudy was as blonde as her children, but she wasn't a fashion diva like her eldest daughter. Instead, she opted for jeans, boots and a Washington State University sweatshirt. No fake nails for her either.

I'm getting rid of these too, Lilly decided, looking at her fingers. *I know Veronika likes them, but she gave this body to me. I won't harm it, but I have my own tastes and I'm sure she'll be okay with that. I'll ask her when I get back to Baker City.*

Jenny straightened in the chair. "Are you ready for lunch?"

"Yes, if you are." Lilly pointed to the menu on the nightstand. "The nurse said to call down and order whatever we wanted. What would you like?"

"You're the one who should choose." Jenny patted Lilly's hand. "I wonder if they have grilled cheese. That was always your favorite when you were sick."

"And chicken noodle soup." Dominique came through the door carrying a garment bag. She hung it in the closet adjacent to the bathroom. She must have been to the realty since she was dressed for success in tailored slacks, a cream turtleneck sweater and ballet slipper shoes. "You threw such terrible tantrums if Mom made tomato soup for me."

"Oh, I'm sorry. That was an awful thing to do."

"You were a little girl." Jenny kissed Lilly's cheek. "And everyone has their favorites. Your brother always demanded Vegetable Tortellini."

"And you spoiled us rotten." Dominique went to the other side of the bed. "You should have told us to eat what was on the table, not prepared three different kinds of homemade soup. No wonder, we're awful adults."

"You're not awful." Jenny shook her finger at Dominique. "And it wasn't any trouble. Don't you remember our 'soup' days? We'd make batches of everyone's faves and stock the freezer."

"That was brilliant." Lilly wondered if her own mother would have done something similar. She probably wouldn't have let her child choose a different accompaniment to her sandwich.

At the orphanages, the nuns had always served whatever was available and refusing to eat something meant extra chores. It was better than being in some of the foster homes when the parents definitely didn't spare the proverbial rod—corporal punishment was the norm—and being deprived of meals wasn't unusual.

No wonder, I ran away to the downtown Seattle library whenever I got the chance. And I certainly never shared it was my sanctuary.

Nick MacGillicudy arrived two hours later with a slender blonde woman in a black jacket, navy shell and matching slacks, toting a leather briefcase. He introduced her as Bree Hawke, an ace attorney who knew their father.

"That isn't much of a recommendation." Lilly leaned back against the pillows. "Why did you bring her?"

"To run interference for you." Bree gestured toward the door. "Close that, Nick. On your way out. Your sister and I need to talk in private."

"Sounds like we need to go with him." Jenny rose to her feet. "Granted, nothing you can say about my ex-husband will come as a surprise to me. We fought for months over custody during our divorce."

"Why?" Bree asked. "Herman never has struck me as the paternal type."

"Child support," Nick said. "He didn't want to pay it. My father never has been good about paying his share. Like I told Ronnie, when I worked for him, my paychecks always bounced, and I caught the fallout in town."

"And I have my share of horror tales." Dominique folded her arms. "Ronnie's doctor is worried about her memories. She didn't recognize our mom last night."

"I fell and bonked my head yesterday," Lilly protested. "I'll be fine. I want to go home."

"Where is that?" Bree asked.

"Baker City. The hotel."

"Oh, honey." Jenny hurried to hug Lilly. "We haven't lived there since your dad's grandparents offered us a place to stay when I left him. You weren't even five years old."

"We've been visiting it a lot in the last few weeks." Dominique shared a look with Nick. "Ronnie comes in the evenings after she finishes Dad's project. We're decorating for Christmas."

"We're going to put up the trees this weekend. I can't miss that." Lilly slipped out of Jenny's embrace. "Okay, so things get a bit fuzzy sometimes, but it doesn't mean I'm not okay."

The door opened to reveal Rob Hendrickson and Mac.

"Ready for company?" Rob nodded at Bree. "Hello, stranger. How are you? It's been a few weeks since the Haunted Town celebration. Cat misses you. This is Mac MacGillicudy. He's partners with Dominique and Veronika. They're restoring the hotel."

"And Veronika's also working on the town library." Mac carried a small box to the nightstand. "I made cookies."

"Chocolate chip?" Dominique asked. "Those are Ronnie's favorite."

"Whoops and I thought it was my special Peanut Butter Blossoms." Mac winked at Lilly. "At least, that's what I heard. My bad."

"Oh no. Those always smell so good." Lilly lifted off the lid and saw the peanut-shaped cookies decorated with two upside-down chocolate kisses and several chocolate chips. "I can't wait to try them. And you made enough for me to share. This is wonderful."

The new guests and the cookies distracted the lawyer and Lilly promised to see her the next day. After Bree left, Rob finessed the situation with some help from Mac. He took Veronika's family to visit the gift shop and the cafeteria.

"What's going on?" Lilly focused on the man who'd originally welcomed her to town. "Why are you here?"

"Because Cat sent me." Rob crossed one leg over the other, faint amusement seeping into his dark eyes and onto his rugged features. "She talked to Veronika at the café and decided I should bring you up to speed on how to deal with folks who'd never believe you got a second chance at life, Lilly."

"I didn't fight her for this body." Lilly glanced carefully at the door before she gazed at him again. "She wouldn't take it back. She wanted to leave it behind. And—"

"I know. The same thing happened to me." Rob lowered his voice. "I came with Cat to this hospital when her husband died after their truck crashed outside of town. He did the same thing even though I ordered him to get back into his body. I wanted him to live."

"It's what I told Veronika too."

"Frazer insisted on going to see what comes next." Rob shrugged. "He didn't love Cat or the girls. I did, so I took the opportunity the

Universe or God or whoever's in charge offered me. And I'm so grateful to be with them."

"My turn to say that I understand." Lilly took a deep breath and felt her ribs throb. "Now, how do I handle the fact that I don't know everything people think I should?"

"You do what Cat did for me. You claim to have dissociative amnesia caused by the trauma inflicted from your fall down the stairs. It will explain the gaps in your memories. As soon as you get to Baker City, go to the cocktail lounge and have a heart-to-heart with Veronika."

"And she can bring me up to speed."

"Right. She did tell Cat that Herman blackmailed her into being Liam O'Leary's secretary for the past couple weeks. Veronika said the guy's a total lecher. It was a struggle to keep him at arm's length, and he kissed her more than once, tongue and all. Cat's his daughter and she told me she wasn't surprised. Liam's last wife divorced him because he cheated on her, lied constantly and didn't even tell her that he had a vasectomy. He tried to make her think it was her fault they couldn't have children. Guy deserves another beatdown, but Cat said I couldn't do it again."

"Some of the ghosts said you two had other issues with him. He was supposed to be the town medium, but they didn't like him. It's why they waited for Cat."

"As soon as she won the guest ranch, he did his best to steal it from her. He and Herman want it to be part of a gravel pit."

"And Baker City too."

"Exactly. We're not going to let them destroy our home, Lilly."

"I can help with that. It's my home too."

"We're counting on it." Rob put his hand on her shoulder. "Let's talk about what else you can expect now."

"Food." She giggled. "I love chocolate. And scrambled eggs. Jenny went downstairs to the espresso stand and brought me a mocha because the coffee here is awful."

"Mom." Rob squeezed her arm. "Call her, Mom."

"But she's not my mother."

"Do you want to stay in the hospital for weeks or months?"

"Of course not." Lilly stared at him. "You're right. I need to act like I'm Veronika or I'll be here forever. The doctor will think I've lost it, and my brain is as scrambled as those eggs. So, she's my mom now. Dominique is my sister and Nick's my brother."

"Right. Linda's your cousin. So are Pop and Dray."

"Oooh! I work in a Carnegie library. It's mine now."

"There you go. You're getting the hang of life. What else?"

CHAPTER SEVENTEEN

On Friday morning when he arrived at the hospital, Mac found Herman MacGillicudy in the hallway arguing with Dr. Aubert. He demanded to see Veronika, but it apparently wasn't happening. The physician was more stubborn than the banker expected. "I've told you. My patient is an adult. She's thirty-two and she's not impaired in any way. She has rights and she's refusing to see you."

"I don't know what's wrong with her." Concern heightened the color in Herman's ruddy features, and he took a step closer to the doctor. "She's my baby and she loves me. Why is she being this way?"

"The doctor may not know yet, but we do." Mac strode forward, remembering his conversation with Cat the previous day. "You pimped your daughter out to your best friend. Now, take a hike or I'll help you find the door."

"What?" Herman gulped for air. "You're lying. You have to be. Liam needed office help and Veronika agreed to do it. He paid her."

"Go." Mac stepped nearer. He didn't have to put his hands on the older man. The threat was understood and Herman scuttled in the direction of the exit.

"Should I run a rape kit?" Dr. Aubert stood in front of the door. "We did another CT scan this morning."

"She fought him off more than once. If she'll agree to stay with me at the family hotel, I have a construction crew who will keep Herman and his cohorts away." Mac glanced through the window and saw Veronika, no it was Lillian, talking to Jenny and Dominique. "Chief O'Connell is still investigating. He suspects something more happened at her apartment and hopefully, she'll remember exactly what led up to her accident."

"That makes sense." Dr. Aubert opened the door. "You have another visitor."

"Mister—" Lillian stopped speaking for a moment. She blushed, then smiled at him. "Mac. We finished off your cookies last night. They were delicious. Everyone loved them, even the nurses. Did you bring more?"

"Since you're going home, I didn't think of it. I'll bring some when you're back for a check-up." He'd grown accustomed to her Army uniform. It surprised him to see her in a bright red sweater that clung to her breasts and slender waist. Faded blue jeans emphasized the curve of her hips and long legs. She wore lace-up running shoes and someone else must have tied them.

He also suspected either Jenny or Dominique had braided Lillian's blonde hair. She didn't wear any makeup, not that she needed it to highlight her face or bright blue eyes. He'd never seen Veronika without it, more confirmation she was gone. "Who is taking you to your place?"

"Nobody. We talked about it and I'm going to the hotel. Mom and I can stay in the left wing. I want the locks changed on the apartment at the library and I need time to adjust."

"Plus, we want Bree to get a restraining order to keep my dad and Liam O'Leary away." Dominique glanced at the clock on the wall. "Come on. Let's get moving. She's meeting us at the hotel if she gets out of court early this afternoon. Otherwise, it will be tomorrow morning. I hope you have more cookies at home, Mac."

"Always. I only brought two dozen Blossoms. There's more of those and I also made some holiday ones. They even have sprinkles." Mac held the door for them. "Let's do this."

Lillian paused near him. "Are you okay with me imposing on your hospitality?"

"It's your place too, remember?" He touched her cheek gently and caught a whiff of jasmine perfume. "I'm glad you suggested it. If you hadn't, I would have. I want you somewhere safe."

"And then, you can kick butt and take names if anyone comes after her," Dominique told him. "I'm counting on you and Jim to protect her."

"We will," Mac promised.

"You'll like Jim, Mom. Dommi thinks he makes the sun rise and set." Lillian headed out the door while Dominique squawked protests. "He served with Mac and the two of them are rough, tough soldiers but Jim doesn't bake cookies for us."

"Oh, come on. He brings fried chicken and salads from the mercantile deli when it's his turn to cook," Mac teased. "And picks up Dommi's favorite cheesecake at the bakery."

"He sounds nice." Jenny tucked her arm through Lillian's. "Now, stop harassing your sister. She's been worrying nonstop about you."

"I know, but she doesn't need to fret anymore. I'm going to be okay."

"And much more careful," Dominique added.

"You know it," Lillian said.

Lilly wanted to ride with Mac in the SUV, but she opted for discretion being the better part of valor as Shakespeare said. She went with Veronika's mother in Jenny's older Jeep instead. On the drive to Baker City, Lilly contemplated how long it'd take her to become familiar with driving. She rode the buses in Seattle from her apartment to work and back again when she was a nurse. Once she volunteered after Pearl Harbor, she'd rarely done it in the Army since her duties revolved around the hospital and most of their supplies were delivered.

Maybe, she could pretend this was one of the things she hardly remembered how to do and have Mac help her 'refresh' her skills. There would be so many things she didn't know how to do in this contemporary world, but she couldn't wait to try them. One of them would be playing with the exercise equipment in the basement gym.

Lilly wondered why the windshield wipers swishing back and forth didn't distract Veronika's mother. How did she manage to remain focused on what she was doing, regardless of all the other vehicles on the highway?

As they pulled into Baker City, Jenny followed Dominique's newer Jeep to the hotel. "Let's get you settled and then your sister and I will go to your apartment. What do you want us to bring back? Do you have any perishable food?"

"I don't remember. If I do, it goes into the refrigerator here and Mac can use it." Lilly yawned. "It will be nice to sleep for longer than a couple hours. The nurses were very nice, but they kept waking me up."

"That's always the way when you're in the hospital, especially if they think you might have a concussion. What else do you want?"

"My clothes and there are some old books in the living room I keep meaning to read. Frank Madison, the president of the Baker City Business Association said I could have them. Except for my TV, the rest of the furniture and the dishes belong to the town, so they stay there."

Mac had chosen two connecting bedrooms for Jenny and Lilly. She debated saying she wanted privacy, but the queen-size bed looked so inviting. She removed her shoes, then curled up for a nap. Dimly, she was aware that Jenny lingered long enough to cover her with an extra blanket from the closet. Exhaustion claimed Lilly and she faded off to sleep.

When she awakened three hours later, she was starving. It was a new and different feeling. She sat up cautiously, pushing the blanket aside and spotted her shoes next to a chair by the dresser. At some point, someone had entered the room long enough to put Veronika's small smart TV on the bureau. Wait a minute. Now, it was Lilly's flat-screen.

She found a pair of comfy, ankle-high slippers in the closet and eased into them, smiling at the pink bunny heads on the front and the puffy little tails at the back. She went across the room and tried to float through the door. She bumped into the solid barrier instead. What was that about?

A second, then a third try failed as well. Lilly heaved a sigh. *Of course. I'm alive. I have a body again. It doesn't do what mine did. I have to act like a human.* She twisted the knob, and the door opened. She left the bedroom and headed through the hallway to the hotel kitchen where she found Veronika's mother. Whoops, I have to remember Jenny is my mom too.

Jenny turned from where she unloaded clean plates from the dishwasher. "Mac made an incredible chicken salad for lunch and there's artisan bread too. I'll fix you a sandwich."

"I can do it." Lilly opened the fridge, glancing around the nearly empty room. She saw another gray Pacific Northwest day outside the windows. Rain poured down, soaking the parking lot and the assortment of cars and trucks.

Lilly smiled and gave a little wave to Florence who stood watching. "Where is everyone?"

"Mac went to his study to work on his book. Jim and the rest of the crew are on the second floor of the left wing. They want to get it painted before quitting today. Dominique had to go to her office. She has three deals pending. The lawyer called and she'll be here first thing tomorrow."

"I don't know how much Bree Hawke will be able to do." Lilly removed the covered bowl, a jar of mayonnaise and a head of lettuce from the refrigerator. "I agreed to work for my dad's best friend, and I walked off the job when he got disgusting."

"It's called sexual harassment, honey. Nobody has the right to put their hands on you without your consent. You know that."

Lilly nodded agreement. "Well, I want an attorney's advice. I like the idea of living here with Mac and Jim—"

"Donal and I will be here too." Florence drifted closer and glanced at the wooden breadbox on the counter.

The lid slid up and Lilly winked at her friend, hastily grabbing the loaf of sourdough bread. She'd seen Mac make it with his special starter, organic flour and sea salt. Now, she'd get to taste it, not just smell it.

"What's the plan after you eat?" Jenny asked. "I already put away your clothes. Do you want to watch TV?"

"No, I've got work to do. Mac's on deadline and I need to edit the last six chapters of the new book. We don't want his agent landing on the doorstep before New Year's, demanding the manuscript."

Jenny put the last two cups away. "Are you serious? Honey, you can't interfere with a writer's creative process."

"I never do that." Lilly spread mayonnaise on a slice of bread. "But somebody needs to fix his books when he goes astray. That's my job."

"How long have you been doing it?"

Lilly popped the lid off the bowl and didn't answer. She wasn't going to lie about the past, but Rob Hendrickson was right. Nobody would believe she'd come back from the dead to replace the real Veronika and Lilly didn't want to wind up in an insane asylum while she tried to convince strangers of the truth.

She pretended her lunch required all her attention. The shredded chicken salad looked amazing with chopped celery, pieces of green grapes and walnuts. Oh, she definitely looked forward to her sandwich.

Mac frowned thoughtfully at the words on the monitor in front of him. He was stuck in what Lillian would call a plothole. Maybe a walk would help. He turned his head, looked out the office window and gave up on that idea when he saw the rain. He'd go check on the progress in the left wing. He'd jump in and help with the new floor tile in the bathrooms. Physical labor always got his creative juices stirring.

"Mac, do you have a minute?" Jenny stood in the doorway. "I'm worried about Veronika."

"What's wrong?" Mac pushed back from the desk and stood. "Is she still asleep?"

"No, she's in your apartment. She insisted on going there as soon as she had lunch." Jenny wrung her hands. "I didn't know how to stop her. She wouldn't listen when I said she shouldn't invade your privacy."

"It's okay." Mac strode out of the office and down the main hallway, rather than cutting through the ensuite into his suite. When he entered the living room, he saw Lillian sitting at the small desk, staring at his closed laptop. "What is it? Didn't you want to read the latest installment?"

She nodded, then glanced over her shoulder at him, tears sparkling in the blue eyes. "Of course I want to, but I don't remember how to find it."

"Let me help you get started." He continued across the room, lifted the lid, and pressed the power button. "Once the computer fires up, use the mouse to go on the Internet before you load the manuscript. You'll need it for research."

When Jenny left the two of them alone, Mac lowered his voice. "What's really wrong, Lillian?"

"This is so different. Before I looked at the screen and was able to change things by concentrating on them," Lillian murmured. "I feel so stupid."

"There's nothing stupid about you." Mac rested his hand on the back of the chair. He couldn't resist the urge to kiss her forehead, and she smiled at him. "I'll bet you have to use the TV remote like I do when you want to stream your favorite shows."

"I never thought of that when I received this opportunity. I had to walk to the kitchen."

"And how did you get there before?" Mac chuckled. "You've certainly been in it several times talking to me."

"I just thought of where I wanted to be, and I ended up there." She rubbed the back of her neck. "I have so much to learn. How do I make changes or add text to the book?"

"I'll show you, Lillian."

"Lilly. You call me, Lilly and I'll remember to call you, Mac." Her smile widened. "Of course, if you do it in public, everyone will think you're the crazy one, not me. Then, I'd better be Veronika for a while until I come up with a way to let people know I'm Lilly."

"Fair enough." Mac clicked on the icon for word-processing. "Now, we pull up the full manuscript and remember to save your changes."

"How do I do that?"

"I'll show you. Are you coming with me to the meeting at the church tonight?"

"I can't. I don't have any suitable clothes." Lillian grimaced. "I looked in the closet and Veronika doesn't have anything I could wear. Her skirts are so short. And the dresses barely have bodices. Just the idea of patching most of her jeans makes my head hurt. This was the only pair that wasn't ripped to smithereens."

"Oh, sweetheart." Mac laughed heartily. "You've seen how clothes have changed in the last eighty-some years. And what you're wearing is just fine. If it keeps raining, you'll want a jacket."

She scowled at him. "You'll get tired of telling me things I should know."

"Not in the next eighty years." He debated really kissing her and decided it was too soon. "Now, do some work before dinner. Tell me what you think of using the victim's wife as a red herring, rather than the killer."

"Oh, that's much better than having her be convicted of murder." Lillian nodded approval. "Nobody wants the kids to lose another parent."

"Glad you agree. Now, you can catch up on the book while I figure out what to make for supper."

"You don't have to cook tonight. Veronika's mom is making spaghetti." Lillian glowered at him. "If she messes up your kitchen, you're not allowed to whine or whinge."

"I won't. Tell you what. While you work, I'll watch TV and then I'll be here if you have any questions."

"Fine, but choose something with a real story, not one of your 'shoot everybody dead' cop shows. I hate listening to those."

"No worries. I'll pick one of your favorite costume dramas."

Being dead didn't change Veronika's enjoyment of hanging out in the cocktail lounge. Granted, she hadn't met all her relatives yet, but irascible Newt O'Leary told her that he thought he was her great-grandfather on her mother's side, but she might need to throw in another 'great' until they found the O'Leary family bible. It listed all their Baker City relatives. He'd shared the ghostly rules with her, and she promised not to break them.

It turned out playing pool wasn't against them. Moises Pride, a former soldier, taught her to use her mind to rack the balls, and then how to play without a cue. Newt joined them and so did Zeke Garvey, another Army Ranger. They'd barely finished a third game when Linda MacGillicudy began opening up the lounge for the living customers. She went through the room, lifting the chairs off the tables while one of the waitresses, Jacinth Sweeney followed, a damp cloth in her hand.

Veronika joined Raven Driscoll-Barlow, Brigid McElroy and her great-grandmother, Florence MacGillicudy at their table. "What happens now? We can't do much in here on Friday night. The living Baker City folks will fill up the place as usual and Chief O'Connell and his sons provide country music so they can dance. Heather McElroy may turn up to sing with them."

Raven, a thin, dark-haired wraith in camouflage fatigues and combat boots, grinned back at her. "There's choices. We can head over to the bakery with Zeke. He likes to visit when his wife is setting up for the next day. She brings their kids to help, and the baby babbles at Zeke."

"Summer O'Neill has late night holiday sales at the feedstore," Brigid said. "We can go there. Moises and her youngest play ball—"

"No way! I don't go to the feedstore. Not now, not ever." Veronika shuddered at the idea. "What else?"

"Come with me." Florence rose to her feet, a plump woman in a flowered housedress. "We'll join Mac and Lilly at the church for their meeting. You need to talk to her and warn her about the man who killed you. We don't want him adding her to the list of victims."

CHAPTER EIGHTEEN

Several tables filled the community room at the church. A kitchen area was in the right corner and Reverend Tommy was setting up the coffee urn on the counter when Lilly entered with Mac. She hadn't met him in person before, but she'd enjoyed his sermons over the past two weeks. A rugged blond man about the same age as Mac arranged chairs around a long table.

A tall, dark-haired man in cowboy attire of jeans, a western shirt, and a denim jacket sauntered in the door carrying two boxes of doughnuts. He nodded at Mac. "Hey there. Glad you made it."

"Thanks, Bendigo." Mac cupped Lilly's elbow, guiding her in the direction of the chairs. "This is Veronika. First-timer."

"Good. We need more women. Glad you're here." Bendigo put the cartons in the middle of the table. "Alcoholism is an equal opportunity disease."

Other people filtered into the room, two women following Jack Madison. They seemed to recognize Lilly although she didn't know them. Perhaps Veronika had. The living members had barely taken their seats when the ghosts arrived. This time, Lilly knew some of them. Three loggers, Newt O'Leary, Florence and Veronika MacGillicudy.

Instead of the minister taking charge, it was the older, bigger man with prematurely gray hair. He introduced himself as Jared. He said he was an alcoholic and the secretary of the Baker City A.A group. Next, he asked for a moment of silence and then everyone except Lilly repeated the Serenity Prayer. After that, he recited the basic purposes of the organization. They were here to share their experiences, strengths and hopes with each other to solve common problems and help others recover from alcoholism. The only requirement for membership was the desire to stop drinking.

Visitors were asked to introduce themselves by their first names. Lilly carefully used Veronika's and saw the new ghost smile in agreement. The meeting continued with Jared reading from a large book and then he encouraged people to share their stories about what made them choose sobriety. Toward the end of the hour, he asked Lilly if she felt comfortable speaking. She started to refuse, then saw Veronika come closer.

"Say yes. I want you to tell them what happened to me, why I'm a drunk."

Lilly took a deep breath and copied what she'd heard the others say as an intro. "I'm Veronika and I'm an alcoholic."

"Welcome, Veronika," everyone else chorused, the living and the dead. "We're glad you're here."

"I've been drinking since I was four years old—" Veronika waited for Lilly to repeat that and then went on. "Nobody in my family knew—"

"I did," Florence said. "I saw you sneaking drinks from the bottles in the drawing room when you lived with us and refilling them with water so your mother wouldn't know. Of course, I couldn't tell anyone except Donal because I was already dead. And since you were a favorite scapegoat in your immediate family, I wasn't going to *The O'Leary* back then."

Lilly rested her hands on the table and kept her gaze on the blonde woman who'd traded places with her three days before. "I hid it as much as I could."

Nobody interrupted but she saw understanding nods, then

continued with the story Veronika told her, careful to use a first-person narrative. "My dad took us to the feedstore to pick up cat food. He and my mom had separated and my brother, sister and I were living with Mom at the MacGillicudy family hotel. While Dad shopped, the three of us played hide and seek. I heard one of my dad's friends arguing with a woman. He didn't see me hiding behind bags of cat litter. She said something he didn't like, and I still remember him saying, 'no woman ever tells me no'."

Mac covered Lilly's hand with his and she gripped his fingers. Then she continued with Veronika's tale. "I don't know who she was. She was in front of a closed door to the basement. He hit her. She fell backwards, through the door and down the stairs. I heard her thud all the way."

"Was she all right?" Jared asked.

"No! She fell, just like I did three days ago." Lilly scowled at him. "Only nobody helped her. Mac wasn't there to call 9-1-1. The first responders didn't come. And when I told my dad, he spanked me for lying about his best friend. It's happened again and again. No one ever believes me."

Tears streamed down Lilly's face, and she shoved back the chair, jumping to her feet. She ignored the stabbing of her ribs and hurried for the door. She wished she could wrap her arms around Veronika and hug the ghost, the way no human ever had. "I'm sorry."

"For what?" Veronika floated beside her. "It's not your fault. And at least, you got the truth out there for me. I've spent too many years hiding it and being afraid of my father, his minions as Dommi calls them, and his friends. Thank you for being so brave tonight."

Lilly looked up at Mac when he caught up with her. "I'm sorry."

"I'm not. I'm grateful you told us. Please come back."

She stopped and stared. "You believe me?" She lowered her voice to a bare whisper. "Believe her?"

"Of course, I do. We all do." Mac put his arm around her. "Come back and share the rest."

"What are you talking about? I already did."

"There's more." This time it was Durango who spoke. Warmth

filled his rugged features and cobalt blue eyes. "My wife's aunt disappeared twenty-eight years ago under mysterious circumstances. Dick O'Connell has reopened the case but so far there hasn't been much trace of Lucy McElroy. She hasn't used her credit cards or paid taxes for almost twenty-eight years. None of her daughters have heard from her, and neither has anyone else in town."

"And your dad sent his campaign manager to threaten Frank Madison unless Dick stopped his investigation into Frank's first wife's disappearance, Durango." Bendigo stood and held Lilly's chair for her. "Sounds like we have a clue, but you'll have to decide to tell Dick because we can't let the police chief know anything you said. What happens in our meetings, stays here."

"But all of you believe me?" Lilly looked at the people sitting around the table and saw the confirmation on their faces.

"You need to tell them that I wasn't drinking on Wednesday. I'd walked off the job at Liam O'Leary's on Tuesday when he tried jumping me again." Veronika stood beside Lilly. "He came to my place with a bottle of whisky. He claimed he wanted to apologize, then grabbed at me and gave me that same speech about 'no woman telling him no'."

"There's more," Lilly said, repeating the story. "I pushed past him, the bottle broke and splashed whisky all over my clothes. He shoved me. I fell down the back stairs. He walked past me and left."

"That explains a lot." Mac put an arm around her shoulders. "I smelled the booze on you, but it wasn't on your breath when I was doing CPR."

"The doctors at the hospital ran tests because they had to be careful what drugs they gave me. There wasn't any alcohol in my system."

"Are you safe?" Reverend Tommy leaned forward. "I don't know if you should stay in the apartment at the library where you've been living, Veronika."

"It's why I've moved into the hotel for the time being."

"And we'll look after her," Mac said. "My mother tells me not to share gruesome stories about my 'sixty-second solutions' but it doesn't mean I can't still use them."

"So can we," Bendigo said, looking at Durango. "Let us know if you need someone to watch your six."

"I will, but it's my best friend's job and he's staying through New Years."

The meeting closed a short time later and Lilly walked out to the parking lot beside Mac with Veronika and Florence trailing behind them. "You didn't ask his name when I first started telling my story. You waited—."

"I knew as soon as you said it was one of your father's friends." He unlocked the passenger door for her. "It was Liam O'Leary, wasn't it?"

"Yes."

"There's no statute of limitations on murder." Mac held the door. "If we can find the body, we can tell Dick O'Connell and he'll be able to run tests to confirm what happened."

"How do we find it?"

"I'm not going to the feedstore." Veronika yelled. "I'm not. I'm not. I'm not!"

"You don't have to," Lilly told the ghost. "We'll go. You've done enough. You told the truth. Now, enjoy haunting the town with the rest of the spirits."

"You're not telling me to move onto whatever comes next?"

"Why would I? I didn't when I came home from Italy after I died in World War Two."

Once they were safely in the Jeep, Mac glanced sideways at Lilly. "Veronika was at the meeting, wasn't she? And that's how you knew what happened to her."

Lilly nodded. "And it gives me the explanation I need for the lawyer tomorrow. I don't know if she can really get a restraining order or not. I wonder why Durango's father tried to stop the investigation."

"Liam O'Leary is supposed to be the big money man around here and that buys a lot of influence." Mac slid the key into the ignition. "Yes, we're supposed to maintain anonymity in our group, but Baker

City is a small town and everyone knows everyone. Durango's father is Senator Tex Hawke."

"Even if he knows Liam is a killer, Tex will help cover it up in exchange for beaucoup bucks." Lilly fastened her seatbelt. "Let's go home. I think you should teach me how to make popcorn with that fancy machine of yours. Then, I can eat it, not just smell it while I watch *Call the Midwife*."

"You'll have to see it in my apartment. I talked to Ted Fenwick today and he'll come back tomorrow to connect the Internet in your room and the rest of that wing."

"That works. Then, you can check my corrections in the book." She heaved a sigh. "It was much easier when I used my thoughts to edit the story. It's harder when I have to type them on the keyboard."

"You're preaching to the choir." Mac laughed and drove toward the hotel.

They found Jenny, Dominique and Jimmy watching the large TV in the lobby. Jimmy hit pause on the remote, stopping the crime drama they were streaming. "How was the meeting?"

"Good." Lilly's bright smile warmed her face. "I'm going again. Everyone was really nice."

"That's great." Dominique reached over to the small end table by the couch. "I forgot your purse in my car when I picked up your stuff. You probably want to charge your phone. I heard it going off."

"Why didn't you check it?" Lilly asked.

"Because it was in your purse and I don't invade other people's privacy, not even my little sister's."

"I wouldn't have minded, but I'll take care of it." Lilly looked up at Mac. "Will you show me how to block callers? I don't want to speak to my father or any of his friends. Reverend Tommy is right."

"What does he say?" Jenny tilted her head to one side. "I haven't been to his church in years."

"He told me parents are supposed to protect their children, not abuse them." Lilly took Mac's hand. "Let's go make that popcorn. I want to hear what you think of the changes I made to the book."

"Works for me." They started out of the room, but Mac stopped when Jenny flagged him down. "Go ahead and I'll meet you there."

Lilly nodded, collected her bling-covered, large western style purse from Dominique and headed for the kitchen.

"What is it, Jenny?" Mac folded his arms and waited.

"Veronika has had a problem with alcohol for a long time." Jenny glanced at Dominique and then at Jimmy. "I don't think she's on a speaking acquaintance with the truth after making up so many stories for years. She means well, but—"

"I'm sure people who knew me when I was drinking would say the same thing about me." Mac shared a glance with Jimmy. "I fell into a bottle after my last tour. Survivor guilt. I lived when I lost a half dozen men. Busted up a bar with a few too many civilians who talked when they shouldn't. Nobody died, but those men spent days in the hospital and I faced charges because the Army wasn't happy with me. Penrose convinced our C.O. I should go to meetings, pay for the damage and find a different outlet. It's when I started writing my first book."

"You were self-medicating, just like Veronika's been doing." Jimmy hugged Dominique. "Glad she managed to share some of what she's been through."

"Me too." Dominique pressed her head against his shoulder. "Maybe, someday she'll be comfortable telling me what's been going on with her."

"Maybe." Mac left them and heard the show resume.

In the kitchen, he discovered Lilly sitting at the island, emptying out her purse. It may have started as Veronika's, but it wasn't hers now. It belonged to Lilly. He hadn't grown accustomed to her being alive, not the strawberry blonde woman in a World War Two uniform who haunted him, day and night. He still liked the way she filled out the red sweater and blue jeans, her golden-blonde braid hanging down her back.

"What are you looking for?" Mac watched her open the wallet. "Is something wrong?"

She shook her head. "Just curious. I checked the phone and Veronika, I mean I had a text from the Haunted Hair Emporium in town. She has an appointment tomorrow or rather I do for a dye job. I'm going to have them remove these fake nails too. They make it hard to type."

"Well, it's your decision." He couldn't say it was her body, and she should do what she pleased. He never knew when someone might overhear. Like she'd said earlier, they'd both be treated as if they were crazy if someone heard the truth about the switch between Veronika and Lilly. And most people would decide they'd undoubtedly fallen off the wagon since both of them were supposedly alcoholics.

"Oh, good heavens. This is totally strange." Lillian held out the driver's license. "Look. Veronika's middle name is Lillian."

"No way." He stared at the official Washington State document. "That's bizarre."

"Not really. If you want to know what's truly outlandish, it's the fact my middle name is Veronica too. It's just spelled a little differently."

"This is a weird, weird world." Mac watched her replace the license in the wallet. The expression on her face reminded him of Lilly at her most mischievous. "You have something in mind, don't you?"

She nodded. "After what happened on Wednesday afternoon, I feel like a new person. I want a new name. I think I'll go with Lilly."

Mac chuckled. "I'm sure I can remember that."

"I'm sure you can too." She slid off the stool. "Okay, Mister MacGillicudy, teach me how to use that newfangled machine of yours to make popcorn."

"Only if you call me, Mac."

"I was holding out for Horatio."

"Don't even go there." He turned, surprised to find her close behind him. "What are you doing?"

"Something I've been thinking about for the last three years." She brushed his lips with hers.

He rested his hands on her waist. "Later, Lilly."

"Why?"

"Because you're still recovering from that fall. I don't want to hurt you when I take you to bed. Let's wait until the doctor agrees you're a hundred percent better."

"Sounds like I have questions to ask when I see her next week." Lilly smiled at him. "Now I know it's on your mind too."

He shrugged. "Okay, call me a perv. It has been since I saw that picture of you."

"Really?" She rested her hands on his chest. "So, would I be a perv if I said I enjoyed watching you write and swear at the computer when the book didn't do what you wanted."

"It wasn't the book. It was the characters, especially the smart-ass secretary who kept giving my hero and me such a hard time."

"And you enjoyed it. You really enjoyed it when I changed her."

He laughed, pushed her away gently. "Come on, Miss Lilly. I'll make that popcorn for you and then we'll go look at how you've complicated our work in progress."

CHAPTER NINETEEN

Lilly fell asleep during the third episode of *Call the Midwife*. When she woke on Saturday morning, she noticed Mac covered her with a blanket before he went to bed. The calico cat and the half-grown kittens curled up next to her. Lilly petted them, marveling again at how soft their fur was. Pushing the throw aside, she slowly sat up, feeling her head start to ache. She needed a cup of coffee and possibly a couple of aspirins.

She remembered the doctor saying there might be a few more alcohol withdrawal symptoms over the next few days, nausea, tremors, anxiety, hallucinations, and seizures. Her body was accustomed to liquor, and it would take a while to get used to life without it. *The last time I drank a bottle of wine with the other nurses was more than eighty years ago, but that isn't something I can tell anyone.* It made perfect sense she'd need to adjust to being alive again after being dead for so long.

She found Jimmy and Dominique making breakfast when she walked into the eat-in kitchen. She dropped a pod of coffee into the brewer, put a cup in place and turned on the machine. "Once I have some caffeine, I'll jump in and help."

"Works for me." The sandy-haired, former soldier grinned at her while he peeled oranges. "I'm not much of a cook, but thankfully your sister has decided to rescue me. She's put me in charge of the fruit salad."

"Mom is having fits because you didn't sleep in your room last night. I told her you were a grown woman and could jump Mac if you wanted. We're very distant cousins, barely related. And when I reminded her that first cousins are allowed to marry in some places, it didn't go over well." Dominique cracked eggs into a shallow dish and beat them with a fork. "I'm making French toast. It might not be the gourmet version that Mac creates, but it will be edible. Where is he?"

Lilly picked up the mug, holding it in two shaking hands. "Asleep. He's a night owl so I'm sure he worked hours after I conked out during my show."

"I haven't heard that phrase in a while." Dominique added milk to the beaten eggs. "It was one of Great-Grandfather Donal's favorites."

"That must have been where I learned it." Lilly carefully carried the cup to the center island and sat on a stool.

Mac had told her that physical alcohol withdrawal symptoms normally peaked around 48 to 72 hours after the last drink and lasted a week or two. He'd said some of the members at his different A.A. groups reported them going on for months, but they were more psychological. She shouldn't have to worry about those once her body grew accustomed to being without liquor.

"After you drink your coffee, you should hit the shower and change your clothes. Mom's going to lose it when she realizes you're still wearing what you did yesterday."

Lilly nearly said she was an adult and didn't answer to anyone but herself. She opted for discretion and nodded agreement. "I don't recall where the hair salon is in town. Do you know? I have an appointment before lunch."

"I'll drop you after we see the lawyer." Dominique stopped concocting the mixture and turned around. "Nick and I talked about life and Dad while you were in the hospital. Nick said the only paychecks that ever bounced were the ones Dad gave him. And it made Nick's name mud all over town when he passed on the pain. He was tired of being embarrassed all over Baker City."

"That's awful. No wonder he was mortified."

"Don't you remember Dad doing the same thing to you? Maxine Garvey kicked you out of the mercantile for writing bad checks."

Lilly blinked. That was news to her. Poor Veronika. Okay, time to come up with a reasonable story. She'd use the one Mac provided. "My memory is a bit goofy. I have gaps, so you'll need to remind me when I forget things."

"That makes sense." Jimmy continued slicing oranges into a bowl. "Mac used to have blackouts when he was drinking and kicking tails all the time. He had more than one concussion back in the day and I'd tell him what happened during one of his raging fits. Otherwise, he'd be trying to solve the mysteries of why he had bruises and the occasional broken bones."

"Well, Nick and I decided you may need a bit of run-around money until you get to Lake Maynard and close the account at Dad's bank. You can pay us back once you're on your feet."

"Thank you."

Bree Hawke drove into the gravel lot at the old MacGillicudy hotel and parked in the lot next to a pair of Jeeps and a vintage pickup. Her new client didn't need to know that her attorney knew more than most people suspected about Herman MacGillicudy, the banker in Lake Maynard and his best friend, Liam O'Leary, the crookedest investment consultant in the county, if not the entire state of Washington. They were two of her father's longest lasting sycophants.

Senator Tex Hawke was a quintessential chameleon, the perfect politician who said whatever his constituents wanted to hear, who never sullied his tongue with truth. Her mother, Estelle Hawke was his cheerleader and helped with every nefarious scheme. Few believed she actually had five grown children. Elijah Roberts, the weasel who served as Tex Hawke's campaign manager and loyal dog's-body always accompanied them everywhere.

Bree knew her father wouldn't be shocked if he learned Eli had offered to pay for law school back in the day if she shared his bed. The surprise would come when Tex heard she'd turned down his long-time friend. Like her younger sister, she'd been sexually active forever, not that she'd had a choice as a child and young teen when her father traded her and her siblings for political favors. Bree counted herself lucky she hadn't ended up pregnant.

Now, she'd interview Veronika MacGillicudy and take the woman's statement. With any luck at all, the other woman would agree to let it be added to the case Bree and one of the county prose-cutors were building. Meanwhile, they'd do their best to protect Veronika from her father and Liam. If there was a way to include any more names of Tex's various minions in the restraining order and keep them away from her client, Bree would.

She collected her briefcase and laptop from the passenger seat of her SUV before she opened the driver's door. Halfway to the porch, one of the French doors opened and she saw Mac MacGillicudy. He carried himself as if he were still in the military. It reminded her of her older brothers and the mercenaries who worked for her cousin. Flecks of gray threaded through Mac's short dark hair, and a close-cropped beard emphasized the firm jaw and rugged features.

Faded blue jeans tucked into his combat boots. She saw the collar of a blue shirt under a black sweater with epaulets. "Good morning. I came to see Veronika."

"We're having coffee in the kitchen, but you two can talk in my office. I know you'll want privacy." Mac held out a hand, offering to take her belongings. "She's decided a new life requires a new name and she's using her middle one, Lilly. Hope that doesn't create a problem."

"Hey, I go by Bree instead of my full one, Brazos. My sister-in-law only calls me that when I annoy her by spoiling her four-year-old twins totally rotten."

Mac chuckled. "Isn't that a requirement for aunts?"

"I think so."

Mac made sugar cookies while Lilly and Dominique met with the lawyer. Their mother remained in the kitchen and helped him, cutting out a variety of holiday shapes. Jimmy had taken Ted Fenwick to install new equipment in the left wing of the hotel. Soon, each room would have access to the Internet and that meant the TVs and landline phones would work.

At the business association meeting last week, Frank Madison discussed the need for more cell towers. With the start of winter, people would discover their smart phones didn't work in Baker City. Mac had suggested they use it as a promotional tool to attract visitors. Many guests might enjoy the opportunity to unplug from a tech-dependent world.

"I understand why my daughters have problems with their father." Jenny arranged Christmas trees, reindeer and Santa cookies on a baking sheet. "He's emotionally unavailable, but I don't know that a judge will see that as a reason to grant a protection order for Veronika."

"Lilly. She wants to be called Lilly now." Mac slid the tray into the oven. "And he set her up to be assaulted by his best friend."

"Oh, I'm sure Herman didn't expect that to happen. Veronika, I mean, Lilly has always been his favorite."

Mac allowed the silence to build between them, wondering how to tell Jenny the stories he'd heard last week. He decided to wait. Instead, he rolled out more dough on the counter. She continued to cut out various holiday shapes and place them on the next cookie sheet. "Did you grow up in Baker City?"

"Yes. Dominique told me that this is your first visit. What took so long for you to decide to meet your relatives?"

"Life. My mother is a veterinarian. She worked at a few different clinics before she found one where she wanted to stay, and she became a partner. She specializes in horses. I grew up in Colorado, enlisted in the Army when I graduated from high school and stayed."

"Didn't you want to go to college?"

"It was a no-go." Mac heard the timer and switched trays in the oven.

He wouldn't tell her about his mother preferring his stepbrothers and sisters or that there wasn't enough money for him to pursue higher education. While his stepfather met his physical needs, providing food, clothing and a roof over his head, the man said he didn't see the need to 'gush over the tagalong kid' who came with his new wife.

Mac figured on using his military benefits to go to college at some point, but the Army took more time than he'd expected, so he chose to attend online classes whenever he had the opportunity. He'd eventually earned a bachelor's degree in English. It helped him learn the techniques of writing good stories.

"So, who is your mom? Do I know her?"

"I'm not sure. Her name is Donna MacGillicudy-Galsworthy."

"Donna MacGillicudy?" Jenny stopped and stared. "Of course, I remember her. We went to high school together and we hung out when both of us were home from college."

"What did you do? Baker City isn't that big."

Jenny laughed. "Oh, there were always parties in Lake Maynard. We went together because neither of us had anybody serious."

"I heard she dated Aiden O'Leary."

"For a while, but that ended when he was drafted. He wasn't going to Canada. He joined the Marines." Jenny shook her head. "He looked amazing in his 'dress blues' – super hot. I was amazed when Donna didn't wait for him —."

"She always wanted to be a veterinarian."

"Oh, I'm not talking about that. I'm talking about her dating Liam once his brother left for boot camp."

While she waited at the salon, Lilly skimmed through a book of hairstyles. So many choices, she thought, as she admired the different pictures. Veronika's golden blonde mane fell almost to her hips, too long for Lilly's taste. She certainly didn't go out in public looking unkempt. It'd cause too much censure, and the head nurse would have verbally chastised her when she arrived at the hospital. *I always took pride in my appearance even before I volunteered for the Army Nursing Corp after Pearl Harbor.*

Lilly had opted for what people referred to as a 'middy' when she was alive. Once she curled it, her hair either floated above the shoulders or right above the collarbone in length. Although, it still had a wave in the front, she swept it back from her forehead, so it'd lie smoothly under her hats.

A tall, curvaceous brunette in faded jeans and a purple sweatshirt paused nearby. "I heard you were in the hospital last week, Ronnie. I hope you're feeling better."

"So far, so good." Lilly wished she had more of Veronika's memories. Obviously, this stranger knew her, but it was a one-way street. "I'm sorry, but I still have gaps after falling down a flight of stairs. I've forgotten your name."

"I'm Quinn Murphy-Chapman and I own this place." Concern filled the woman's dark blue eyes and face. "Are you sure you want an appointment today? If the chemicals bother you, we can reschedule."

"I'm ready for a change-up." Lilly closed the book and put it back in the rack. She reached for her phone. "Since I can't find what I want in this, maybe I'll pull it up on the Internet."

"What inspires you today? A new color? A different style?" Quinn nodded a greeting at the receptionist. "Does Haisley know Veronika is here?"

"Yes, she's just finishing up her last appointment, Quinn. She'll be out in a few minutes."

"Good." Quinn turned back toward Lilly. "Tell me what you want while I wait for my sister-in-law to arrive. Tate's home and Sully's meeting me here. After I do my paperwork, we're going to lunch at Pop's before she has to go home to the twins."

"Mac and I watched *A League of Their Own* yesterday, and I really liked some of Geena Davis' and Lori Petty's hairstyles. I want a 'middy' like theirs if that's possible."

"It's been a while since I've seen that movie. I should stream it for my daughters, so they learn about women playing baseball during World War Two when the men were off to war." Quinn gestured toward the phone. "Show me. If Haisley can't do it, I will."

"You hardly ever cut hair anymore," the receptionist pointed out.

"It doesn't mean I can't," Quinn said. "I just get tired of doing the same styles all the time. This sounds like a fun challenge." She eyed the pictures on the phone. "Are you going back to your natural color, Ronnie?"

"I think it'll be amusing to be a redhead for the holidays." Lilly studied the other woman. "I want real nails, not these artificial ones so is there time to have these removed? And since I've chosen a new lease on life, I'm also going by my middle name, Lilly. I hope none of this is an issue."

"Not for me. Let's get started, Lilly."

Almost three hours later when she left the salon, Lilly felt like she was her old self, the one she'd never expected to see again in a mirror. Veronika's hair was a brighter, more coppery red compared to Lilly's strawberry-blonde hair, but she liked the shade. It curled to her shoulders and looked absolutely wonderful. Her fingernails were back to normal too, but she'd allowed the technician to apply clear polish.

She strolled down the street, catching an occasional glimpse in a store window. For a moment, she contemplated stopping at her sister's real estate office, but the town hall drew Lilly's attention. She'd go there and see Dick O'Connell, tell him what she'd discovered last night at the A.A. meeting and learn if he'd investigate a cold murder case from so long ago.

When she walked into the Baker City police department, Lilly nodded to the brown-haired officer sitting at the reception desk, ready to greet visitors. He looked as if he were in his mid-thirties. He wore a dark blue uniform, and she saw the nametag on his shirt, Sam

Montgomery. Equipped with a pistol belt, radio, and other police paraphernalia, he was apparently ready to go on patrol but hadn't left yet.

"What do you want, Veronika? Why are you here?"

"To see Chief O'Connell." Lilly kept her tone courteous although she wondered how he recognized her. She didn't know him, but that was nothing new. "Is he here?"

"He's busy." Sam scowled at her. "Are you going to file a complaint about me pulling you over last week?"

"Why did you?" She raised a brow and decided to play dumb. "I was on my way —."

"To the Baker City Saloon for happy hour."

"But I hadn't gotten there yet." She kept her gaze locked on his. "So, what got your knickers in a twist? The fact I turned down your invitations?"

He flushed, anger mounting on his face. "You were friendly enough and let me buy you drinks until you learned I was a cop. Then, you cut me dead."

"I have standards." She shrugged, remembering what she'd heard the other ghosts call some of the visitors to Baker City. "I don't date flatlanders either."

At the sound of footsteps, she glanced at the hallway to what must be the private offices and spotted Dick O'Connell coming toward her. His eyes widened for just a moment when he saw her coppery red hair.

"Hi, Chief. Do you have a few minutes? I'd like to talk to you."

"Of course." He glanced at Sam. "Go ahead and do your rounds. I'll take care of any walk-ins. Thanks."

After the other officer left, Dick drew up a chair by the front desk for her. "What's on your mind, Veronika? Do you remember how you fell down the stairs last week?"

She nodded. "Yes, but first things first. I'm making changes and one of them is going by my middle name, Lilly. Will that be an issue for you?"

"I can remember that." After he sat down, he pulled a pad of paper out of a desk drawer. "The stairs, Lilly? How did you fall?"

"I didn't." She held up her hand. "I know Mac found me and you brought your kith and kin to save the day and me. The O'Connells have been the town peacekeepers and first responders forever. But I wasn't drunk, and I didn't fall. Liam O'Leary pushed me."

Dick stiffened in his chair. "Why?"

"You believe me?"

"I'm a cop. I'll want evidence. Why did he hurt you?"

"Because I told him, no. And that's something he doesn't take from a woman." Lilly paused. "Any woman. He doesn't realize I remember seeing him kill one when I was little. And I'm not telling him!"

CHAPTER TWENTY

Because the Christmas trees he'd ordered had arrived, Mac picked up two tall evergreens at the mercantile. Now, they just needed to decide where to place them. It'd be too warm near the fireplace, but he liked the idea of placing the one in the lobby under the three-story skylight in the rotunda. If he set it up before Dominique and Lilly returned, it'd be a moot point. He wouldn't have to tell them he was the 'man in charge' and listen to Lilly's response or discover how she'd reprogram his TV and computer to teach what she thought he needed to learn.

"It should be in front of the picture windows. Then, you can tie it in place, so the cats and the kids don't knock it down."

Mac froze, slowly glancing around. He was alone, except for the insubstantial old man who stood behind the reception counter. He was a dapper looking gent in a well-tailored, black suit, with a vest, and a tie. "Who are you?"

"Donal MacGillicudy. My wife, Florence, and I talked. We decided it was time for you to meet us. We were the first members of the family to have the hotel."

Mac looked, but didn't see anyone else. "Where is she?"

"Either preparing the drawing room because the ladies come for tea tomorrow or in the kitchen admiring those cookies you made. She thinks you should pick up some holiday tins at the feedstore."

"Don't you mean the mercantile?"

Donal chuckled. "No, Maxine Garvey is one of our local Grinches. She thinks selling a few trees and some packages of mistletoe is enough. Summer O'Neill is the one who goes the extra mile when it comes to holiday doodads. She already put out the old sleigh her daddy and grandaddy and great-grandpa used to drive around town to deliver gifts to needy families for their children."

"Doesn't she need snow for that?"

"Oh, we'll have some in the next ten days. We usually have white Christmases here. If not, she'll finagle a way to put wheels on it and get around Baker City just like her—"

"Daddy, grandaddy and great-grandpa did," Mac teased.

"Exactly."

Ted Fenwick wandered into the lobby, a cup of coffee in one hand and a frosted snowman cookie in the other. While he munched and drank, he waited for Mac to finish fitting a sturdy tree-stand on the trunk of the evergreen. "I remember seeing the big tree here through the picture—"

"I heard. It gets tied in place. Do you know where I find some string or twine?"

"In my truck. I'll grab it." Ted gazed around the room. "I heard you talking to someone. Who was it?"

"Donal MacGillicudy." Mac stood. "Aren't you going to give me a hard time for talking to people nobody else sees?"

"Not in Baker City." Ted finished his cookie and put the cup on an adjacent table. "I'll get the baling twine. I always grab some out of the barn at home. It comes in handy. With that and duct tape, I can fix anything."

"Sounds about right," Donal said, after the twenty-something left. "It's why we've always counted on the Fenwicks to fix what's broken."

"I thought they only did tech support." Mac stood and lifted the twelve-foot tree, ready to move it into place. The smell of freshly cut pine filled the air. "What else do they do?"

"Anything you want." Donal nodded at Lilly when she came into the lobby behind Ted. "You look lovely, Miss Lilly."

"Thank you, Donal." She tilted her head to one side, eyeing the tree. "I don't know if that will be big enough, Mac. Perhaps, you should ask Maxine to find a taller one."

"Everyone likes a comedienne." Mac shifted slightly so he could see her.

She wore a white blouse tucked into khaki slacks and low-heeled shoes, but it was her hairstyle that caught his attention. A lovely shade of dark reddish-blonde, it reminded him when he'd first seen her as a ghost. Parted in the center, she'd brushed the waves back from her forehead. It curled down to her shoulders but wasn't below her shirt collar.

"So?" She lifted a dark red brow. "What do you think?"

"You're a knock-out, Lilly." He pointed toward the paper sack she carried, noticing she had the artificial fingernails removed. It was her choice, but he preferred the natural ones she sported. "What's that?"

"Mistletoe." She winked. "Fair warning. I'm going to catch you under it more than once."

"Well, if he's reluctant, you can catch me, Ronnie." Ted began to untangle the twine. "Why is he calling you, Lilly?"

"It's my middle name and a new life requires a new name." Lilly patted his arm. "No offense, Ted, but I'm going after what I want. And from now on, it's Mac."

"Because you see dead people too. *The O'Leary* is coming out in you since you almost died this past week." Ted's attention remained on the green string he held. "What about you, Mac? Are you an O'Leary too?"

"Starting to seem that way. I'll ask my mother when I talk to her tomorrow."

Lilly sorted through the boxes of ornaments, removing vintage bulbs, glass shaped snowflakes, snowmen, reindeer and various Santas. She texted Dominique and asked her sister to pick up several tinsel garlands and strings of lights for the two trees. Mac had said tonight's recreational activity would be decorating both Christmas trees.

Jenny came into the lobby and did a double-take. "Veronika, what on earth happened to your hair? It's so short."

"Quinn Murphy collects human hair for a charity that makes wigs for cancer patients so the first thing I did was donate mine." Lilly glanced at the older woman and reminded herself to be courteous to Veronika's mother. "Then, I chose a color and cut I liked."

"But it's so short. You've made some garish choices over the years. I'll never forget the time you went with that burgundy for your prom. It was almost purple."

"It was a bit wild." Lilly unwrapped an angel tree topper, setting the newspaper aside. "I liked it."

"And then you decided to go emerald-green for the summer because it matched your new bikini." Jenny huffed a sigh. "I never knew what to expect. You changed your boyfriends more often than your earrings. And now, you've decided you want a new name."

"It's still mine." Lilly flashed a quick smile at Mac and Jimmy when they sauntered in from the drawing room. "I think we should announce your 'high teas' tomorrow at church, Mac and tell everyone you're starting them in January. Ladies and girls only. I'll wrap up gift samplers of cookies for you to give away."

"I don't have enough of them." Mac wandered over to look at the arrangement of decorations on the long, low coffee table. "I'll have to make more."

"You can do it when I'm editing the newest chapters tonight." Lilly put the angel next to the snowflakes. "Did you two agree on where we're putting the mistletoe?"

"Not yet." Mac's slow grin teased and tantalized her. "Penrose wants to help because he intends to drag Dominique under it."

"No dragging necessary. I know my sister." Lilly rose to her feet. "Did you bring down a stepladder from the left wing of the hotel?"

"It's in the hallway. I'll get it." Jimmy turned around and led toward the main doors. "I really like your hair, Lilly. It's cute."

"Careful, Penrose. I don't share."

"Yeah, I've heard that before."

"Wait a minute, Mac." Jenny held up her hand. "You and Veronika are related. You can't date."

"It's a bit unusual." Lilly recalled what she'd learned from Donal about the MacGillicudy family history. "Actually, it's do-able because we're third cousins, twice removed, only they didn't 'remove' me far enough. I know a handsome man when I see one. Mac's great-grand-father was a cousin of my great-grandfather."

"I'm more closely related to Mindy who had the riding stable outside of town until last spring." Mac took the bag from Lilly. "Ready?"

"I know who Mindy is." Jenny sputtered. "I still don't like it."

"You'll change your mind when I start popping out Mac's babies." Lilly left the shocked woman behind. She took Mac's hand and waited until they were out of earshot. "Am I a total harridan if I admit I don't much like Veronika's mother?"

"Dominique says your brother is her favorite." Jimmy proceeded to set up the ladder. "Shouldn't you be referring to her as your mum, Lilly?"

"I guess, but she annoys me." Lilly remembered the story the woman who'd had her body told on Friday night at the A.A. meeting. "I don't think she provided much support after I saw that murder."

"You mean after I did." The ghost of Veronika floated through the main doors of the hotel, Florence beside her. "And even if Nick claims she loves me, I still don't believe it. Nothing I did ever suited her, so I gave up trying to please her."

"That makes perfect sense." Mac flicked a sideways glance at Lilly. "It may come as a surprise, but the other ghosts in town are introducing themselves to me. And once they talk to me, I can see them."

"Careful, Sergeant-Major" Jimmy drawled. "If anyone else hears you, they'll think you're off the sobriety wagon. The only ghost I know you've been talking to was the one on Thanksgiving." He stopped, stared at Lilly. "It was—"

"Me," Lilly agreed. "I'm glad you've opened your mind, Jimmy. Now, I won't have to keep pretending with you."

"Has Dominique realized it yet?"

"I don't think so." Lilly took the bag from Mac and opened it. "Things may change when Chief O'Connell continues investigating that murder he thinks I saw."

"I did see it," Veronika said.

"I know, but you can't testify so I will." Lilly peeled back the covering on the artificial mistletoe. "And later, Mac and I are going to the feedstore and see what there is to see. I don't understand why the murder victim hasn't shown up in town."

"Well, if you're brave enough to find her, you can ask her."

Since being in Baker City, Mac had time to become somewhat familiar with the town. It included the Baker City Mercantile, Pop's café, two bars that he definitely avoided, the church, a cemetery, and a vintage schoolhouse. More cedar shake buildings of varying sizes lined the streets and of course, the hotel that took up more than a city block. It was only the second time he'd been to the large barn on the right-hand side of the main drag. A sign painted on the building proclaimed, "Summer's Feed and Tack."

He parked his Jeep beside the police chief's cruiser. "I wonder why Dick's here. I hope there isn't any trouble."

"He could be investigating Veronika's story. I told him about the murder this afternoon."

"That took courage." Mac slid out of the driver's seat and walked around the SUV to open her door. He appreciated the fact Lilly still used the kind of manners popular in her day and waited for him to escort her inside. Of course, he was smart enough not to say so.

Close to the doors, they saw an old-time red sleigh waiting for Santa. Mac noticed it was designed for a team of horses to draw it, rather than reindeer. Still, it was extremely cute. Inside, the store, wrapped gifts were piled under a flocked Christmas tree. As they drew nearer, he spotted the professionally designed tags describing who was supposed to receive the presents.

Display racks of outdoor clothes, gloves, riding boots, and barn boots were to the left. Shelves of gifts and souvenirs, including a few used paperback novels on a spinner took up the front right corner. Holiday decorations, ornaments, brightly colored wrapping paper, packages of ribbons and even more seasonal items took up another section. Pet gear, horse tack, medicine, and farm equipment filled the back-half of the store. Feed was through the back door in the adjacent warehouse.

"Let's browse." Lilly led the way to the Christmas supplies. "We need boxes and those little gift bags for your cookies."

"We'll do it soon." Mac spotted Dick O'Connell coming toward them, accompanied by a slender brunette. "Looks like the chief wants to talk to us first."

"All right, but then we're going to shop."

Lilly advanced on Dick who was still in uniform. "You didn't find anything." Her flat tone made it a statement, not a question. "Did you?"

"Not yet." Dick gestured to the woman beside him. "This is Summer O'Neill. She took over the place from her father a few years ago. And he had a new concrete floor put in the basement a long time ago."

"I was about five and he let me help rake the dirt and prep for it." Pity filled Summer's face. "I'm sorry, Veronika. There's nothing like what you think you remember. It must be a dream or one of those memories the headshrinkers might have tried to implant when you were in rehab."

"No, it's not. I know what I saw." Lilly lifted her chin. "My mother's an O'Leary. May I look downstairs and see what I find?"

"Does she have *The O'Leary Gift*?" Emotions slid across Dick's weathered features—curiosity, wonder, concern and a trace of fear—before he took a deep breath. "Is she a medium?"

"No, but I am since I fell down the stairs last week." Lilly took

Mac's hand. "May I go into the basement? Is it all right if Mac comes with me?"

Summer nodded before the police chief answered. "Of course. Let me know what you find. Keep your jacket. It's always cold down there, but it's a basement."

"I'll show you." Dick walked beside Lilly and Mac, ushering them toward the back of the store. "I grew up in this town. I know better than to discount what I hear from the O'Leary family. What about you, Mac? Are you talking to the dead too?"

"Only if they talk to me first. Then, I see them." Mac shrugged. "I call my mother on Sundays so I'm going to talk to her about my biological father again. He may be one of the O'Leary clan too."

Florescent lights in the basement revealed rows of shelves filled with supplies. Accompanied by Mac and Dick O'Connell, Lilly went up one aisle and then a second. She worked her way toward the furthest corner where she saw tools lining the wall. Someone had set up a work-bench in this area.

"If you tell me what you want, I can help find it." A tall redhead in jeans, a flannel shirt and cowgirl boots floated toward them. "Of course, it'd depends on if you actually listen to me or not."

"Why wouldn't we listen?" Lilly eyed her. Vibrant red hair cascaded down her back to her waist. She was gorgeous with high cheekbones, a pointed chin, and huge green eyes. "We're only here to find you."

"What?" The ghost stared at them. "I've been stuck down here forever. Nobody saw him kill me—"

"Actually, someone did, but people didn't believe her because she was only four years old."

"Oh no. I'm so sorry. That's a horrible thing for a baby to see."

Lilly thought about what Veronika would say and channeled the other woman. "I wasn't a baby. I was four."

"Well, it's a baby to me." The woman glanced at Mac. "Don't you agree? My youngest girl is only three, and I definitely wouldn't want her to see what happened."

"Why did you stay here?" Mac shifted from one foot to the other. "Why didn't you go find the other ghosts or talk to *The O'Leary* who was here before Cat took the job as town medium?"

"I can't leave. Don't you think I've tried? The bastard who killed me imprisoned me here with my bones. He was an O'Leary, and he told me he had the power to control the dead. He was taking over the job from his mother."

"Well, he didn't get it. He's not one of the actual O'Leary's who serve as mediums in Baker City." Lilly planted her fists on her hips. "You're a spirit. You can go wherever you want. Talk to Rob Hendrickson and his wife, Cat O'Leary if you don't believe me. She's the other medium here."

"So, Liam never got the opportunity to have the power he wanted?" Baffled, Lucy narrowed her gaze. "Is this other woman related to him?"

Lilly nodded. "She's his daughter. She has the dude ranch outside of town." She gestured to the silent cop standing next to them. "Now, where exactly are you buried? It's why Chief O'Connell is here."

"I can hear you talking to someone," Dick said, "but I haven't heard her name yet. Who is she?"

"Lucy McElroy-Madison." The ghost pointed toward the large white refrigerator and the matching freezer nearby. "You'll have to move those to find my body. They were brought here a couple years ago. The gal who runs the place keeps extra dog food there for people who want to feed the fancy stuff to their pets. I haven't seen Trevor O'Neill or his brother for a while."

"People around town say Summer bought her father's feedstore when he retired." Mac put an arm around Lilly's shoulders. "Do you have any idea how long you've been here, Lucy?"

She shook her head. "Not really. I've tried and tried climbing those stairs but whenever I do, I find myself falling down them and repeating my death over and over." She looked at Lilly. "You're a grownup now, so it must have been at least twenty years."

"Twenty-eight years, almost twenty-nine." Lilly saw the other woman fade away, then reappear. "Come on, Lucy. We're leaving."

"I told you. I can't go. Liam O'Leary is the seventh son of a seventh daughter, and he said I have to stay—"

"He's nothing," Lilly interrupted. "The ghosts in town refused to let him be the Baker City medium because he's a scumbag and his daughter, Cat, runs things. Mac and I share the *O'Leary Gift* too. We're taking you out of here."

CHAPTER TWENTY-ONE

Back upstairs Chief O'Connell headed toward the cash register where Summer waited for them. "They did it. Lilly and Mac found her. Lucy McElroy-Madison."

Summer stared at the three of them, obviously not seeing the ghostly woman who stood next to Mac. "How could there be a body in my basement? My father would have called the cops if he'd seen it."

"He didn't know." Lilly stepped close enough to pat the feedstore owner's hand. "Lucy says the area was cleared, dug down, and most of the dirt was already compacted. Nobody knew she was buried under the subbase before the construction company poured the concrete."

"And she's been there ever since." Summer shuddered. "That's horrible. I'm not refusing to let you finish your investigation, Dick, but I need to contact my father. He holds the mortgage on the store. He has to approve of any renovations, and you know what my family is like. They'll raise holy hell if I just have the cops in here."

"It's okay, Summer. I want to get a search warrant before we start. I'll ask the county to bring in their cadaver dogs too and then a court order to dig up the body. I don't want Lucy's killer to go free. And he'll hire an expensive lawyer to get him off even though there isn't a statute of limitations on murder." Dick glanced at Lilly. "Is it all right with Lucy if we proceed with the exhumation after Christmas?"

"Hey, I'm out of the basement and I want to see my daughters. I'm sure Frank replaced me with one of his sluts before I was gone a week. He certainly had enough of them calling the house."

Lilly blinked and toned down Lucy's response. "She says it's fine. We're taking her to the cocktail lounge to meet the mayor and learn the rules."

"What rules?" Dick held up his hand. "Never mind. I'm sure it's ghostly business and not something I need to know. Meanwhile, I'm trusting the three of you to keep this on the downlow. I don't want Liam to get a hint that we know anything he's done. How safe are you, Lilly?"

"I'm staying with Mac at the hotel." Lilly pressed close to him. "And Bree Hawke is getting me a restraining order on Monday morning. She says she'll see to it that you have a copy and then you can arrest him if he shows up here."

"After Liam tried to abduct his granddaughters last Halloween, Cat O'Leary has one too. Granted, he's more afraid of her husband since Rob kicked his ass all over the cocktail lounge and of course, I made sure I didn't see a thing."

"You're my kind of cop, Chief." Mac laughed. "Let's go, ladies."

"Tell Pop I'll be there in time to start the live music with my boys in two hours."

"We will." Lilly started for the door with Mac and Lucy, then stopped. "Whoops, I almost forgot. I need to buy some holiday gift bags so I can give away samples of Mac's cookies at church tomorrow."

"Take them," Summer said. "No charge for *The O'Leary* who found Lucy after all this time. Dick, is Heather coming to sing with you tonight? She always claims the music lessons with her Aunt Lucy inspired her dreams to be a country star."

"It depends on how Heather feels. She's seven months pregnant, you know."

"Did she marry Durango Hawke?" Lucy demanded. "She was always crazy about him even when they were little kids."

Lilly relayed the question. Both Dick and Summer nodded.

On the way to the door, Lilly snagged two packages of small plastic gift bags. "You'll learn all the news when we get to the café. If it's too busy with the living enjoying Saturday night, then the dearly departed may certainly come to the hotel."

"I couldn't agree more." Mac ushered them toward the Jeep. "I'll enjoy meeting the rest of the former townsfolk."

The clouds had parted, and the rain stopped while they were in the feedstore. Moonlight lit the parking lot. Lucy stared up at the stars glittering in the night sky. "It feels like forever since I've seen the sky and a nearly full moon."

Lilly followed her gaze. She didn't correct the other woman or tell her that it was in what was considered a Waning Gibbous phase. It meant more than half the surface was illuminated, but the light would continue to decrease as it moved from a full moon towards a new one. *I spent too much time researching odd facts at the library before there was an Internet. Of course, what else was I going to do for nearly eighty years.*

Lucy heaved a sigh. "I hope everyone understands why I lost it when I saw Liam's car here. I had to tell the freaking pervert what I thought of him!" She strolled beside Lilly. "He jumped Chloe, my fifteen-year-old daughter, and she fought him off. She cried and blamed herself for accepting a ride home from the mercantile. She begged me not to tell her dad. I wish I had. Frank would have killed him. He was a lousy husband, but he was a good father."

"Weren't you angry about his girlfriends?" Lilly asked. "I always knew Mac would find someone else, but it doesn't mean I liked the idea."

"Okay, this sounds as if there's more to the story than you being the kid who saw me killed." Lucy waited until they were in SUV. "Dish. Just the facts, honey."

"I guess I should tell you everything." Lilly drew a deep breath. "Otherwise, it's going to totally freak you out when you meet the real

Veronika MacGillicudy. She's the one who saw Liam kill you and he attacked her last week."

"Then who are you?"

"First Lieutenant Lillian Boyce. I died almost eighty years ago during World War Two and Veronika gave me her body when she was done with life."

It only took a few minutes to reach the café, and Mac was surprised to find a parking place on the street near the cocktail lounge entrance. When he guided Lilly through the door, he spotted a bunch of mistletoe hanging from the beam overhead. "Why do I think you've been here already?"

"Not me." She laughed up at him, amusement crinkling her blue eyes. "That was Moises Pride's contribution. He really enjoys the holidays, and the mayor put him in charge of the ghostly reenactments of *A Christmas Carol* this year."

"You'll have to tell me more about that later." Mac drew her close. "Meanwhile I have a few ideas of my own."

"Do you want me to tell you the truth about mistletoe?" Lucy inquired. "It's a parasitic plant that grows on trees and is spread through birds' feces. The berries are poisonous too."

"Wow, another trivia expert." Lilly beamed at her. "I'll meet you here and we can watch Jeopardy and shout out the answers."

"Sounds fun." Mac lowered his head, and his mouth claimed hers.

She melted against him. Her hands clutched his shoulders, and her lips parted beneath his. He kissed her the way he'd wanted to, longed to ever since the first time he saw her picture. He slowly lifted his head. "Too bad about your cracked ribs."

"You're telling me." Lilly squeezed his hand. "Come on. We'll introduce Lucy to the other ghosts and then I'll let you buy me dinner."

There were only a few people in the cocktail lounge. Mac noticed

Jack Madison and Ted Fenwick playing pool, but neither of them were drinking beer. Two bottles of soda sat on a table nearby. Lilly nodded to them and then walked across the room to the cordoned off booth in the corner and the sign on the table that read, 'Reserved for Mayor O'Connell.'

She stood still for a moment, before she spoke. "We went to the feedstore and found—"

"Me," Lucy said. "I'm Lucy McElroy-Madison. Mac and Lilly brought me here to learn the rules before I go home and break a few things over Frank's head."

"You can't do that, Lucy. Well, actually you probably can but it isn't a good idea when he's moved on and there are innocents who will suffer." The mayor, a middle-aged man in a dark suit, a black fedora on the table in front of him glanced at Mac. "Who are you? Thanks for finding her. We've been wondering where she was for a long time."

"Dang near thirty years." This time it was the gray-haired man in a red plaid shirt that jarred with the orange suspenders holding up cut-off, logging jeans who joined the conversation. "I'm Newt O'Leary."

"Mac MacGillicudy. And I think I'm one of your descendants or I'd have to be dead to see and talk to you."

"Makes sense." Newt drifted to his feet. "Join us, Mrs. Lucy and we'll share what's been happening with your family while you were gone. Why did it take so long for you to arrive?"

"Liam O'Leary trapped her in the basement of the feedstore after he killed her," Lilly said. "He claimed he had total power over the dead because he was the new medium."

"Not after he tried to kill his daughter sixteen years ago." Newt shared a glance with the mayor. "He shoved her down a flight of stairs at his mother's wake, then dumped Cat's body in a gravel pit along with her dog. I took Aiden there when the dog came and got me after she died."

"He tried to murder his own child?" Lucy gasped. "He's worse than I thought."

"We didn't know what he'd done to you," Mayor O'Connell said. "Newt asked me to hold a meeting for all the ghosts in Baker City. We voted on whether we wanted Liam to be our contact with the living."

"We didn't," Newt said. "It was unanimous. We'd wait until a new O'Leary showed up in town. We didn't expect it to take years for Cat to arrive with her daughters, but nobody complained."

"We'll let Lucy tell you about what he did to her," Lilly stepped closer to Mac. "Since we're both starving and Mac promised to buy me dinner, we'll check in with you later."

Two hours later, when they arrived at the hotel, Mac saw the brilliant lights from the Christmas tree in the picture window of the lobby. He drove around to the parking lot behind the building. He ushered Lilly through the back door into the kitchen. "What's the plan for tonight? The book? Packaging cookies for tomorrow?"

"Well, first I think we'd better check in with the relatives and Jimmy." Lilly shrugged out of the fake leopard-print jacket and dropped it on a stool by the center island. "After we do that recon thing, you guys talk about, we'll do what we have to do."

Mac chuckled and followed her. He always enjoyed it when she was the woman in charge.

Dominique glanced over her shoulder at the sound of footsteps. Had her mother changed her mind about going to bed early and decided to join them to watch *Die-Hard*? It took a moment to recognize her younger sister. Veronika, no she wanted to be called Lilly now, had totally changed her appearance. She'd frequently complained about being the only redhead in the family and constantly visited the local salons in Baker City and Lake Maynard for dye jobs during the last twenty years.

Their mother had grounded her more than once when she saw the latest bizarre color, but their father had just laughed and given Veronika money for another visit to her favorite stylist of the month. The barely shoulder-length cut suited her. So did the slacks and long-sleeved, white blouse tucked into the high-waisted pants. Mac couldn't take his eyes off her. No wonder Jenny kept railing about the two of them at dinner even though they were long gone.

Dominique didn't blame Lilly and Mac for escaping once the four of them finished decorating the two trees. Who wanted to spend their evening dealing with constant complaints? "So, what have you two done tonight? Lilly, you missed Nick. He stopped by with that cashier's check after he closed your bank account. Dad asked why you didn't do it, and Nick told him that your lawyer advised against it. You have to keep your distance, or the restraining orders will be null and void."

"Thanks for the rescue." Lilly sauntered over to take the check. "Mac, will you take me to Lake Maynard on Monday? We should have a bank here in Baker City, but we don't."

"Not yet." He slid an arm around her waist. "I'll bring it up at the next BC Business Group meeting. And we need to figure out what I should be paying you for editing the books."

"Nothing. I love doing it." Lilly leaned against him. "You're the one who does all the hard work."

"We'll argue about it later." He dropped a kiss on top of her head. "The books wouldn't be as popular without you and Gwen would throw a fit if my sales figures dropped."

"That's for sure," Jimmy agreed. "If she made less money from her share of your income, Major Talbot would kick your sorry—" He stopped, seeing the censorious glare from Lilly. "Okay, she'd kick his sorry tail—" Another pause when she planted her hands on her hips. "All right, she'd chew his ears. Is that any better, ma'am?"

"It will do for now. I don't like potty mouths and you two will be hunting snipe in the parking lot if I hear any more of it."

"He's the one who offended you, Lilly." Mac pointed out. "Why am I in trouble?"

"Because I know how soldiers talk, and I've certainly heard enough from the pair of you." She glowered at him. "And it wouldn't be fair to send Penrose out in the dark without you. Since I don't like your 'shoot everybody dead' movies, I'm going to pack those cookies for tomorrow. Don't worry, Dommi. I'm not taking all your favorites."

Once she left, Dominique turned her attention to Jimmy. "She's gotten weird since that fall last week but you don't have that excuse. Why are you calling my baby sis, ma'am? What's that about? Since when doesn't she like Bruce Willis? She's always insisted on having a movie night with me and streaming the entire *Die-Hard* franchise during Christmas."

"People change when they experience traumas. Mac and I did when we came home from the war. We're not the same kids who enlisted fresh out of high school."

"I think there's more to it than that. Meanwhile, you've got the remote, Jim. Are you staying or going, Mac?"

"Oh, I'll stay a while. I like *Die-Hard*."

"Okay." Dominique waited until he settled into the recliner. "Just a FYI. My sorority sister's partner calls moving on without a destination in mind, a bass-ackward's contingency. You can't just go from—you have to go to!"

"Makes sense," Mac agreed. "What brought that up? Oh, wait a minute. I'll bet your dad talked to Nick about convincing us to sell him the hotel."

"Pretty much. Turns out he's been chatting with your mom, and she told him that you have wanderlust in your veins. You'll move on after New Year's."

"Your dad better be careful what he wishes for." Jimmy pointed the remote at the flat-screen. "If Mac goes, your sister will too."

"I could say she'll stay here because they've only known each other a few weeks, but I'm beginning to doubt that." Dominique glimpsed the look the two men shared, but neither spoke. She was right. Something strange had happened to her little sister and nobody was talking.

Well, there was more than one way to learn the truth and Dominique pressed her head against Jim's broad shoulder. He'd spill the secret before morning.

After Bruce Willis successfully defeated the terrorists and rode off into the sunrise with Bonnie Bedalia, Mac left Jimmy and Dominique to watch the second installment of the Die Hard. He found Lilly humming along with swing music on the radio when he entered the kitchen.

Several gift bags sat on the center island, each holding three to four cookies. She'd been very productive in his absence. Doris Day's lovely voice filled the room inviting them to take a 'Sentimental Journey' with her.

Mac walked across to Lilly and held out his hand. "Dance with me."

A smile flitted across her face and landed in the blue eyes. "It's been years —."

"For me too." He drew her into his arms. "I took classes, so I'd know what was popular in the '40s."

"I can teach you the *Lindy Hop*."

"I'm counting on it."

The next morning, Jenny joined them for church saying she looked forward to seeing old friends and acquaintances. Lilly reminded herself that everyone thought she was Veronika and this was her mother. Before Dominique and Jimmy joined them in their pew, Lucy arrived. Lilly nodded when the other woman beckoned to her. "Excuse me. I'll be right back."

In the restroom, Lilly waited while the ghost floated back and forth across the room, her rage mounting. "That man spent a fortune on his Taj-Mahal stable, probably what he got from the life insurance he had on me. White board fences, seeded green pastures, gravel and paved driveways, an expanded huge indoor riding arena and horse barns to the three-story house where he and his new wife live."

Lilly folded her arms. "Lucy, it's like what Newt said last night. You've been gone nearly thirty years. The living move on—"

"He married that slut, Ginger Nevins. Granted, she was more discreet than the rest of his whores. She never called the house, but I still knew all about her." Lucy waved a hand and water poured from the faucets into the three sinks. The toilets flushed, although nobody was in the stalls. "She destroyed my kitchen two years ago. Golden brown wood cabinets, light granite countertops. a matching center island and stainless-steel appliances."

"It may not be your style, but it sounds nice." Lilly walked over to the counter and turned off the faucets. "Lucy, as people say now, chill out. Did you visit your daughters?"

"How could I?" Tears filled the emerald-green eyes, ran down Lucy's cheeks. "They're adults. They don't live there anymore, and Ginger didn't say a word about them. She kept talking about updating the master bedroom and ensuite. Frank pointed out they'd just done it last winter and she said it was time for a change."

"Hmm, makes me wonder what he did. Why is she nickel and diming the man? Whoops, I can't say 'to death' since he's alive. How much do you want to bet he's been on a left-handed honeymoon with someone else? Once a cheater, always a cheater."

Lilly stopped speaking and held up her hand when the door opened and Ann Barrett entered, accompanied by her daughter and the Hendrickson twins. "Hi. Are we having what Dommi calls a potty party?"

The comment prompted giggles from the girls and Sophie nodded to Lucy. "Hi there. I'm Sophie and this is my sister, Samantha." Then, she glanced at Lilly. "Our momma wants to talk to you, Miss Lilly and Mister Mac said we'd find you here."

"Cat isn't the only one." Ann ushered dark-haired Devon toward one of the bathroom stalls. "Dad says he wants to have a crew paint the library during the Christmas break. If you're not comfortable supervising them after your accident last week, he'll arrange for my stepmom, Ginger to do it."

"I'll do it." Lilly didn't look at Lucy who drifted toward Ann, a tremulous smile on her spectral features. "Did he order appropriate colors for a Carnegie library? We want the interior to be accurate, or Dominique will have fits. She's already applied for the building to be included on the state register as a historical landmark."

"He's here and you can talk to him about it." Ann gestured to the twins. "If you don't need to use the bathroom, we'd better get back or we'll be late for the service."

"We'll come with Miss Lilly," Samantha said. "We want to talk to the new ghost in town."

"The one that's with her, not Miss Lilly. We already know her," Sophie added.

"New ghost?" Ann raised her eyebrows. "What are you talking about? That's Veronika MacGillicudy. Why are you calling her, Miss Lilly?"

"Because a new life deserves a new name," Lilly said, narrowing her gaze on the twins. "Since I fell down the stairs last week, I'm using my middle name, Lilly. And almost dying means I now have *The O'Leary Gift* just like the girls and their mom do."

"That's because your momma is an O'Leary too," Sophie said. "What about your real mom, Mrs. Ann? Was she an O'Leary?"

"No, she was a McElroy."

"Like Captain Heather?" Samantha asked. "Ally and Toney's mom?"

"Actually, my mom is her Aunt Lucy." Ann guided Devon to the sink to wash her hands. "And we have to get moving or we'll miss what Reverend Tommy has to say."

"That's my baby," Lucy announced when Ann and her daughter headed out the door. "And I'm going with them. I'll catch up with you O'Learys later."

CHAPTER TWENTY-TWO

After the service, members of the congregation headed for the reception area and joined in the gathering. Mac collected a cup of coffee and an apple fritter before he snagged one of the smaller tables. He enjoyed watching Lilly and Dominique circulate with the sampler packs of cookies. At the end of the sermon, Reverend Tommy had announced 'high teas' for the women in town would start at the hotel on Sundays in January.

Meantime, there were more upcoming holiday events to celebrate like the gingerbread house contest at the bakery, a cookie decorating party and exchange at the day-care, midnight sales at the feedstore on Friday and Saturday nights, and Summer O'Neill accepting gift donations for the sleigh at her store. Dominique had invited everyone to attend a holiday celebration in the hotel drawing room next Sunday night.

Virginia Thompson, the minister's wife, worked her way around the room, reminding people about the tree-lighting ceremony at dusk in the restored city park that night. She paused at Mac's table. "You're making a difference here. Is it all right if I put posters on the bulletin board about your meetings?"

"They're not mine. They're for everyone who needs them." Mac gazed at the stately woman with silver-streaked dark hair. "You have plenty of room here."

"Good. Tommy says he wants to add some meetings during the day because nights aren't easy for some folks."

"Makes sense." Mac watched her walk away, turning his attention to Jimmy when his friend joined him. "I think you're really enjoying it here. You haven't said anything about going back to Seattle or mentioned checking on your house or the tavern."

"I never thought I wouldn't miss them." Jimmy frowned thoughtfully. "This place feels like the home I didn't know I wanted. And Dominique is different. I don't want to leave her in three weeks."

"Then, don't." Mac took a swallow of coffee. "We still have the right wing of the hotel to update and the second and third floors of the main building."

Jimmy rubbed his jaw. "Got kind of a crazy idea. How would you feel about taking on another partner? If I sell my property, I could invest the proceeds here in Baker City. I'd split them between the hotel and that theater."

"Sounds like a winner." Mac nodded his thanks when Dray brought around the carafe and topped their cups. "I need to talk to Lilly and Dominique about it, get them on board." He gripped Jimmy's shoulder for a moment. "I'm glad you want to stay."

"What's going on?" Lilly arrived, Dominique behind her. "We're already picking up a few reservations for January's teas and Linda suggested you do a big Sweetheart thing for couples in February."

"You should tell them about Ann Barrett's offer." Dominique leaned over to kiss Jimmy. "She's bringing the teachers tomorrow after school to work on the hotel library. The holiday break starts this Friday, and she wants Lilly to teach some literacy classes at the hotel until the town library is up and functional."

"I told her I can do that." Lilly nibbled at a sugar dusted doughnut. "And she wants me to consider taking a job at the school. Lisa Jensen was hired for a position at Fort Darby, the new Army Reserve base in Liberty Valley. She'll handle the paperwork for Harry Colter, answer phones and deal with any day-to-day dramas when he's busy. She starts after New Year's, so she won't be returning to the school."

"What did you tell Ann?" Mac trailed a finger over Lilly's cheek. "You can always say we keep you too busy at the hotel. We have a book deadline, and you've also got your duties at the town library."

"I told her I'd think about it." Lilly laughed. "Her daughter, Devon, promised she wouldn't let the munchkins in the class bully me like they do Ms. Lisa."

"Ann's husband said Ms. Lisa is one tough officer." Dominique reminded Lilly. "The woman is a combat vet. She kicks butts and takes no prisoners when she's at the fort, but then she's telling grownups what to do, not little kids who manipulate her."

"They won't do that to me." Lilly sipped her cream laced coffee. "But I'll have to go shopping and buy some suitable clothes. Do you want to come with me, Dommi? You have such fantastic taste."

"Okay. That's it!" Dominique glared around the table. "What is going on, Lilly? You've been nicer to me in the past few days, then you have my entire life. And you always criticize my taste. You never want to spend time with me. And you've always gone after whichever guy I'm dating."

"I've grown up." Lilly wrinkled her nose. "It's about time, don't you think?"

"Or you could just tell me the truth."

"We could." Mac met Dominique's blue gaze. "You've been putting two and two together, but it's not for public consumption."

"Then, I'm not insane. She is like a different person." Dominique froze in her chair. "This is the first time she's come to church in years. On her eighteenth birthday, she said she wasn't going to let Jesus get her and had a big fight with Mom."

"Wow, I was a total spoiled brat." Lilly finished off her doughnut and stood. "Be back in a minute. It's amazing any of you came to see me in the hospital. You should have left me to rot."

"Where are you going?" Dominique demanded.

"For another doughnut. Virginia said I could have a second one after everyone else got them and I see another of my favorites calling my name. Anybody else want more?"

"I'll take a second apple fritter if they have one and Penrose will want a maple cruller."

Once Lilly was out of earshot, Mac focused on Dominique. "Stop playing detective. I told you that we'd share when it was just us at the hotel. You can't tell your mother. She may be from Baker City, but I doubt she'd believe it."

"You'll tell me about it this afternoon before the tree lighting ceremony."

"We will." Jimmy nudged her maple bar closer. "Now, I have something else I want to discuss with you."

Lilly placed four pastries on a paper plate and glanced around the room. She spotted Veronika hanging out with the other ghosts, including Lucy McElroy-Madison and walked toward the group clustered in a corner. "I have a question about your relationship with your sister, Veronika."

"What relationship?" Veronika shrugged. "Dommi was the typical middle child. She was utterly invisible. Mom loved Nick best, and I was Dad's fave."

"Were you friends at all? I'd have loved having a real sister. Sometimes the other orphans and I pretended we were family, but we weren't."

"I adored my brothers," Lucy commented. "I had one older and one younger, but I was the princess because I was the only girl."

"Same here," Raven said. "It was weird at my best friend's house. Her stepbrothers were the favorites, and she was ignored. You should tell Sully about Dominique being treated the same way, Lilly. The two of them have more in common than they know and it's not just Tate Murphy."

"Isn't he Sully's husband?" Lilly asked.

"Yes, and Dominique's high school sweetie. They split when he went in the Army, and she left for college."

Lilly looked at Veronika who appeared totally happy with the rest of the spectral entities. "Dommi and I are going to be friends."

"Good. She deserves a sister who loves and respects her. Thanks, Lilly."

At the hotel, Mac sought the privacy of his office. After he closed the door, he settled in the rocking chair. Dominique and Jimmy were in the kitchen discussing his real estate proposition. She was going to bring her sorority sister into the loop since Claire Rocklin had more than one brokerage in Seattle. Lilly was in Mac's apartment working on book edits. Jenny hadn't returned from a late lunch at the café. She wanted to visit with her friends because she planned to head home for a few days, then come back to Baker City for Christmas.

Mac pulled up the contact list on his smart-phone and found his mother's number. She must have been waiting to hear from him because she answered immediately when he called. "Hi, Mom. How was your week?"

"All right. I'm almost done shopping and now it's just all the wrapping, cooking and finishing the last-minute decorations."

He switched to the video-chat option and studied her face. The makeup barely hid the shadows under her eyes, and she was pale under the spots of blush on her cheeks. He didn't comment on how tired she looked.

"What about you?" Donna rubbed her chin. "Where are you going for the holidays?"

"Nowhere, Mom. I'm staying here."

"You can't. You'll never be happy in Baker City. Herman MacGillicudy is willing to give you plenty of money. Sell that albatross and move on."

"Not my trip." Mac rocked back and forth for a moment in the old chair. "I'm staying here. Why does it bother you so much?"

"Because the town is dying, Mac and you deserve so much more."

"We're rebuilding it. I'm going to suggest we have a grand opening for the hotel next year once it's ready. Will you come for the celebration?"

"Hell, no! And I want you out of there. Leave now!"

"No." Mac kept his gaze on hers. "Is my father here? Is that why you want me to go?"

Silence grew between them, and he saw fear and concern mingle on her face. "Mom, I've met Aiden O'Leary. He seems decent. He doesn't know I'm his son, does he?"

For a moment, hope filled her brown eyes, then she shook her head. "He's not."

"No, he isn't." Mac wished they were together in the same room so he could hug her. "Mom, it's okay. I know."

She winced. "I was so stupid, Mac. And I never wanted you to know the truth."

"What? That my mom went to parties? Of course, you did. You were in college and home on break. Hey, I hit the bars a little too hard with my buddies. Got wasted a lot."

"I was drunk. I passed out in an empty bedroom. When I woke up, he was—"

Mac's free hand knotted into a fist. "Liam O'Leary."

"Yes. I tried to get away, fought him and he hit me. He said, 'no woman ever told him, no' and—" Donna drew a ragged breath. "Back then, it was a case of 'boys will be boys', and I wasn't brave enough to go to the cops and tell them he raped me."

"When did you know you were pregnant?"

"I was in denial for a few months. There were options, but I wanted my baby. I never blamed you for his actions. I know some women do, but he was so different from the rest of his family. The O'Learys are good people, Mac. I was afraid of him, afraid of what people would say. I never told your stepfather what happened either. I let him think I was just a college girl gone wild, but I stepped up and took responsibility for my actions."

"What Liam did wasn't your fault."

"I was impaired. You didn't get your weakness for alcohol from him. It came from me."

"Alcoholism is the gift that keeps on giving." Mac recited. "Fifteen generations."

"I don't know how many of my relatives were drinkers. Anyway, I was very proud of you when you stopped. Do you still go to meetings?"

"Yes. We started them here in Baker City. I'm staying, Mom. I'm the son of a seventh son whose mother was a seventh child. I have the *O'Leary Gift*."

"He does too."

"He may have it, but the ghosts here in Baker City rejected him. He doesn't have any power here in town, but I do."

"And you're staying there."

"Yes, but we will come visit next time I'm on tour."

"Who is we?"

"Lilly and me. She's a very distant cousin, Jenny MacGillicudy's daughter. I'm going to marry her, Mom."

Donna's lips trembled into a smile. "Tell me about her."

She'd finished her corrections on the chapters. The tree-lighting ceremony wouldn't start for another two hours, so she had time for a new project. When she went through the kitchen, she saw Dominique and Jimmy at the table, papers spread out around them. Lilly left the two of them and headed into the pantry to grab two trash bags.

Once in her bedroom, she began to sort through the clothes in the closet. She'd never be comfortable wearing such short skirts or lowcut dresses. She'd donate them to a thrift store in Lake Maynard. She'd keep the shoes she liked. She added the leopard-print coat to the pile on the bed.

Someone tapped on the door, and she answered it. Mac stood in the hallway. She took a step toward him, tilted her head, looking up at him. Then, she kissed him. "How's your momma?"

"We had a heart-to-heart talk." He reached for her. "It was difficult."

She slid her arms around his neck and pressed close, her cheek against his flannel shirt. "Tell me about it."

"I'm the son of a seventh son which is why I have the *O'Leary Gift*."

"Even if you didn't tell me, I knew you suspected Liam was your father, didn't you?"

"Yes. It was his catchphrase. The one he used last week when he knocked you down the stairs at the library."

"The one I shared at the AA meeting on Friday for Veronika. 'No woman tells me, no!' And when Veronika tried to get away, he shoved her. Just like he did with Lucy McElroy-Madison. And Dick told us about him abducting his granddaughters to blackmail Cat. Newt didn't say it, but I'll bet Liam said the same thing to her when he knocked her down the basement stairs when she was a teenager."

"I'm going to have to tell her that I'm her half-brother, aren't I?"

"Yes, but I'll go with you." Lilly rested her hand on his bearded cheek. "It's all going to be okay, Mac. We'll see to it."

"So, why are you packing? We don't have a book tour for months."

"I'm not really." She followed his gaze. "I told you I didn't share Veronika's taste in clothes. We'll drop these off tomorrow at the thrift store and then I'll have room in my closet when Dominique and I go shopping. I'm going to tell her who I am and what happened to Veronika."

"She's already starting to figure it out, so I don't think it will come as a total surprise."

Lilly took a deep breath. "I just hope she understands Veronika volunteered to give me her body. I didn't steal it."

"Oh, she will." Mac smoothed her hair. "She's been asking me and Penrose leading questions."

Lilly's mouth teased his for a moment. "We're not going anywhere, are we?"

"Oh no, Miss Lilly. We're here for the duration. We have a lot of work to do."

"Like what?"

"Writing books, rebuilding a town, opening this hotel and a happy —."

"Oh, a happy forever after. I'm so ready for that."

"Forever." He kissed her. "I can go with that too."

THE END

THANK YOU FOR READING

Did you enjoy this book?

We invite you to leave a review at your favorite book site, such as Goodreads, Amazon, Barnes & Noble, etc.

DID YOU KNOW THAT LEAVING A REVIEW...

- Helps other readers find books they may enjoy.
- Gives you a chance to let your voice be heard.
- Gives authors recognition for their hard work.
- Doesn't have to be long. A sentence or two about why you liked the book will do.

ABOUT THE AUTHOR

Josie Malone lives and works at her family's riding stable in Washington State. She's taught children to ride and know about horses so long that she often discovers she's taught three generations of their families. Her life experiences span adventures from dealing cards in a casino, attending graduate school to get her Master's in Teaching degree, being a substitute teacher, and serving in the Army Reserve all leading to her second career as a published author.

Contact Josie at:
josiemaloneauthor@outlook.com

Find her on Online at:
www.josiemalone.com

Join her Newsletter:
https://sendfox.com/josiemaloneauthor

facebook.com/JosieMaloneAuthor
x.com/josmaloneauthor
instagram.com/josiemaloneauthor
goodreads.com/shannonkennedy
amazon.com/Josie-Malone/e/B006HC9VMI

ALSO BY JOSIE MALONE

Seattle Lost Lovers

Rainy Day Rescue (Coming soon!)

Baker City Hearts and Haunts

My Sweet Haunt

More Than A Spirit

Family Skeletons

Ghost of the Past

Kindred Spirits

Merry Ghostmas

Ghost Writer's Inn

Summer's Last Call (Coming soon!)

Liberty Valley Love

A Man's World

Cowboy Spell

The Marshal's Lady

Hero Spell

A Trail Through Time

Time In Between

Kitchen Witch

Undercover Priestess (Coming Soon)

War Witch (Coming Soon)

www.ingramcontent.com/pod-product-compliance
Lightning Source LLC
Chambersburg PA
CBHW050517260626
47157CB00004B/1364